CHRYSALIS

APOCALYPSE CHRONICLES
BOOK 5

DARREL SPARKMAN

ROUGH
EDGES
PRESS

Rough Edges Press
An Imprint of Wolfpack Publishing
9850 S. Maryland Parkway, Suite A-5 #323
Las Vegas, Nevada 89183

roughedgespress.com

Paperback ISBN 978-1-68549-313-4
eBook ISBN 978-1-68549-312-7
LCCN 2023939565

The book I was writing to save the world lies fluttering at
my feet
As the wind sifts through countless pages,
Distracted sheeple mime sonorous beat
Ignoring words of freedom's sages
We are lost, too blind to see

CHRYSALIS

PROLOGUE

THE TALL, extremely thin man stood watching the waves come into the beach near Gulfport, Texas. Dressed in a touristy Hawaiian shirt and cutoff jeans, he looked like a typical vacationer. He stood next to a wooden bench at the very end of the pier that stretched out into the Gulf of Mexico. Leaning on the rail, he noticed there were very few anglers around him. Even the few left were gathering their tackle and leaving. Liam laughed softly to himself because it was a familiar scene. He got that a lot. People just didn't like the looks of him. It was his eyes. People always told him it was his eyes.

Liam Sandoval, hell, he couldn't remember his real name, thought it was funny that the name he was using now was a mix of Irish and Mexican. He didn't resemble either of the nationalities. Soon he'd be heading south and would have to pick another name. He chuckled again. Maybe Ralph Gomez or Mohammed Smith. The possibilities were endless.

Hearing the scuff of a step behind him, and the

squeak of dress shoes, he knew his contact had arrived. The man was obviously not dressed as a local.

Liam turned and extended his hand to the short, nattily dressed man. "Well, met."

"Well, met." The man shook his hand and then took off his fedora, looking Liam over as he did. "I see you've gone native."

"I like my creature comforts."

Idiot, Liam thought. It must be a hundred degrees here, even with the gulf breeze, and this man was dressed as if he could turn his office thermostat down to sixty. But he was the best at what he did, and that is all that matters.

"Teddy," Liam said. "It *is* Teddy for now, isn't it?"

The man inclined his head in affirmation.

"Since our orders were for you to never contact me unless we were five minutes ahead of Armageddon, I take it all the pieces are in place?"

"Unbelievable, isn't it?" Teddy smiled and then continued. "The American economic wheel is grinding to a halt, even as we speak."

Liam shook his head. "It's so soon. All the projections pointed at ten to twenty years down the road. There are so many things left to be done."

"Hell," he continued. "I'm not ready. I'm still trying to break in my third wife."

He couldn't believe the size of the grin on Teddy's face. The man's florid and sweating face held the fervor of a zealot.

"It's a miracle. I truly didn't think we'd see it in our lifetime. What we didn't count on were the politicians of the United States. They did our job for us. What a marvelous stroke."

"Explain that to me," Liam said. "Oh, I know all the theories and projections—the propaganda that is pushed at us, but how? How did it happen?"

"It's so very simple. For the last fifty years or so, the progressives have controlled education in this country. They were hiding in plain sight, calling themselves Democrats and Republicans. Once they were in leadership in both parties, the game was over. The true liberals and conservatives could do little about it. It's kind of funny. They call themselves progressives. We call them communists. Thanks to them, education began churning out citizens ranked at the twentieth and thirtieth level compared to the rest of the world. In a word, they're stupid. From these ranks, new teachers come to the schools and colleges, and they teach the same drivel taught to them as students. The conception of this was brilliant. This action coined the term, sheeple. And the politicians, the people that run this country, come from that educational pool."

"The government schools teach the sheeple that they deserve a free pass in life, that they're entitled to everything. People or organizations not conforming to this line of thought are accused of racism. Now we're at the breaking point because over half of the people in this country get a government check for their existence. If you take away the very rich, who don't work for a living or know how to, then only a very small portion of the masses actually produce anything. Most of the rest either make their money, or get their money through electronic means through the internet and speculation."

"So," Liam asked. "How do you interrupt that? The internet is a very redundant system. If you drop a server in one city, another picks it up, sometimes in another country."

"Patience," Teddy said, obviously enjoying his lecture. "I'm getting there. Let me ask the question. What will bring this country to its knees? What circumstances other than the stupidity mentioned already?"

"Okay, what about foreign invasion? Or it could be runaway inflation and the price of fuel?" Liam closely watched Teddy shake his head at all of these.

"Food," he said with a sly smile.

"Although," Teddy continued. "Some of your points are valid and contribute in their own way. Although the progressive government has tried to disarm the people on numerous occasions, the United States still has the most well-armed populace in the world, with the possible exception of Israel. So, invasion is out—at least at the outset. That could easily happen later."

"Fuel is the kicker. Speculation and poor manage-ment have driven the fuel price up to the point hardly anyone can afford to drive. Years ago, in his first term, the President finally got his Congress to curtail most drilling operations in the United States. This was under the guise of protecting the environment, of course."

"Since no new refineries have been built since the late seventies, the existing refineries are running at maximum capacity. So, to fill the ever-growing need they now must ship in crude oil for their own refineries, plus ship in refined fuel from other countries. It's insane. The Saudis stopped shipping months ago because of our stance on Syria. I know that other sources have now stopped ship-ping oil. It's only for a couple of weeks, they say. And this is just for negotiation for goods and services. For once, the United States is feeling the boot of sanctions from other countries."

"I can never understand how a country so rich in energy can refuse to use it, preferring instead to buy that energy from those who hate them. There must be some kind of mental illness involved in that."

Liam stopped Teddy for a moment and went to a vending machine. After gazing at the different choices a moment, he shrugged, bought a couple—amazed the machine still took dollars. His mind was swirling from all the ramifications of what he was hearing. He'd been undercover for years, infiltrating groups that were trying to bring about the downfall of his country. His job was to cause delays, slipups, and interference in their plans while protecting his mission and identity. He thought he'd done a good job, until now.

Handing a soft drink to Teddy, he waved at him to keep going.

"The United States," Teddy continued after draining half his bottle. "Is now tapping into its fuel reserves to ride out this little hiccup in the supply chain. It's not just a slight delay, as one politician put it. What they don't realize is that fuel won't start flowing again until we tell it to."

"So, the price of fuel is going through the roof. The people are pissed. They've been pissed before. What's the big deal?" Liam asked.

"Liam. Liam. Liam. How soon you forget your economics. The United States ranks near the bottom of all industrialized countries in education. Have you been going to school here? What delivers over ninety percent of the food to the stores? How do most of the frozen food, perishables, and canned goods get from one point to another?"

Inwardly he felt sick but grinned and said, "Now, I have it...big rigs. Tractor-trailer units."

Teddy smiled back at him. "That is correct. Right now, food is almost too expensive to buy because of the cost of fuel. Supply companies pass the cost of fuel to the consumer. It's increasingly hard to find diesel fuel. What do you think will happen if no food deliveries arrive because of a lack of fuel? Grocery stores normally carry three to four days of food on hand and the hub storage depots have two to three weeks supply stored. Some of these hubs are fifty miles from a major city. Unfortunately for the Americans, the majority of homes have only a few days of food on hand."

"So, how do you think it will play out?" Liam asked as he took another swig of his soft drink. As soon as he lifted the bottle to his lips, an ever-present seagull floated effortlessly by, just to see if he had some tidbits to share. *You may inherit this earth soon, bird.*

Teddy shrugged. "There are a lot of variables, different locales will act differently, but it should start within a few weeks. In some locales, it's starting already. It will affect people across the economic spectrum and not necessarily with the people who get food stamps, commodities, and benefits."

"It's normal for people to take their government checks and go to the store to buy food and get cash for change. That money will stop coming in. When they go for their free food from the community service organizations, the supply will eventually dwindle to nothing. The riots will start then. People will start to get hungry. They won't be afraid, just angry. In their heart of hearts, they suspect and think that people are keeping food from them. They can't conceive that there's no food. After all, it must be somewhere—it always has been."

"The rich and upper middle class will have a little buffer, but not much. Actually, the rich will suffer as quickly as the poor will. No one will deliver their food. Restaurants won't be open and grocery stores will be empty. What will they do? Even with money, you can't buy something that isn't there. Within a month of the initial shutdown, millions of people will be on the move. And ultimately, millions will die."

"What about the military? Do you think they'll try to get control?"

"How can they? Oh, they'll try to deliver food, probably by food drops. There's still a huge supply of aviation fuel. But they'll fail, and those efforts will be concentrated on larger cities where there are millions of people. Once they give out most of their MREs and packaged food, the military will be hungry, too. And, believe me, they'll give the food away. Even a hardened soldier can't stand a small child asking for food and crying."

Teddy took another drink from his bottle. "And," he added. "Finally, there's the *coup de grâce*."

"Which is?" Liam asked, finding it hard to continue showing interest.

"All the folks in the Midwest, or a good portion of them, are going to lose power. And communication will be down."

"How will that be accomplished?"

"A few dedicated individuals at strategic locations. They're all zealots for the wrong reasons, but very useful."

"Won't the satellites keep working?"

"China has been experimenting with SAT killers—laser beams and pulsed sound waves to disrupt command and control of the military. An accident will occur and they will report it to the United Nations. It will be very regrettable, of course."

Liam couldn't stand it any longer. "My god, can it be so easy to plot the death of my nation?"

"It's very easy when those in charge plot their own death." It seemed Teddy's mind finally caught up with what Liam had said. "Wait, what did you say...your nation?" Teddy's voice ended abruptly as he got to his toes and gave a gasping grunt.

Liam's hand grasped the haft of a long blade that sliced just under Teddy's sternum.

Teddy coughed. He'd tried to react when he heard the snick of the knife opening but had been slow. His belly muscles tensed, trying to repel the invader, but gave up the fight. One hand gripped Liam's arm, but the strength was fading. His gaze met those wild, killer eyes.

"You bastard. Why? We had you vetted. You've killed Americans." His voice was fading. Trying to speak, he coughed up blood. "...all for nothing...too late. It can't be stopped."

Liam thought of his dying country, of the death and destruction that she'd endure. His own failure was a bitter pill. "No," he said. "Not for nothing."

Liam was supporting Teddy's weight now, mainly with the knife. With a twist, he finished the job with a classic figure seven and left Teddy leaning over the railing as if he was sick. Aided by gravity, blood streamed into the water below. He wiped as much blood off his arms as he could with a handkerchief, then picked up a pole and bait bucket filled with bloody pieces of fish. That should cover the blood on his arm if anyone noticed.

As he walked off the pier, he told one of the few anglers left nearby, "Not my day for fishing, I guess." He nodded toward Teddy. "I wouldn't bother my friend for a while. His stomach is bothering him."

Once away from the pier, he pulled out his SAT phone. *Dammit. No signal? Already?* Glancing at the sky as if he could see the offending satellite, he shook his head. There had to be a way to alert his bosses. But whom would he tell? He couldn't just walk into the local FBI office and say, "Hey, bad things are going to happen." Liam had been undercover and off the grid for too long. His credibility was with very few people, and they were inaccessible.

From the President on down, everyone was suspect. And it was already happening. Right now. Like the old saying in the Bible, it was too late to moan and complain because the Philistines were already among them.

He looked up and down the street bordering the beach. Everything looked normal. There were hardly any vehicles, of course. The fuel crisis had taken care of that. But people were moving about normally with no sign of panic. *Nero fiddling, indeed.* And they didn't even know there was a fire.

Abruptly making a decision, he headed toward his home and his wife, walking with a long, distance-eating stride. Thank God there were no children. They could be at the border with Mexico in a few hours. His wife had always wanted a long vacation.

He was thinking of a nice coastal town on the eastern

coast of Mexico. He already had precious metal and jewelry stashed in several different places, ready for retrieval. They wouldn't starve. A steady diet of fish and vegetables was infinitely preferable to what was going to happen here.

"We're in a hell of a mess here. Inflation is hitting my people so hard, they're coughing up bones."

—Senator John Kennedy (R-LA)

ONE

COLTON BLAINE and his wife Jennifer were getting ready to go up the street to a friend's home for a neighborhood barbecue. As he sat on the bed, thinking about the evening ahead, he knew the word friend was not accurate. George and Amber were her friends, not his. Their bedroom reflected this same division. From the paint on the walls to the frilly and flowered bedspread he was sitting on, the bedroom had little in it that was his—including his wife.

He watched as she stood nearly naked in front of her closet, dressed in a shiny black pair of pumps with four-inch heels and black lace top thigh highs. The straps on top of the shoes were black lace tied in a neat bow around her ankles. After a moment of going through most of the hangers, she chose a black party dress, raised it above her head and dropped it down over her slim frame, wiggling her hips to get it to fall. It shimmered down and finally came to rest. It had just enough sequins to be more appropriate in a dance club with the big, rotating ball light fixture hanging from the ceiling. The hem was about mid-thigh, and the top cut low with a modified *V* that fastened behind her neck. The back was open down to her butt. It was a beautiful dress, and he remembered paying big bucks for it. Her long, blond hair covered most of her bare back.

He cleared his throat. "No underwear?"

"I can't wear underwear with this dress, and you know it. You could see everything." Her voice was soft, controlled exasperation.

"That's kind of the point, Jen. You can see everything."

She patted him on the cheek. "It's just a party, Colt. Besides, we never go dancing anymore, so I have to wear it somewhere."

"I don't understand why you're doing this," he said, not liking the complaining sound of his voice. "Most everyone else will be dressed in jeans or cutoffs and pullover shirts, including me. It's a barbeque, for Christ's sake."

His ensemble was a brick-red polo shirt, tan cargo shorts, and running shoes. "We're not going to a ball, you know."

"You're such a wimp." She grinned at him. "I'm doing it because it's fun and nice to feel alive. Amber said we should both dress like this and put on a show tonight for all you guys." She did a slow pirouette. "You know the saying. If you've got it, flaunt it."

"Besides," she continued. "Most of the other women there belong in cutoffs and T-shirts—or a sack. They couldn't wear this dress on their best day."

He thought about the parties they'd attended in the past. Block parties were the norm for their small sub-division in the south of Springfield, Missouri, with everyone hosting their own party on occasion. Their street had twenty houses on it, but there were fewer families around than a month ago. At last count, half the families were gone with more leaving every week. Of the ones left, quite a few were in the same fix. Jobs had dwindled in the last year, prices on just about everything had gone up to the point only the very rich could afford to buy anything.

It was amazing. Last year the news reported that more than half the people and families were on government assistance. Now, he didn't know of anyone who wasn't looking for help of some kind, except maybe for George, and everyone knew the reason for that. Even in times of crisis, the government employees got raises and benefits while the serfs went without.

The only grocery items available now were from the food banks that would send trucks around to hand out food. It was anybody's guess where that food came from.

Colt could think of many song titles to describe their situation. Like, "Waitin' For a Miracle" or "Something's Gotta Give." The possibilities for song titles were endless. Everyone he knew socially, and in what was once business circles, was out of a job. Even if someone were lucky enough to have a job, most companies were emulating Europe and putting people on a three-day workweek to save money. There just was not enough commerce going on to keep workers busy. He knew the only reason they were going to the party was that George worked for the local government in the tax division, so he still had access to food and liquor. After all, the Internal Revenue had its hands in everything from health care to bilking money from anyone it could. Why shouldn't they have food?

Watching his wife put the final touches to her ensemble, what little there was of it, he knew the economy was not the only crisis facing him. *As if the world going to hell was not enough.*

"Look, Jen. How about laying off the booze when we get to the party. Last time, things got out of hand and we've enough problems without adding to them."

Her gaze met his in the mirror. "Oh? And what problem would that be?"

"I don't like you acting like some street whore. Is that plain enough? It's bad enough you dress like one. You're a wife and mother, for God's sake."

"Hey," she said angrily. "I don't get out of the house much anymore. It's not going to hurt anything if I blow off a little steam and have some fun."

Colt thought about that a moment and then shook his head. "Well, it's nice to know where I rank in the grand scheme of things since you know it hurts and embarrasses me."

He knew he was whining but couldn't seem to help it. They'd both been out of work for several months and were trying to stick it out until the big turnaround happened. After all, the President said the recovery was on the way and they were building back better. At least, the last time they'd heard from him. There hadn't been a newspaper put out in six months, but the internet had a lot to do with their closing. Television stations had gone off air three weeks ago. The only internet available had been through satellite phone connections, and that had stopped a couple of weeks ago. Information technology in the Midwest was in a total blackout.

Colt's everyday routine was going through the neighborhoods looking for work, offering to do anything to bring in a little money for food. This last week he found no one had money and wouldn't trade food for work. If anyone had food, they were keeping it. He had to range farther every day because he'd given up trying to find any kind of job in stores. Knowing he had a wife and two kids at home made his plight desperate enough to find himself standing in food lines hoping for a handout. It was hard for him to imagine how things could be any worse. His pride had left the building with Elvis.

Jen, on the other hand, had to stay at home and watch the children. That was another casualty of the slowdown of the economy. Public schools weren't open. The few schools that stayed open were private, and those schools couldn't afford to provide buses for the kids because of a lack of gas, or afford to pay to feed them while they were at school. Moreover, safety and security at any school was nonexistent.

He finally responded to her. "So, come with me. You don't have to stay cooped up in the house. We can get someone to watch the kids and you can look for work and food along with me. Besides, we aren't talking about your getting out of the house, and you know it. You and George put on quite a show at the last party."

Jen's voice climbed a couple of octaves. "I can't help it that I got boozed up and then got carried away a little bit. It happens. You gotta loosen up, Colt." She smiled at him slyly. "I'm sure Amber would help you do that."

Colt wasn't blind and knew why Jen was always trying to push him toward Amber. He'd thought about it, but not long. Amber was beautiful, and the exact opposite to her name with black hair, dark eyes, and a creamy complexion.

"No. Not a chance."

She shook her head and then said in a more conciliatory tone, "Look, this may be the last party for a while, maybe forever for all we know. It helps us to forget the way things are. That's not a bad thing, you know. We've lost more neighbors just this week, and since we can't re-supply booze at the store, we might as well use up George's while it lasts. It's all good if you'd just open your eyes and see it."

Colt said with a resigned sigh, "You can't party forever, Jen. Tone it down. It's possible to have fun without losing all your morals. All I'm asking is for you to show a little respect for yourself and your family. Act like you wish to be *my* wife for once and not looking to trade up."

———

LATER THAT EVENING, Colt slouched in a canvas deck chair, watching George Beckman grill some burgers and pork steaks. The kids were running around the fenced-in yard and having a noisy good time. George worked for the IRS, or HSA, or some other alphabet soup organization, and somehow had a good supply of food and beverages on hand for the rest of the neighbors to enjoy. No one really cared where he got it, or how he got it, as long as he shared.

The wives were huddled at one end of the pool, although with the low temperatures common for the first week in April, the water was too cool for swimming. Jen and Amber had their heads together and were deep in conversation. When Jen saw him looking at them, she raised her glass in salute. As he predicted, the two women were the only ones in party dresses. Amber looked like she was on her way to Hollywood and the Academy Award show.

"So, Colt?" George asked. "You're the internet expert. What's the deal? We've got electricity and an internet connection, but nothing happens when we try to log on, so we can't get any work done. We contacted the National Guard unit in town and the airport, but they have the same problem. Even Homeland Security can't contact anyone through their network. It's like a giant blanket has been thrown over us."

Colt snorted into his beer. "Hell, you're with the government. Why don't you tell me what's going on since you people control everything? I haven't had a network to work on in weeks. From what I've been able to find out, most of the servers are down and the overseas connections are locking us out. The internet, at least here in the Midwest, is dead."

"Well, something has got to give," George said. "We're about out of everything and can't get money transactions to work. Even the banks are limiting withdrawals, and a lot are closing. Hell, money isn't worth squat anyway. It's kind of spooky. I heard one rumor that all the banks are about to close. Any money they have on hand might as well be cut-up newspaper."

Adam Johnson spoke up. "Guys, I talked to several people today and heard enough bad news to scare us. I heard there hasn't been a food delivery to the local stores in a week. George's steaks won't last forever, so we're getting out tomorrow while there's gas in the van. We're going to visit the in-laws on their farm in Ohio."

"How are you going to get anywhere?" Colt asked, curiously. "When I looked earlier today, the interstate was jam packed with traffic in every lane. The drivers may think they're going to go somewhere, but the sad fact is they're barely moving. Cars run out of gas and just sit there blocking the way. I wouldn't want to be stuck out in that crowd on the interstate and not be able to get home."

Colt had walked over to the local Walmart supercenter during the day to check on a possible food shipment and found the interstate jammed. He'd crossed the divided highway several times, checking on different food stores. Cars were sitting right where they ran out of gas and stalled vehicles littered the median. With the median full, there was no place to push the stalled cars, so traffic didn't move.

"You know what worries me?" Colt continued. "Like Adam just said, in all the traffic I've seen, I didn't see one delivery truck."

"Look," Johnson said, picking up the last thread of conversation. "We'll use side roads and take the scenic tour to get out of here. The map shows all the county roads. As soon as we get out of Springfield, I think we'll be okay. I think we've enough food stashed away to make it. All we have left to do is hit the road. Of course, we wanted to sample George's free food before we left." Johnson looked around with a grin. "So, anyone want to buy my house, cheap?"

George laughed. "Buy it with what? If I *had* any money, the bank wouldn't let me withdraw it."

"I'd take gasoline, or food."

Shaking his head, Colt stood and walked to the end of the patio, staring and listening into the night. He could see flashes of light and what he thought sounded like gunfire off to the north. *What the hell was going on? Gunfire?* From the glow in the sky, there was a huge fire on the north side of town. He had trouble processing the images his eyes were sending his brain. The image was like a news clip of night fighting in the Mideast countries.

A fleeting thought crossed his mind about Rome burning and Nero fiddling, but he couldn't keep that thought going. Maybe things will improve in a week or so. Someone had to know what was going on and how to fix the problem. It was just a matter of finding the right person.

Finding a way to keep Jen out of George's pants was a bigger concern for the moment, or vice versa. *And right on cue.*

"Ah," George said, coming up next to him, waving his arm at the night sky. "Don't pay any attention to all that, the natives are just restless tonight. Maybe the gangs will kill each other off. There would be more food left for the rest of us, don't you think?"

"Besides," he continued. "The kids went inside to play board games—the food is ready and the women are restless." George turned back to the other men. "Let's party, guys. Colt, I don't know how you let Jen out of the house tonight wearing that dress."

Colt put his hand on George's arm. "I've already told Jen, and I'll tell you. Keep your hands off my wife."

George looked at him a moment, then laughed. "Well, now. I guess that will be up to her. Loosen up, man. Don't spoil the fun. We have a party going and willing women who want to play. Hell, tomorrow we may all be dead."

He was getting the same message from everyone—party today because tomorrow may be too late.

If it came to it, Colt was not sure he could take George in a fight. The last fight he could remember was in grade school. After the way Jen had been acting, he was not sure there was anything left to protect. Suspecting it was already a lost cause, he crossed the yard and pulled his wife aside.

"It's time to go home, Jen."

"What? Why?" she answered hotly. "We haven't had any barbecue yet, and the party is just getting started."

"You know damned well why. I'm not going to stay around and watch you play patty cake with George and Amber, and who knows what else you've planned."

She violently shrugged his arm off. "We were hoping to get you involved tonight, but I guess that's out. If you don't want to watch or play with us, then I guess you'd better take your righteous ass home. No one will force you to stay, and you might as well take the kids with you when you go. But I'm staying here."

Colt looked at her long and hard. He didn't have to look around to know everyone was staring at them. "Have you got things figured out for when I leave? I won't put up with this."

Startled, she glanced over at Amber, then back at him. As she stared at him, her expression slowly settled into a mocking smile. "As a matter of fact, I do. Amber has been telling me of some possibilities, and it sounds very interesting. Besides, you don't have the balls to leave me, and I know you won't leave the kids—we both know that. So, if you don't want to party with us, just go home. Maybe I'll be home later to take care of you."

A cold knot formed in his stomach. When he started speaking to her again, she turned and walked away.

Colt shook his head. In a way, she was right. Call him a wimp. Call him whatever. Like a fool, he was still trying to play by the rules, even though he was not sure just what the rules were anymore.

When he went inside, Timmy and Annie were half-asleep and didn't offer any objection to leaving. They'd played themselves out. He gathered Annie up in his arms, and holding Timmy's hand, walked up the street to their home. They were both dressed in sneakers, jeans, pullover shirts, and a light jacket. At least they didn't have to worry about getting cold during the early spring night. He had a thought that Jen didn't have a jacket or cover-up, but promptly threw that thought out. He suspected she'd stay warm.

Deep in his soul, Colt knew he should have left this marriage a long time ago. The disrespect had started even before they both lost their jobs. The little things she did seemed inconsequential to her but stood out to him, like always cutting him off when he tried to speak. When they were in public, it was as if she couldn't stand it if he finished a sentence. Their friends thought it was cute, the sign of an old married couple. In reality, she was finishing his sentences with her thoughts, interceding in the conversation before he could give his opinion. Not surprisingly, their opinions were rarely the same. When he tried to talk to her about it, she always threw it back at him with the comment, "What, I don't get an opinion?"

On other occasions, her lack of respect for him was apparent. At social functions or even at the mall, when she talked to men she knew, she'd always had her hands on them, patting their back or rubbing their arms. With some men, ones he'd previously called close friends, she always stood close to them in what psychologists called their personal space and close enough that for either person to move, they'd have to rub against each other. If she held a man's arm, it was always rubbing surreptitiously against her breast. To him, that was cheating and stealing. Those intimate moments given to someone else should be his.

He'd have put that down to jealousy on his part, except that she never initiated any physical contact between the two of them, only with others. She told him it was his responsibility to do that, not hers. What bothered him was the degree of intimacy that must have preceded the action for her to act that way toward other men. The physical contact was automatic and familiar. Things were going on that he didn't know about or was too stupid to see.

Regardless of her actions or the pain they caused, he had a wife and children and felt deeply responsible for them. Promises and vows still meant something to him. He wanted to hold it together, if for no other reason than the two children. It was not their fault the adults around them were stupid. Someone had to provide for them.

The cold knot wouldn't leave his stomach and left him nauseous. He had an inner ear infection once, and the dizziness felt was about the same as now. His was a mental dizziness and he was out of options. Everything was spiraling out of control and he couldn't think of a way to get it back.

———

BETH WILSON STOOD next to her old red Ford pickup. She looked back at her house and gardens, wondering if she'd see them again. For the last few years, after her husband had left her, she'd been growing organic vegetables and selling at the different farmers' markets in Springfield. Her family owned several hundred acres, but she and her brother were the only ones left and she only used about ten acres of it. The rest was scrub brush, trees and pasture. It was hard work, and there wasn't much money in it. However, it was a living she loved doing and at least she had food.

She'd convinced herself that leaving was the right thing to do, but it was a hard sell. Earlier that day, she'd opened the gates to the pens that held her goats and a couple of feeder calves. She put out every bit of hay and feed for forage, knowing the animals would leave when they ran out of food. Chickens, turkeys, and geese could take care of themselves.

The raised beds were all worked up and ready to plant, but the starter plants were still in the lean-to greenhouse where they were raised because it was early April and the threat of frost was very real. In some beds, the potatoes were up and Cole crops were half grown. Cabbage and broccoli didn't care about the frost.

She shook her head. *Damned shame.* Her lips curled slightly when she watched her Guinea hens running around squawking at their new freedom. The local welcoming committee of coyotes and dogs would undoubtedly take care of the slow ones. Beth mentally shrugged. *Sorry, guys.* Their release was the best she could do for them.

Beth remembered looking in the mirror that morning and wondering for the thousandth time why her husband had run off with another woman three years before. Since then, those three years had taken a toll on her. She saw more wrinkles on her face. She'd call them laugh lines or crow's feet that framed her gray eyes and had a scattering of freckles across her nose. Her hands were strong and calloused, and she couldn't remember the last time she'd painted her nails or been to the beauty salon.

Looking at her reflection, she'd shaken her head at her farmer's tan. In her case, the tan stopped where her usual scoop neck sundress started. Her ex-husband had tried to get her to wear shorts and a T-shirt while working, but they were too tight and confining. Of course, he'd also tried to get her to go topless. *The rat, like that was going to happen,* but she couldn't face that kind of sunburn. But, on a hot summer day, there was no way to beat the air circulation of a cotton summer dress. She called it wind where you need it.

Her arms were tan, but the usual gloves kept her hands a lighter shade. The funniest part was the white feet, then tan legs up to skirt level, then white up to her chest. It was strange looking, but she didn't owe anyone an explanation, and no one saw it but her. She still couldn't find any gray in her auburn hair, but at twenty-nine didn't expect any.

She'd turned back and forth in front of the mirror, critically checking herself out. Aside from the strange tan, she thought she still looked good. Well, pretty good. She was slim, and her breasts still didn't sag. But, with her frame, she didn't expect they would. *Well, not too much.* At barely five feet tall, she'd endured all the names like munchkin, shrimp, and the myriad short jokes. Still, his leaving had shattered her ego for a long time. *What ran him off?* She hadn't looked at a man romantically since.

A week ago, her brother had sent her a message on the satellite phone he'd given her. He'd told her things were coming apart and thought she'd be safer with him. The fear was that people would be leaving the city in droves and a lawless element would go with them. He didn't have to say much more. They'd already discussed this possibility several times. Arnie was a sergeant in the local National Guard unit. If he thought she needed his protection, things were serious.

Beth took a deep breath and savored the fresh air moving through the mixture of pine trees and oak. It was a good place, and she loved it. With a final look around, she jumped into the cab of the truck. The gas gauge showed about a quarter of a tank. That would get her to the armory in north Springfield. Past that, she had no idea. Her brother was her only family, and it was time to be together. Driving toward the city, she could see smoke rising from several areas.

Safer? It didn't look safer.

TWO

COLT GLANCED at his watch when he saw Jen come dragging home from down the street. It was ten a.m. Incongruously, he thought the one thing that was the most useless now, namely a watch, would probably still be working when the only thing left in the world were insects. When you've no schedule to keep, a watch isn't worth much.

She crossed the yard and stumbled on the tall grass, not mowed since the gas confiscation. Her appearance confirmed the old saying, 'rode hard and put away wet.' The ripped hem of the party dress, Medusa hair, and her missing pumps and thigh highs were mute evidence of the night she had. Colt was having trouble assimilating the fact that looking at his wife made him sick.

"Have fun last night?" he asked sarcastically, louder than normal.

She flinched and held her head with both hands, not meeting his eyes. "Oh god, please don't yell at me. I need a shower, and then we can talk."

"Yeah, I'll just *bet* you need a shower, and I'm afraid

the time for talking is past," he said bitterly. "If you can find the energy, take care of the kids for me. I'm going to check with the bank this morning about this damned eviction notice."

She looked at him with bleary eyes. "What eviction notice? What in the hell are you talking about?"

"Some dude walked up and delivered it this morning. It says we have to get out, now. I swear at the last hour on earth there will be a bank trying to take your money."

"Shit." Her voice was listless as she moved toward the stairs.

IT WAS AMAZING THAT, in a city the size of Springfield, with very little fuel, no deliveries of anything that he'd seen, and no functioning mail service that somehow this piece of crap paper had made it to him. He knew his anger was over the top, but it seemed as if all his trouble over the last year, and especially in the last few days, had centered his focus on this one letter.

Colt stood before the bank manager and felt as if he were leaking anger from every pore in his body. He'd walked into Citizens Bank carrying the eviction notice. Only one person was behind the small service counter and she was busy shredding volumes of paper. No other customers were in the building. The woman could easily see that he was mad, so she just pointed toward a large office in the back corner of the building without saying a word. Colt thought her eyes couldn't have been bigger even if he were robbing the place.

His tennis shoes squeaked on the polished floor when

he stepped into that office. The bastard didn't even ask him to sit.

So much for pleasantries, he thought. Unfolding the paper, he showed it to the man. "What can you possibly gain by kicking us out of our home? I have a wife and two kids. You're putting us on the street."

The manager finally looked at the paper, then spoke to him as he leaned back in his chair and shook his head. "Mr. Blaine, you knew this was coming when we foreclosed. You haven't paid on your mortgage in over six months." He held up his hand. "Look. I know you and your wife lost your jobs months ago, and unemployment payments are exhausted. Hell, son, the government is broke. The bank is holding foreclosed properties that aren't worth a dime with no hope of recovery. I'm sorry. Many people are hurting right now. I have bosses, too. My hands are tied."

Colt waved the paper at him. "This makes no sense. There are empty houses all up and down our street. I don't think there's been a home sold in Springfield in the last six months, maybe a year. Do you have a buyer for it? Have you processed any home loans at all? In case you haven't noticed, the economy has tanked." He paused as he looked at the name placard on the front of the desk. "Mr. Sims, there's no work anywhere."

"Our policy states…"

"Mr. Sims, you know damned good and well, we never got a dime of unemployment. As soon as the government unfreezes all the retirement accounts they confiscated, I'll have access to some funds and we can pay the mortgage. Eventually, they'll start paying the unemployment they owe me. Please." Colt stood, shoulders slumped, and with desperation said softly, "For God's sake. Please."

The banker's gaze flicked over Colt's shoulder and he heard a step behind him. Turning, he saw a security guard standing with his hand on his sidearm.

Colt wadded up the eviction notice and threw it at Sims. "You son of a bitch."

Sims waved the guard forward, dismissing Colt. "Yeah, I get a lot of that lately."

———

STANDING OUTSIDE THE BANKING FACILITY, he hesitated to call it an actual bank since it was just a hole-in-the-wall auxiliary in a strip mall, he took a deep, calming breath. It was April fifteenth. He was sure there wouldn't be a single dollar of tax money sent to the IRS today, or any other day, for that matter. Not for a long time.

A voice spoke behind him. "Excuse me, sir."

Colt turned and saw the security guard had followed him out of the building.

"What?" His reply held more anger than he intended. It was not this guy's fault.

"Look," the guard said. "I know you have an eviction notice, but it's just a piece of paper. The police department or sheriff's department carries out an eviction. I know for a fact that isn't going to happen."

"How do you know that?" Colt asked.

"I'm a police officer," the man said. "Or at least, I was. Most of us just walked away from the job last week. No pay and we have families to feed, just like everyone else. Do you see any patrol cars on the road or hear any sirens in the distance? You don't and you won't. There are a few patrolmen left assisting the Guard. But that's it. So what I'm saying is, you don't need to worry about eviction. It just ain't going to happen."

On impulse, Colt reached out and shook the man's hand. "Look, I'm sorry I snapped at you, and I know this isn't your fault. Thanks for the information. It helps my peace of mind, I guess. I kind of suspected it, but the notice just made me so damned mad."

"Yeah," the security guard said. "It seems like everyone is mad about something nowadays."

"Why is this bank still open? It must be the only one in Springfield still operating."

"Yeah, the guy's an S.O.B., but you gotta hand it to him. He's still trying to do his job. And you're right. Most of the banks are closed. Once they get the records shredded, Sims will be out of here. I don't know why he sent the notice. It's as if it was one of his last official acts for the bank. That's his wife inside, by the way, and as soon as they finish, I'll escort them home. He promised me food for pay. We'll see. It's getting to be a hell of a world, isn't it?"

Colt shook his head as he waved to the suddenly talkative guard and started walking toward the subdivision where they lived, just south of the James River Freeway. It was midmorning, so he should be able to walk the distance and be home by noon. He was walking because his lawnmower, the SUV and his wife's minivan had nothing in their fuel tanks but air. Colt was seriously thinking of stealing a bicycle.

The only vehicles moving on the road were military, and to his way of thinking, that was ominous. A few days before, the authorities had gone door to door confiscating gasoline. Parked vehicles, regardless of owners being present, were all siphoned empty, along with mowers, lawn tractors and anything else that had fuel in it. They cited a new ordinance that prohibited the hoarding of gasoline. Non-compliance meant jail time, but with no guarantee of food while incarcerated. They could sure as hell lock you up, but feeding was optional. Fights over gasoline were commonplace.

First, he'd stop at Wally World to see if they'd received the expected food shipment. Colt looked up and down Glenstone Avenue before he crossed it. He hadn't seen a tractor trailer rig in days. Of course, he didn't know how they'd get here anyway. There were more vehicles than potholes on the road, and they displayed the same ability to move. The most interesting thing he'd seen was the use of snowplows to clear a path down the roads. If no path existed, the big trucks used by the National Guard just drove through yards to get where they were going.

The few local store employees said the government was promising a shipment of food soon. If nothing else, they'd send the famous MREs—Meals Ready to Eat. From what Colt had heard, those were about as tasty as cardboard wrapped in tinfoil. Supplies of dried foods were skimpy. It wasn't a good situation, but he wasn't too worried. Not yet. They had canned goods left at home, but another couple of weeks would deplete that supply. It wasn't much of a cushion.

Colt and his wife Jennifer had both worked for large corporations in the city. They fired her almost a year ago to the day, along with most of the personnel at her job. A few months later, his company had simply closed its doors, giving the employees thirty minutes to vacate the property. Both he and Jen had held high paying jobs, but now there was no demand for IT professionals or computer geeks. Out of habit, he pulled out his smartphone and checked the signal. No signal was available. There was still electricity at his home so they could charge the phones, but for some reason, the towers weren't functioning, so there was no signal. He couldn't call anyone and wondered for the hundredth time why he was carrying the thing because he just didn't need a calculator, any other app, or camera all that bad. Without internet access, that is about all he had. On impulse, he threw it away. Surprisingly, that small act made him feel good. He'd always wanted to do that.

Looking around, he noted the wasteland of abandoned stores and vehicles. This week has brought about great change in this part of the city. Big box stores, like Lowe's and Home Depot, stood abandoned, their parking lots littered with vehicles. The fire department had come through and siphoned all the fuel from them. If anyone objected, there were police and army escorts to deal with. The stores were closed, but the doors were open. No one was building anything, but all that wood was good for kindling and fireplaces. There was no money to pay for it, so people just took it. Colt had heard that a gang tried to take control of Lowe's, but had lasted less than a day. The citizenry was just as well armed as the gang.

As he walked by several dozen closed stores and entered the huge parking lot of the Walmart Supercenter, he stopped and stared. The food truck they were expecting must have come in. He could see fighting around the docks at the rear of the store where the trucks unloaded. At the front of the store, there must have been a thousand people trying to get inside the store. From where he was standing, he could see the crowd surge toward the door. Several military vehicles, parked around the perimeter, didn't approach the mob. Colt had the thought that maybe the soldiers were just as hungry as everyone else and might be in the forefront of the group. As he watched, he saw a man struggling through the mob to get out the door carrying a plastic shopping bag. The man and his bag disappeared under a mass of fighting, kicking people.

Bypassing the melee at the store, Colt crossed the interstate. It seemed to him the plight of the city multiplied in intensity every day. Last night they had a party and barbecue. Today he was witnessing food fights.

Every direction he looked, there were smoke trails climbing into the sky. From the direction of most of them, the fires had to be in housing additions. Maybe he should do that with his house. Let the bank repossess that.

Two houses on his street burned last week. They never knew if the owners had burned them when they left, or if vandals and gangs had done it.

Before crossing the James River Freeway, he stood and looked to the west. The freeway looked the same as Glenstone Avenue, covered with immobile vehicles. He thought about checking the Sam's Club building or the other grocery stores close to it, but decided it would be the same everywhere. Besides, everywhere he looked were throngs of people. More than he'd seen on any other day. It seemed like everyone was moving. Singles, couples, and many families holding hands to stay together. There didn't seem to be any particular direction of travel for anyone. They were just moving about, going nowhere.

Watching all the people, Colt had a queasy feeling in

his stomach. Springfield has around two hundred thousand people, and Colt suddenly realized they were all getting hungry—all of them, with no relief in sight. If relief was coming from anywhere at all, it needed to happen now.

Colt started jogging toward his home. One of the columns of smoke looked like it came from his neighborhood. That was just one of his fears, and he realized that lately, his fears were stacking up pretty high. He hated to leave Jen and the children alone, but there was not much choice.

Picking up the pace, he ran easily toward his neighborhood. The local government council on physical fitness, hell, there was a council on everything, should be proud of him. He was not overeating, and running every day. At least he was staying in shape.

THREE

COLT AND JEN lived at the end of a cul-de-sac housing addition of single and split-level homes. It was just south of a newly abandoned farmer's market and up against the nature preserve. The dense growth of trees surrounding it made the neighborhood very private. Until the last few weeks, the homeowners kept every yard carefully trimmed and landscaped. Thanks to an overzealous homeowner's association, every yard had the same amount of trees, similar landscaping around the homes, and even the same type of grass for lawns. It was a cardinal sin to leave a car outside its proper garage.

When he jogged onto his street, thankful he and his wife were long-time runners for exercise, he saw the fire was in the next addition over.

As he approached his house, he waved to a neighbor who sat in a lawn chair on his front porch, a shotgun cradled across his knees. Seeing no reason to hurry home now, he changed direction and went over to talk to him.

"What's up, Ralph?" Colt asked. "What's with the cannon?"

It wasn't that Colt was unfamiliar with firearms. He'd spent some time at the range inside Bass Pro and played in a few paintball contests on a couple of occasions, back when the world was normal. There just wasn't any reason to own a weapon, or to have one in the house.

The man didn't say anything at first but pointed across the street. Squatters were staying in a vacant house across the way. There looked to be about a dozen of them. As he watched, a couple of men came out of the house and stared at them. Even from a distance, they looked dirty and unkempt. There were no threatening gestures or words, but it didn't take much imagination to see the implied threat was there.

"Those guys just moved in over there this morning," Ralph said. "The first thing they did was come and demand I share food with them. They sent some woman over to ask for it. I guess they thought I couldn't refuse a female." He laughed. "I told her to get lost."

Colt looked from the squatters to Ralph. "I didn't know you owned a gun, Ralph. Are you sure you can use that thing?"

Ralph grinned at him. "I stole it from the neighbor's house next door. They've been gone for a few weeks, so I don't think they're coming back. As far as using it, I think I can figure it out. Hell, if I fire it, maybe the noise will scare them away."

"Did they threaten you? Why are you holding the gun?"

"Not in so many words. But there isn't much doubt in my mind they want to get inside my house. Besides, I don't think the folks at 9-1-1 are taking calls, so it's up to me." Ralph snorted. "Right now we're having a staring contest. I'm shakin' in my boots."

Colt looked at Ralph's bony feet nestled in flip-flops, laughed, and told him to be careful. Continuing to his own home, he glanced toward the house the people had camped in and could almost feel the eyes watching him. When he finally walked in the door, Jen was standing by the living room window watching the squatters across the street.

She turned to him and spoke. "Remember that conceal carry course I wanted you to take when you were practicing at Bass Pro? Now, I wish you had."

He gathered her into his arms. She stood rigidly for a moment, trying to push him off, and then finally relaxed. He hugged her briefly, trying to reassure her, but she gave him little response. That was her normal reaction for the last few months. He often chided himself for trying.

"You could have taken the course, too, you know," he said lightly. "After all, you know that instructor who offered the course to us was looking at you, not me."

"It's your job to protect the home, not mine," she said as she went toward the back of the house where there was a minor war going on between the five and six-year-old.

Colt went around the house, latching all the windows and locked the back door.

Jen came back into the living room. "I was over at Amber's house after you left this morning."

He stopped what he was doing. "Great. I suppose George was there?"

She nodded and said, "Where else would he be?"

He just stared at her. *Where else indeed.*

Finally, she said, "We're just friends, Colt. I wish you could see that."

"He's just a friend that gets almighty familiar with my wife. You also don't discourage it."

Jen put her hands on her hips. "Dammit, Colt. I wish you'd stop with this jealousy thing. It's just a little dirty dancing and harmless grab-ass, that's all. George and Amber are very tactile and loving. It's just their way. Anyway, we were talking and George doesn't think this economic downturn, as he calls it, is going to end. He thinks we're in for a really bad time."

"Well, good for George," he said. "You're scared enough without him adding to it."

Jen finally noticed what he was doing. "I don't suppose you noticed there are no lights?"

Colt stopped closing up the house. They hadn't been using the lights very much, so it hadn't occurred to him anything was wrong.

"No, I didn't. I just figured you'd turned them off. Don't tell me," Colt guessed. "The electricity is off?"

"Yup. Right after you left this morning. That means there's no air conditioning, so you need to re-open the windows."

"Dammit," Colt said, thinking they'd need to eat the food from the freezers before it spoiled. "What's left in the big freezer?"

"Uh, melting ice cubes?"

"Really? I thought we had stuff in there. What about the refrigerator?"

"Same answer, nada." She put her hand on his arm and he looked down at the rare occurrence. "Colt, it's getting bad. I know you've been spending all your time trying to find work and gathering food. You may not know it, but we're down to canned green beans, peas, and ravioli. And we don't have much of that."

"I'll go out again in the morning," he said, although he was not sure where he'd go. "I heard there might be a food truck at Walmart again tomorrow. The trip today didn't work out so well. Who knows, people may start bringing stuff into the farmers' market."

She said, "I saw Ralph going into some of the vacant houses today. We should do that, too. See what we can find."

"That's stealing."

"Dammit, Colt," she exploded. "This is serious. We may not have enough food for another week, and you're worried about stealing?"

He pulled her to him again. This time she didn't relax.

"Get your damn hands off me," she said angrily. "Every time I get upset, you think a hug is supposed to fix everything? Well, it won't. Not this time, Colt."

He was worried, too, but didn't want to show it. Worry, like fear, is contagious. Trying to lighten the situation, he said, "You could try breastfeeding. Maybe we could try to get your milk going again."

She looked at him incredulously for a moment, and then her expression softened. "You've been trying to do that for years. It hasn't worked yet...and no, I'm not going to get pregnant just to get my milk going."

He couldn't help it. Ever an optimist and despite her actions lately, Colt loved his wife and still held out hope for them. Even after two children, she didn't look much different from when she was in college. They'd met at Missouri State and hit it off right away. Both loved computers, information systems, and keeping in shape. Before the babies came, they'd run together every morning. He'd normally lag behind on the run, just so he could watch the morning sunlight sparkling in her blonde hair as her ponytail bounced in syncopated time with her rear end. He loved it, and she'd glance behind once in a while and grin at him. Life was good, or it had been. For the last few months, their relationship had hit bottom. He initially put it down to the stress, and couldn't blame her. However, every time he thought about her friendship with George and Amber, he was less sure. If she needed comfort, it should be from him and not someone else. Under all his denial and excuses, he knew something was going on.

––––––––

THE POUNDING on the front door startled them. He motioned her back and went to the door.

"What?" he yelled without opening the door.

A woman's voice came back to him. "We're your new neighbors. Can I talk to you a minute?"

Colt thought about the gang of squatters across the street. "You're talking now, what do you want?"

Jen brushed by him and pulled the door open, giving him an exasperated look.

"My husband isn't very neighborly. What may we help you with?" she asked politely.

The woman standing on their porch looked to be in her late twenties, with dirty brown hair and a sweatshirt and jean shorts. She was tall and beanpole thin, and her eyes were continually on the move with an occasional head bob as if she were dodging flies. He wondered if she was on drugs, with her eyes tweaking, or twerking, or whatever the hell they called it now.

"My friends and I need help." She spoke in a raspy, staccato voice. "We've been going around to all the neighbors to see if there's any food to spare. We're all out."

While talking, the woman was craning her neck, trying to peer into the house. Colt moved over to block her view. Although her voice was mild, Colt could see anger and hardness in her face at his action.

"I'm sorry to hear that. We've hardly enough for ourselves and our children," Jen said. "Food is really scarce everywhere. I'm sure you know that."

"Well, okay. I mean, if that is the way you want it," the woman said. "Are you sure about that? We have babies to feed, too."

Sighing, Jen said, "Wait a sec," and turned to go to the kitchen.

Colt tried to stop her. "Jen, we shouldn't..."

She brushed by him, muttering, "Don't be an asshole."

He and the woman stared at each other. Looking beyond her, he could see several men and a couple of women watching from their yard. They just stood there, no one sat or walked around. They just watched and Colt didn't see any kids.

"You're not very friendly," the woman said, bringing his gaze back to her. "We'll remember that."

"Well, remember I walked all over town looking for food. You're just walking across the street."

Before she could reply, Jen came back with a couple of cans of ravioli. "Here, take these. Maybe this will help."

"I know you have more," the woman said, taking the food. "Next time, my boyfriend will come over with some of his friends. Maybe you'll be more generous then." She looked Jen up and down. "I'll bet some of the guys would like to get to know you, missy. Maybe when hubby is gone?"

Jen gasped, and Colt said, "We don't want any trouble, lady. But you've got all the food we have to give. We have children to feed, too."

As the woman went down the walk, she stopped and made a gun with her index finger and thumb, and pointed at them. "Pow."

Colt slammed the door.

"Of all the ungrateful..." Jen hissed as she peeked out the window.

————

WITH A BATTERY-POWERED lamp sitting on an end table, Colt was holding Timmy and Annie while trying to read a book to them. It was not easy because it was the kind with the crank handle on the side. Once you wound it up, it was bright for a couple of minutes, but then started losing its charge. It was dark in the house, except for the failing lamp.

"Where are the big lights, Daddy? It's really dark."

Colt smiled at them. Timmy was always the precocious one, full of energy and curiosity.

Annie chimed in with, "Yeah, lights."

"The electricity is out all over the town, guys. It's okay. The lights will come back on. They always do."

"Why?" Timmy asked.

He downplayed it into something they could understand. "It happens, sometimes. Remember when we have thunderstorms, sometimes the lights go out for a while?"

Jen walked from window to window, holding an

aluminum baseball bat. It was their sole home defense weapon.

"It looks like they're going into all the empty houses, Colt. I can see flashlights. We should have done that a lot earlier. Now, we're going to be left out."

"We'll be okay," he said.

"How?" She came back at him, hot and angry. "How are we going to be okay?" Glancing at the wide-eyed kids, she toned it down. "You're the husband. You're supposed to be taking care of us, protecting us, and getting us food. Look at you just sitting there while I'm swinging the ball bat. Typical."

Colt stared at her without responding. The role reversal was plain enough. She should have been sitting with the kids, but he knew it wouldn't have happened that way, even without a crisis.

With no reply from him, she went stomping upstairs. He didn't want the kids to see them fighting, they were frightened enough. Kids don't have to understand the words flying around them to know something is wrong. Plus, he knew that with the mood Jen was in, arguing with her just made things worse.

Finally, the kids were asleep on the sofa. He covered them up with a light blanket. Lightly stroking their fore-heads, he turned as he heard a forceful exclamation from Jen.

"Shit," she yelled from upstairs.

Jen came down the stairs from their bedroom. She was holding a flashlight, and the light reflecting from the eggshell-painted walls turned her into a wraithlike image from a zombie movie.

Her voice was tight, and he could tell she was wound up like a coiled spring. "I hope you like the way I smell."

"I always do," he said, smiling. "As a matter of fact..."

She shook her head violently. "As usual, you don't understand. You're so lost in your own little world. Listen to me. There's no water, Colt. I can't take a bath."

Colt sat up straight on the couch. "No water? The hell with your bath. What're we going to drink?"

He immediately took the flashlight, went to the garage, and found their stash of water bottles. There were precious few, maybe a dozen from a pack of twenty-four. He lined these up on the kitchen counter. While Jen watched him as if he'd lost his mind, Colt took the trash to the garage and dumped it on the floor, finding more empty bottles. With the empty bottles, he headed for the bathrooms. They had three, and he took the lid off each toilet tank and filled the bottles.

"Have you lost your mind? I'm not drinking water from the toilet. That's...that's unsanitary."

"No, it's not," he said. "I read this in a magazine. This water is as clean as faucet water, unless you've been peeing into the tank. Only the bowl is unsanitary. Besides, beggars can't be choosers. If the city water doesn't come back on, we're in real trouble, Jen. Do you realize that? Everyone will be in trouble." He looked at her for a moment. "I don't think you understand. If there's no water, this is Armageddon-ville."

She turned and walked away, and he could hear her mumbling to herself about water all over the damned planet. It was clear to him she didn't know the difference between lake water, river water, and potable water. Clean water would be hard to find.

He worked late into the night, filling everything he could find with water. It took him a while, but he finally got a garden hose attached to the hot water heater in the garage and filled containers from that. He wasted a lot of time until he figured out that he had to take loose the waterline at the top of the heater to let air in. Once he did that, it was simple. Of the fifty gallons in the tank, he figured that once gravity stopped pushing the water, there was at least twenty-five gallons of water left and drinkable. Exhausted, he was feeling good about the situation and was finally satisfied they had enough water to last for a few days. He took the bat and lay down by the door. Jen had already gone to bed upstairs.

Toward morning, he woke from a fitful sleep, thinking he'd heard a gunshot, but when there wasn't any other noise, he went back to sleep.

FOUR

THEIR HOME FACED THE EAST, and sunlight streaming through the windows woke him from a restless sleep. He quickly glanced around and found Timmy and Annie still sleeping on the sofa, got up and softly padded in his sock-covered feet up the stairs. Jen was sprawled on their bed dressed in a tee shirt and loose jogging shorts that had serious gaposis around the leg. She'd taken loose the ponytail, and her blonde hair softly covered most of her face, full of highlights from the window. In sleep, she looked innocent and beautiful. For a moment, he thought about joining her, *needed to join her*, but decided she wouldn't be in the mood. His fantasy of her innocence would be shattered as soon as she woke and opened her mouth. Hell, she was never in the mood —at least not with him. Armageddon, the apocalypse, the President's idea of recovery, or as he'd read in the magazine article, TEOTWAWKI—the end of the world as we know it—had totally ruined his sex life.

Slipping on a pair of walking shoes, and taking the ball bat, he quietly unlocked and let himself out the front door. Glancing around, he saw Ralph still sitting in his lawn chair a couple of houses away. Cutting across the lawn toward the man, the morning dew on the tall, uncut grass soaked his sneakers.

As he walked, he looked around and didn't see anyone on the street, although he thought he saw a shadow of movement in the squatter's house across the way. He reached out his hand to wake up Ralph and then stopped so quickly he nearly fell over. Ralph was not going to wake up.

Quickly, he dropped to a knee and looked around, thinking about running for cover. Then, he quickly realized that if someone wanted to shoot at him he'd know about it by now. He straightened and looked at the body. One irrational thought that came was that this was the first dead body he'd ever seen, that was not on television or the movies. His parents had died in a car wreck in California a few years ago and he received their ashes by UPS. Jen's folks lived in Florida, and they'd likely never see them again. A cold premonition told him this body wouldn't be the last.

There was a small hole in the middle of Ralph's forehead, with a trickle of dried blood below it. Flies were doing clean up detail on the blood. The shotgun was gone, and his hands remained open as if he was still holding it. Now, he looked like he was asking for something. But someone had turned the lights out for him. His expression was blank. The eyes were open, but there was nobody home. Ralph stared at some unseen marvel... with three eyes. Colt whirled around and still didn't see anyone. Then he remembered the shot he thought he heard early this morning—guess he really did hear it.

Colt was surprised he felt so little reaction. Maybe it

was shock. The door to Ralph's house was standing open and, after taking a quick look around, especially at the squatter house, he walked inside. The place was in shambles. Pictures were off the walls and broken, and drawers were emptied on the floor. One of the pictures remained on the wall and had a hinge on the frame. When moved aside, it revealed a wall safe. Nicks and scrapes adorned the front, but the safe remained closed. Its secrets remained hidden to anyone but a skilled safe cracker.

The kitchen was a wreck, and the cupboards were empty. Utensils were scattered on the floor, plates, and bowls smashed. He looked and found no food anywhere —not a crumb.

On an impulse, he went down the hall to the bathroom and lifted the porcelain lid to the tank. It was full of water. He made a mental note to check all the houses after the looters left. Guess they weren't so smart after all. A second thought came unbidden. It wouldn't take them long to correct that error. He was betting the people across the street didn't represent the 'A' team of looters, so he needed to move fast.

Going back outside, he noticed something that Ralph's body was sitting on. Gingerly he moved the body enough to see it was a large hunting knife. It had a bone handle and stainless steel blade. Looking furtively at the house across the street, he put it behind his belt, under his shirt. Then he brought it back out, asking himself why he'd want to hide the fact that he had a knife.

Watching all around, but mostly the house where the squatters were, he walked back to his house.

JEN WAS awake when he got back. She was trying to figure out something for the kids to eat. Having a sudden brainstorm, he went out the back door and took the cover off the gas grill. If he remembered right, the propane bottle was mostly full. He'd always been better at theoretical barbecuing than the actual thing. They hadn't used it in a long time. He was amazed when no yellow jacket wasps flew out from under the lid, and doubly amazed that the grill fired up on the first try. At least, the first try after he turned on the gas valve on the bottle. He used one burner turned down low to conserve fuel.

Going back inside, he grabbed a box of pancake mix he'd seen on the shelf and handed it to Jen. "Use some of the water from the toilet tank and make batter for pancakes. Use a cookie sheet on the grill to make them on."

He smiled at her as she looked skeptically at the grill. "See? At least for now, we have fire, food, and water. We have all the essentials...well, most of them. The kids will love you."

She finally nodded. "That'll work."

"Say," she continued. "Did you go over to Ralph's? I looked out the window and he's still in that lawn chair. Is he asleep?"

"You might say that." Colt sighed before continuing. "But he's not going to wake up."

She gasped and brought her hand up to her mouth. "He's dead? What happened?"

"Someone killed him early this morning, and then ransacked his place."

Jen stumbled as she backed up and sat down on a kitchen chair. She shivered as if she were cold and then said in a tremulous voice, "Colt, we need to get out of here. We just have to. About everyone else has left the neighborhood, and I think we should, too."

He nodded. "Alright, let's say we leave. Where do we go, Jen? I think we'd be worse off joining the crowds roaming the streets. Out there, we would have thousands to compete with for food and water. At least we have a little food and some security here. I've been out there, Jen. It's not a good place to be if you don't have to be there."

"Look," he continued. "I think the only reason Ralph was killed was because he threatened them with his shotgun. Even if the squatters killed him, I don't think they'll bother us because they know we don't have much. We're in the same boat they are. I think we're safe enough for now."

She took a deep breath, shaking her head and unable to meet his gaze. "I'm scared, Colt. Really scared."

————

HE DIDN'T WANT to leave his family but couldn't think of another way to get things done. An hour later, he headed back toward Wally World to see if the food truck had come in. The morning was clear and warm, although he heard rumblings of thunder to the west. If you discounted the turmoil, it was just a typical April morning in suburbia.

It took him about a half hour to jog to the parking lot. He couldn't believe how relieved he was to see a tractor-trailer truck parked in front of the doors, guarded by a half dozen soldiers in full riot gear. A crowd of what he thought looked like several hundred people surged back and forth, trying to position themselves toward the back of the trailer to be first in line. He started walking faster, hoping they wouldn't run out of food before he arrived.

The soldiers were starting to hand out packages from the open doors at the end of the trailer. Strangely, the crowd was silent. Colt could clearly hear talking from groups of people behind and to either side of him. A pair of geese flew by overhead, honking raucously at the humans below.

Colt stopped his forward rush so quickly he nearly fell over in midstride. As he watched, the crowd swerved all together, looking like a synchronized flock of birds, and ran toward the truck. The sound of gunfire was short-lived as the mob overwhelmed the soldiers. People were pushing each other as they jockeyed for position. They leaped and climbed into the trailer, but once in, couldn't get back out because of the press of bodies behind them. He heard their screaming from his vantage point at the edge of the parking lot as people tried to fight their way back out of the trailer. The scene reminded him of videos of soccer games where the crowds rioted and trampled people to death.

Colt flinched, and ducked behind one of the many divider islands in the parking lot that contained a hump of mulch and a tree in the middle as more firing broke out. An armored vehicle drove into the lot. This one had a machine gun mounted on top and was hosing lead at people as they scattered and ran. The lot was nearly empty in a few moments, except for the bodies. With a sick feeling in his stomach, he estimated over a hundred dead or dying sprawled on the parking lot.

He watched as if he were in a bad dream and couldn't wake up. How did this happen? Was the whole town coming apart while their neighborhood partied two days ago? Did anyone know this was going to happen? The articles he read on the internet had talked about this possibility, but who'd believe it? How oblivious was he? Colt was torn with the fight or flight syndrome. In his case, it was stay, or go home to protect his family. One thought prevailed above all others. He needed food.

More soldiers arrived and started pulling bodies out of the trailer. Some were alive and fighting, only to be quickly dispatched by the soldiers. He was shocked to see some of them were women. Not shocked that they were in the mob, but that the soldiers killed them. To him it seemed way beyond callous. In his old way of thinking, he thought dying in a fight was a male thing.

As he looked around, he thought he'd never seen so much blood in his life. Some of the soldiers moved out among the bodies, dispatching the wounded. It was the most gruesome thing he'd ever seen.

If the Army had declared martial law, how would anyone know? It was not as if they could get a news flash on television or anything. He watched until everything seemed to settle down, and then on an impulse driven by desperation and a growling stomach that hadn't eaten much in two days, walked slowly toward the soldiers. He figured it was worth a chance.

As he walked, he skirted the twisted bodies on the tarmac. The smell of blood and voided intestines assaulting his senses, and he couldn't imagine a slaughterhouse smelling any different. He held his arms above his head. One man seemed to be directing everyone else, so he walked toward him. It was not long before they noticed him.

"Sergeant," someone yelled, and Colt found himself the target of at least a dozen rifles. The sergeant turned and looked at him, then motioned a couple of men forward. "Search him, and then see what he wants."

The two men roughly turned him around and immediately found the hunting knife. One of them held it up, and the sergeant said, "Give it back to him. He probably needs it more than we do."

Colt stood before the soldiers, trying to straighten his clothes after the frisking.

"What do you want, son?" The sergeant's eyes were cold and his attitude said he really didn't have time for this. "I've got to give it to you that took some guts walking up here after this." He waved his arm at the bodies. "As you can see, we're a little busy here."

"Food," Colt said, not mincing words. "I have a wife and two kids. We're running short of food."

"Well, you saw what happened to the food truck," the man said. "The really bad thing is that it may be the last one we see for a long time. Here we are trying to feed these people, and they kill us for it. I lost four good men today."

"I'm sorry about that. These people were desperate and hungry, and obviously didn't trust anyone," Colt said. "I'm not that far along, yet. But I can understand it."

"Well," the man said. "Hell, I understand it, too." He shook his head. "That doesn't mean I like it, and for damn sure doesn't mean I'm going to die for it." The man paused and took a deep breath. "Look, there isn't much left here, but you're welcome to what there is. After all, that's why we're here."

One of the soldiers found a black plastic trash bag and filled it with the MREs. There were dozens of meals. The sergeant handed him the bag.

"Here," he said. "Meals ready to eat. This should last

you a week or better. If you have too much, share with someone. Wish we could help more. You have water?"

"I do. Well, some anyway. I could use a canteen for the water, though."

The sergeant pointed toward the west. "Academy Sports is right down the road. I'm sure they have plenty of them, and the price is right."

Colt lingered. "Sergeant, what's going on? How bad is it? There's looting up and down our street. They killed my neighbor last night. We don't have much water and the power is out." He lifted the bag. "This is about all the food we have."

The soldier looked at him a moment in amazement, then shook his head. "Look, I don't know you and probably won't see you ever again. By the grace of God, you've obviously missed a lot of the rioting that is taking place. You must have a good place to hide. My advice to you is to hunker down and do anything you can to survive. And mister, I do mean *anything*. This situation isn't going to get better."

He pointed at the truck. "You see what's left in that truck? That's all my men have to eat, for now anyway. I don't know if more is coming and I suspect it isn't. Even the military is running out of fuel, so we can't deliver anything or move troops around effectively. Once we can't get around, the gangs will take over.

"The powers that be, if we even have a government anymore, left the Midwest to blow in the wind, so to speak. There's no help coming from anywhere. Any fuel left in the country is diverted to the East Coast. Go figure on that one...the *bastards*. Now, you get on out of here. Take the food and go, and good luck to you."

"Do you have any extra weapons?" Colt asked.

After looking at him a long moment, the sergeant said, "Have you ever fired a weapon? A pistol? Anything?"

"I've done the pistol range at Bass Pro, plus used a shotgun quail hunting when I was a boy."

The man thought for a moment. "I should have my head examined for this." He reached into one of his pockets and pulled out a small pistol. "Here, this is a nine-millimeter. Hell, you probably don't even know what that means." He pointed to a lever on the side. "The gun is ready to fire, cocked, locked and ready to rock. This is the safety—push that down and then pull the trigger, preferably not at your own foot. You have twelve shots. If you run out of ammo, throw it at the bastards and run like hell. Now, you hide this and don't show it to anyone. It might make a difference someday. Don't tell anyone you have it. They'll just steal it or kill you for it. That's all I can do for you."

The soldier looked him over. "I gotta tell you, in this brave new world of ours, a yuppie like you has a very short life span. Good luck to you. You're going to need it."

Colt stood in shock. As he watched, the soldiers were donning simple white masks to try to keep the smell at bay. A soldier offered him one, but he just shook his head. He hadn't expected this, neither the gun nor the advice.

"Thank you, I think."

The sergeant just waved at him. "Guns aren't the problem. Hell, we got all kinds of guns. Food is the problem. That is just something nobody has very much of."

After looking around and hoping no one had seen him, Colt turned and walked toward home.

One lesson he'd learned already. Before going very far,

he took the meals and put them in his pockets and under his shirt. He bulged everywhere from the hidden packages. Hopefully, no one would notice and wonder what he was carrying.

He just looked like a fat man in a starving world walking down the road, whistling past the cemetery.

————

IT TOOK him longer to get back home because he couldn't jog with all his pockets full. Walking up the middle of the street, he saw that Ralph's body was gone, and he didn't see any of the squatters. That was strange.

Walking into his house, he had a tense, scared moment. No one was there. After a frantic search, he spied a note from Jen on the kitchen table.

"Some men came and cleared out the squatters and took Ralph's body away. Amber came by and the kids and I went for a walk."

Some men came. Men from where?

He put the MREs in a kitchen cabinet, then remembering the squatters, took some packages and hid them. Walking out to the front of the house, he stood watching for Jen. She surely wouldn't be gone very long with the kids in tow.

It was late afternoon, and he was about to go looking for them when he saw Jen and the kids walking toward him. A giant of a man accompanied them. He was not a "Jack and the Beanstalk" giant, but was easily six feet eight or nine, and must weigh out at two hundred fifty or so. As they got closer, he upped the estimate about thirty pounds. The guy was ripped.

Colt continued to assess the man. He had a shock of

unruly blond hair on his head, no neck, and the body of a football player on steroids, with small and mean-looking blue eyes...at least to Colt. He had a rifle slung over his shoulder and wore a muscle shirt tucked into fatigue pants.

They stopped in front of him. Colt hadn't met many people that he felt such an instant dislike to. The fact that he was with Jen and the kids just angered him more. "Who's the steroid junkie, Jen?"

The kids ran into the house and Jen, rolling her eyes, said, "Colt, this is Sam Jones. He's a friend of George and Amber's. Sam, this is my husband, Colt Blaine."

Neither man offered to shake hands, just stared at each other. In his mind's eye, Colt thought of two boxers in a stare down. His hand caressed the pistol in his pocket. The man just smirked at him.

"Why are you here, Sam?" Colt asked. "Did my wife," —he emphasized wife—"need an escort?"

The man nodded and continued to grace them with his irritating smile. "She did. There are some nasty characters around."

Colt interjected, "If she'd stayed *home*, she wouldn't have needed an escort."

Sam motioned over his shoulder. "I noticed you let some squatters move in on you and put your family in danger. We got rid of them for you. You can thank me anytime. We didn't want them this close to our camp, anyway."

Colt looked Jen over with a critical eye. They'd been married long enough that he could see the signs; signs that he was usually responsible for producing. Her lipstick was mostly gone and her rumpled hair outlined tired eyes. It must have been a rough day at the camp. "It looks like Jen has thanked you already."

Other than a sharp intake of breath, Jen didn't say anything, or raise her head to look at him.

When Colt kept staring at him, Sam continued with a smug look on his face. "Your wife is a rare, beautiful woman that needs to be protected. You should know that."

"Protected from whom?"

Sam stared a moment, losing his smirk. "Well, I guess I'd better get back to the camp. Jen, you should seriously think about what I told you. Amber and George are on board with us. You should be, too."

On board with what?

LATER, after feeding the exhausted children and putting them down for a nap, Colt sat in the kitchen staring at Jen's back. She was standing, apparently lost in thought, looking out the window into the backyard. Her shoulders were slumped and she kept shrugging them as if she were arguing with herself.

"What's so interesting out there?" he asked, just to open the conversation.

"Hmmm?" She turned around toward him. "Oh, nothing."

"So, where did you pick up Sammy Boy? I heard him mention Amber and George?"

She quickly turned away from him again. *What the hell?*

"Will you at least tell me where you were and what you were doing all that time, or do I really want to know?

Was it just another opportunity to party with George and Amber?"

With what he'd seen happen with the Army truck at the mall and in his own neighborhood, his fear for her and the children was a deep-seated knot in his stomach —and it was a fear on many levels. He wanted to protect her, but he could see he was losing that battle. In fact, he was not sure what tools to bring to begin the fight.

"Colt, you don't need to be so pissy about this and you were absolutely rude to Sam. That was uncalled for."

He couldn't keep the anger from his voice. "Oh, I don't think I was rude. As a matter of fact, I think Sammy Boy and I understood each other very well."

She turned and looked at him for a long moment. "Don't try to get all macho here. You wouldn't stand a chance against Sam and you know it, not one. He's bigger and stronger than you, and he'd break you in a heartbeat."

Jen continued. "When the kids and I got to the bottom of the hill on our walk, I could see a tent city had sprung up along Lake Springfield and the Nature Center. When I went down to see what was going on, Sam came out to greet me. He had George and Amber with him." She glanced over her shoulder in his general direction. "He's a nice guy, Colt. He really is."

Colt couldn't help but wonder why she wouldn't look at him. He did some math in his head and figured she'd been there about four hours, along with his kids.

"And?" he prompted.

Jen took a deep breath. "He gave me the grand tour. It was actually nice, if you like to camp out. Everyone was working at something. It was very organized and looked kind of normal. The main thing is that no one looked afraid. Women were washing clothes, cooking, and bathing in the lake. Some men were standing guard, so everyone was safe, while others came in carrying boxes of food."

"I don't understand the tent city. Why not just take over a neighborhood?"

Jen shrugged. "I asked him that, and he said it was easier to protect. A housing addition would be too spread out."

She glanced back at him. "He offered to escort me back home because he said the streets aren't safe."

"Not safe from whom?" Colt asked sarcastically. "Him?"

"Dammit. What's the matter with you? Why are you acting like this?"

"Oh, well, golly gee. I don't know, Jen. You come back home with some steroid junkie, your hair is messed up, lipstick smeared, and your blouse is buttoned up wrong." It was a shallow "gotcha" victory when her hand went to the front of her blouse. She didn't have buttons. "So, you tell me. What could *possibly* be the matter? I figure that little tour took you about four or five hours. You could have toured half the town in that time. And you still won't tell me what you did in that time, or what he wants."

"Alright. Fine." She was shouting at him. "He wants us to join their group. You heard him say that. It would be safer for the kids and us, plus we'd have security and food until this madness is over. That's his offer."

"That's it? Just like that?" Colt looked at her skeptically. "That's all there is? Why pick us, Jen? There are tons of people wandering around looking for food. He could pick anyone." He continued, "And more to the point, why did he pick you?"

When she didn't answer, he rose and put his hands on her shoulders. "Talk to me, Jen."

She shrugged him off and stepped away. "There are terms to join."

Here it comes.

"For you to join, it's a fifty-pound box of food, then the same amount every week. No one can stay if they don't provide food and goods for the community."

"The community, huh?" Colt shook his head. "Well, that should keep Sammy Boy well fed. What's the rest of it? What do you have to provide to good old Sam?"

Jen looked at him for the first time, and he wished she hadn't. She looked right through him. "Me. Women get in free."

All the permutations of that simple answer assailed his senses. Just from hearing about the camp, the structure sounded like a classic commune with one 'special' guy as the head. All the women would be his to dally with at his leisure. What knotted his stomach and was about to send him outside to puke in the grass? He could tell by looking at her. She didn't tell him no. In her mind, she was already there, and he would not have offered without sampling the goods.

"He was right upfront about the arrangement," she continued in a monotone voice. "All the women there are beautiful and handpicked. Sam says, when all this blows over…"

He couldn't contain his anger. "The hell with Sam and what he says. You're my wife. What did you tell him?"

She looked away.

"What did you tell him, Jen?" Colt could barely speak because he was holding his breath.

Her voice was soft. "I told him I'd have to talk to my husband."

"You didn't tell him, no way in hell? You couldn't even put a name to me. While you were in his tent for hours playing house and being *persuaded*, what were the kids doing? Did you think of them for one minute?"

"I...don't know. Playing, I guess. There are other kids there. Amber's kids are there. When we got ready to leave, one of the women brought them to us."

She continued haltingly. "I know this would be... different. But we can make it work. It's our only chance. Colt, I'm scared and I've *been* scared. You're gone every day looking for food and I'm all alone with the kids. Someone could come and kill us, or...rape me...or, just about anything. We're helpless."

"So," Colt replied. "Maybe we need to form our own neighborhood watch. Get together with the families that are left. We're not helpless. I made friends with an Army sergeant who hands out food. I don't think we'll go hungry."

"You don't think? Maybe? Dammit, Colt, I can't live this way." She was shouting at the end of her sentence.

He couldn't believe what he was hearing. "Is this what you want, Jen? Is being in Sammy Boy's commune your idea of security? Did Sammy Boy take care of you so well in those few hours that you're going to throw our marriage away?"

Colt ended by shouting at her. "You go from being married one day to being a whore the next? I can't believe this. Did you even think of your marriage vows while

Sammy Boy persuaded you? This...this thing is what you want?"

Jen was openly crying. "No, this isn't what I want. I don't want to be afraid all the time, and I want our life back. I want to have a job and money, to go to the movies and out for dinner. I want to go to a concert once in a while. That's what I want."

Trying to calm his breathing, he said, "That is all gone, Jen. We must accept that. When the fuel went away, and the trucks stopped running, it turned us into a third-world country nearly overnight. You might remember that people are still alive in third world countries."

Colt took a deep breath, fighting nausea. "So, will it be you and me or you and Sammy Boy? What're you going to do?

"I don't know," she said softly. "I have to tell him tomorrow."

She already made up her mind. She's gone.

He turned her face to his with his finger on her chin and said coldly, "Understand this. If you go down there, you won't have a husband."

She wailed at him. "If I don't, I'll die—starve to death or be killed. Something."

"Is that the line he reeled you in with?" Colt reached into the cupboard and angrily slammed a green package down in front of her. "See? Here you go. Meals Ready to Eat, menu twenty, spaghetti and meatballs. We won't starve. We can find a way, together. It will be hard, but we can survive. I have enough of these to tide us over until we find another way." He spaced his words out. "Some other way, Jen. You don't have to sell yourself."

"Sam said you'd resist."

Bought and sold. Shit.

Colt just stared at her with his mouth open. "How could you have been brainwashed so quickly. Did he drug you, maybe a little date-rape cocktail? What happened to you? Is he that much better than me, that he turned you into a whore in one day?"

Her voice was mocking and hard. "Nothing has happened to me that I haven't been doing for years, Colt. Get over it. You know what went on at those neighborhood parties. And today at the camp? They treated me very well. It's just that someone is finally talking sense. Unfortunately, it's not you."

Colt stood, shaking his head and not believing what he was hearing. "So, you're leaving me? You're going to chase a little red wagon pulled by Sammy Boy?" he asked softly. For some reason, he couldn't believe this was happening. Reality had left on the train.

"Can't you come?" she pleaded. "Maybe we can get enough food together for your entry?" She didn't look at him.

He couldn't believe he was hearing this. What had happened to his wife? Things had cooled a little between them in the last few months since they lost their jobs. *Hell, actually gone stone cold, but this?*

"For your information, no I did not know you were whoring around." His voice rose. "So if I come along with you, the deal is I get to watch you being used by Sammy Boy, and the rest of his merry men? Then, you come back to me and everything is normal? I can't believe you'd even consider this. No, thank you."

"God, Colt. You make it sound so...so...damn you." She couldn't finish, but stood shaking her head and looking at him with tears in her eyes. "Alright, I'll think about it. We'll see what happens." She sounded defeated. "But, Colt, we have to keep this option open. Think of the kids. We have no food or water...or at least precious little. The camp offers security for us. And the other thing, with the men? It doesn't really matter, does it? How *can* it matter? It's just sex. I'll still be yours."

"What kind of crap is that? You'll still be mine? I don't think you've been mine for a long time. Certainly not after you warmed up to George and who knows how many others, and then met old Sammy Boy."

She tried to stare him down but finally lowered her eyes. When she didn't say anything else, he just dropped his hands and walked away.

What the hell happens now.

He barely made it out the back door and into the grass before he threw up.

FIVE

COLT WAS UP and out of the house at sunrise. From the feel of the humidity, it was going to be a hot day. He was working with feverish purpose now, trying to make things better and somehow show Jen she could stay with him. Sleep didn't come during the night. He kept turning the problem over in his mind. She was the mother of his children, and had made a mistake. Was he better off with her or without her? How could she do that if she loved him? Did she think her behavior was wrong? What was he supposed to do now? He spent the night picking at the scab of her infidelity and morning just revealed a bleeding scab and no answers.

Methodically, he went through all the neighboring houses. He was surprised to find that his was the only family left at home in the housing addition, and wondered where everyone went. It seemed as if everyone took flight at once. The neighbor taking off for Ohio just opened the floodgates. Of course, he knew where George and Amber were—with Sammy Boy.

He continued to search through houses stripped of

food and water. It was strange, but it seemed the looters considered food as what they could eat immediately. They left things that have to be prepared, like mixes and pasta. He could find cereal, but no canned goods. You don't have to have milk with cereal. It works great with water.

Remembering what the sergeant said, food was the big problem. There were plenty of guns and other supplies. Well, he hadn't found any guns yet, but he was sure they were out there. But stuff. Every home was full of everything but food and water. But without food and water, it was all just...stuff.

At one home, he found a fishing vest that had dozens of pockets. It fit pretty well, so he put it on. He checked the toilet tanks and water heaters. If there was water, he stored the location in his mind for future reference. In one house, he found several boxes of cake mix and pancake mix to replace what they'd used at home. In another, he found a six-pack of cola under the sink, back behind the Drano and a couple of rotten potatoes, and two five-gallon propane bottles for the gas grill. The drinks went into his pockets. After he worked most of the morning, he had a sizable pile of goods to take to his house. He also broke into cars and found fiber bars in one of the compartments, along with an assortment of gum, breath savers, and a box of condoms under a seat. *In the car?* He took them all. Borrowing a yard cart from one of the houses, he loaded everything and went home.

A note on the kitchen table said Jen and the kids had gone to the river to bathe, since there was no water here. *A lie.* He had a brief vision of her bathing in the river with all the men around, but quickly squelched it. Surely, there would be other women there. He still didn't like it.

On some level, he accepted the fact she'd been with Sammy Boy. She never actually admitted it, but he knew. Maybe he could live with it. Maybe. What she was doing right now was the thing that churned his guts. He'd read stories about men who shared and liked to watch their wives with other men or women. He wasn't one of them.

Colt decided he could do with a cleanup himself, so he got a kettle full of water from the tank, and put it on the grill to warm. He'd have been more than happy to do that for her and the kids. It took a lot longer to heat the water then he figured it would. Remembering they should always be drinking boiled water, he made a mental note to tell Jen. It had only been a few days, but he was afraid of polluted water in the lake.

Cleaned up and shaved, he waited for his family. He'd put the pistol in the top cupboard so the kids couldn't get to it. The knife was uncomfortable stuck in his pants, even if it did have a scabbard. He set it aside also. *No wonder Ralph wasn't wearing it.*

Stepping out on the front lawn, he looked toward the camp. He could see smoke rising above the trees, he supposed from cook fires. Finally, getting close to dusk he saw them coming. It was just the three of them, with Jen carrying Annie.

She walked right by him and into the kitchen. The kids were excitedly telling him about their adventures and swimming in the lake with the other kids. They finally wound down, and he had them go sit on the sofa to read a book and rest. It took barely a minute for them to fall asleep.

Going into the kitchen, Jen handed him a bag. Inside were a couple of bloody steaks.

"They shot a cow today, so we have steak tonight."

"Let's hope the owner wasn't counting on that cow for milk." He knew it sounded petty, but couldn't help himself. "How did you happen to get the steaks? What's the going rate these days?"

She whirled around. "You have to stop with this...this obsession of yours. You're just going to make both of us crazy."

Stepping close, he reached out and lifted the bottom of her tee, and pulled it up. At the first try, she slapped his hand away. The second time, she just stared at him defiantly as she let it happen. Bite marks and bruises covered her breasts. There was a mark on her neck that hadn't been there when he left this morning. Letting the hem of the shirt fall, he just looked at her. She stared back at him and pointed to the steaks.

"Food."

Colt stepped around her and opened a couple of cabinet doors. The shelves were full.

Shaking his head, he said softly, "Food."

She looked stunned. "How...? Where?"

"The first time people ransacked the houses, they weren't very thorough."

He pointed to the grill. "There's sterile water in the pot. Use it to cook with and for the kids to drink." He closed the cupboard doors. "Do me a favor. Keep the kids out of the water. If that lake isn't polluted by now, it soon will be."

"Aren't you going to eat?" She sounded on the verge of tears. "I brought the steaks just for you."

"Just for me? Just for...? No. I'll find my food the old-fashioned way, foraging and hunting. I'm not going to live off the back of my wife."

As the late afternoon sun shining through the kitchen

highlighted her hair, he looked at her and couldn't understand what she'd become. Memories flooded his thoughts in a kaleidoscope of pictures. Life used to be so good with them. Now, there was a dead feeling in his chest and it just wouldn't go away.

"What are you doing, Jen? I thought you weren't going back to that camp. You said you'd try it my way. What happened?"

"We needed to clean up. All we have here is drinking water. Sam said we could use the same spot they do. They made kind of a beach along the river. Sam said the water is safe."

"Really? Is the bathing spot downstream from where they get their drinking water? Where do they go to the bathroom? Where does everyone upstream go to the bathroom? Do they keep cattle out of the water?"

She held both hands to the side of her head. "I don't know about all of that. They said it was safe. They wouldn't use it if it weren't safe. Surely you know that."

"So, was it just you and Sammy Boy? What about the kids?"

"I was with Sam and Amber." She was studying the patterns on the floor. "The kids just played."

"It was just you, Sam, and Amber? Where was George? How many other men were with you? How many, Jen?"

"Go to hell!"

He looked at her until she finally raised her gaze to meet his. "I'm already there."

Colt got changes of clothes for the kids, and then took water into the front room by the sofa. They were so tired they barely stirred as he washed them and changed their clothes. He hoped washing off the lake water would help but worried more about what they ingested.

For the first time, he thought of escaping the city.

―――――

LATER, he was sitting outside in a lawn chair thinking how strange the world is. Or, maybe not so strange. His yard needed mowing and weeds had overtaken the flowerbeds. The presence of man was supposed to make the world a better place. Conversely, with all the travails visited on mankind and even if most of them died, the grass and weeds would still be growing, the birds singing, and the ants kept marching on.

The sun had set and left the twilight that came just before dark. There was no breeze and he could feel sweat trickling down his neck into his shirt. As he idly swatted at a persistent mosquito, Jen brought a chair out and joined him. She'd changed into long pants and a sweatshirt.

She looked over at him a couple of times, then sighed and said, "Colt, we need to talk about this. I don't want our marriage to end this way."

He looked at her and all he saw was a stranger. "It's your dime, but it's a little late for talking, don't you think? The time for talking was before you whored yourself out to Sam."

"Look," she said, taking a deep breath. "I'm sorry I've hurt you. It was not intentional and doesn't have to be this way. I know you've heard people say it's just sex, and it *is*. For some reason it just doesn't mean anything to me. It certainly isn't like what you and I have."

"Like we have?" he interrupted. "It's more like what

we *had*. You haven't been interested in me for months, Jen."

"Alright, I'll concede that." She looked at him pleadingly and he thought she'd make a great actress. "But I still believe I haven't taken anything from you. You can have me anytime. Right now, if you want me. I'll never deny you. I miss you."

"Oh, goodie." He snorted, shaking his head. "You mean I can share you. Right? And you'll go running back tomorrow? Be still my heart. How can I not jump at that chance?"

"If you really loved me..." she started and then stopped. In the darkness, he could hear her muffled sobs. "It's not all my fault, Colt. Things just happened."

"You're not helping yourself, Jen. It's not your fault? Your choices have caused every bit of this. It looks to me as if you tripped him and hit the ground on your back before he fell."

Although it was dark, he could hear her take a couple of calming breaths. "I haven't been out in the town like you, but I hear things. Our world has gone to shit, I know that. People are dying left and right and no one has control of it. No one can stop it. Most of the time, after you'd leave, I was so scared I couldn't hold my water. You didn't know it, but I actually peed my pants a couple of times. Any loud noise would set me off.

"When I met Sam that first day," she continued. "He showed me what a man should be like."

"As opposed to me."

She continued as if he hadn't spoken. "Colt, you were a good man in a world that is gone. Things are different now. Sam is strong and smart, and takes charge of everything around him. I'm not afraid when I'm with him. He can protect the kids and me and keep us fed. You can call it survival of the fittest, or whatever you want, but Sam knows what he's doing and has planned for all of this. You never did."

"So, this is my fault? Where's your responsibility in all this? It sure didn't take you long to fall out of love, did it?" Colt said. "Why in the hell are you still here?"

"Fall out of love?" She laughed bitterly. "This isn't junior high school. Love has nothing to do with this. I'm taking the kids in the morning and going to the camp permanently. When you come to your senses, you can come and join us there. Sam said you'd be welcome. With all the food you gathered, I'm sure you can get in. Things will be better for all of us there."

He spoke into the darkness. "So, we're through? You've made up your mind?"

Her choked answer was more of a sob. "Yes."

Colt had been afraid of this from the first moment he'd seen them together. He tried to think of something else to say, something witty and profound. His mind was blank.

"I'm sorry I'm such a disappointment to you," he finally said. "I hope you get all your needs filled by Sammy Boy. Or is it the variety that's filling your needs? You have to submit to all of them, don't you? Isn't that part of the deal, everyone shares everything? How many did you have today...two, three, or from the looks of the bites and bruises...ten?"

He could hear her crying, but kept going. His bitterness was out of control. "But, if there's one shred of decency left in you, do me one favor?"

"What?" She sounded startled.

The worst part of her betrayal was the kids. She was

stealing them from him because it was too dangerous to take them with him while he foraged for food and water. He couldn't leave them by themselves. With her going to the camp, they'd have to stay with her.

"Take care of your kids," he said. "Put their needs first. Not yours or those of your new Messiah."

They sat in silence for several minutes, the peacefulness only broken by an occasional sob from Jen. He used to like their quiet times and had always loved how they didn't need to fill the void of silence with words. Finally...

"Colt, I still love you. It may not seem like it, but I do. This just seems to be the best option right now. Look, I know we haven't made love in a long time. I've been distracted...we could..."

His laugh was a bitter pill of anguish and reality. "Is that how you think everyone around you will be controlled? You're going to get skid marks on your back. I'll make a deal with you. I'll think about it just as soon as you bring me lab reports that say you're clean. Have you thought of that? The last few months and everything you're doing now is controlled by your libido. Something put you on hyper drive, and it wasn't your loving husband. Jen, the thought of all those men having you, apparently any way they want you, makes me sick. So, no we can't. Never again."

THE NEXT MORNING, he fixed the kids breakfast on the grill. He mixed pancakes and fried some Spam he'd found. They seemed to be excited about going camping, and playing with the other kids. He didn't know if he'd ever see them again, and it was tearing him apart. With tears in his eyes, he just hugged and kissed them and sent them on their way.

When they left, Jen turned and looked at him. She tried to speak a couple of times, and reached out for him once. He shrugged her away.

"I'm sorry." Her voice was barely audible.

"Sure you are."

Colt tried to think of other things. He dressed lightly, wearing the fishing vest and cargo pants. The number of pockets he could fill controlled his world. He stuffed a couple of plastic bags into his pocket, just in case he found something large. The knife went through his belt at the back, and the pistol in his front pocket. With a couple of bottles of water stashed away, he was ready to face the day. Although, he kept asking himself why bother? To what end?

He spent a couple of hours going through the rest of the homes that he hadn't been to earlier. As he searched the homes, his mind wouldn't leave Jen. Finally, he decided to go to the camp and try one more time to get her to leave. He thought the years they had together were worth at least one more try, and didn't want to give up.

Moving quickly, he walked down the deserted street to the bottom of the hill. Off toward Lake Springfield he could see the tents and campsite. Tall oak trees canopied the site, and a carpet of grass grew right down to the water. It was a good campsite. Most of the tents were the pop-up type he'd seen at Bass Pro and Walmart. He wondered how they'd fare during the frequent spring thunderstorms.

A man stepped out from a stand of trees and stopped him, holding a menacing looking rifle with a long ammunition clip on the bottom. He'd heard them called banana clips. The man looked young, alert, and competent. Colt fingered the pistol in his pocket but knew it would be no contest if he tried to use it. It was a lesson learned. A weapon you can't get to quickly is useless.

"Stop right there, mister."

Their conversation was short.

Colt said, "I need to talk to my wife."

"Your wife?" The man laughed. "There are a lot of wives down there. Not many husbands, but we do have a bunch of wives. Does this wife have a name?"

"Her name is Jennifer. She has two kids with her."

The man looked at him with what Colt thought was pity. "So, you're Jen's husband. I heard about you."

Colt mentally rolled his eyes. "So, how about letting me by?"

The guard shook his head. "I got orders from Sam to keep you out. Look," he continued in an apologetic tone, "there isn't anything for you down there. You need to understand that. Once he gets his hooks in a woman, it's all over but the shoutin'. Don't you see what's going on? That guy attracts some of the most beautiful women I've ever seen. Hell, the rest of us just hang around for the leftovers. My advice to you is to forget it and move on."

Colt was looking over the guard's shoulder when he saw Jen come out of a large tent, about fifty yards away. As he watched, Sam followed close behind her. They were both naked and, hand in hand, headed for the river where several people were playing in the water.

Glancing back toward the camp, the guard saw where Colt was looking. "See what I mean? It's too late. If we still had internet, you could find old Sam on a lot of porn sites." The man snickered. "He's quite the performer."

Colt just stared, not listening to the guard rattle on. He'd seen enough and turned to walk away. The sun was hot on his skin, but he felt cold inside.

Laughing, the guard said, "Sorry, man."

———

WALKING out of his old neighborhood, past the empty houses, he could barely recognize any of his surroundings. Once he crossed the interstate going north, people were everywhere. He couldn't understand why his little pocket of suburbia was almost deserted. Maybe Sammy Boy kept them run off.

There was a small crowd of people at the Walmart parking lot, next to an Army ambulance. Actually, it was just a green truck with a large, red cross hand painted on it. He walked over when he saw the sergeant he'd met before.

"Hey, the yuppie," the sergeant said, grinning. "You're still alive."

Colt replied, "Yeah, mostly. Sort of."

"Trouble?"

Colt shrugged. "You could say that, but not like you think. I used to have a wife and kids. She took the kids and ran off to join that hippie commune down on the lake run by some porn star guru. I guess she thought they'd meet her needs better—toss her salad better or butter her biscuits inside and out—hell, I don't know. So, I guess it's just another day at the office with me sucking hind tit and wondering what happened."

A couple of people were shooed out of the back of the ambulance, followed by a small woman in a print dress. Maybe she was a nurse, or something. She could have been a general for all he knew. A very small and beautiful general.

She looked him up and down. "Well, you look healthy enough. Do you need help?"

The sergeant laughed and said, "Beth, this is..."

"Colt Blaine," he answered for him.

"...and Colt, this is my sister, Beth Wilson. She used to raise organic veggies and crap like that. For some dumbassed reason, when this little crisis started, I thought she'd be safer here in town with me."

Beth laughed softly. "Yeah, that was *not* one of your better decisions. When everyone is trying to get out of town, I'm coming in." She turned back to Colt. "Mostly Arnie is protecting me from meth heads and other addicts that think the red cross on the truck means an unlimited supply of drugs. We don't have any, but they don't know that. We're just trying to help people and we're about tapped out of supplies."

Glancing at her brother, she said, "And I'm not really a nurse. I did a little training before I took up farming."

She continued. "Arnie, I think we're about done here. We can move on anytime."

She spoke to Colt. "We're just going from parking lot to parking lot to see if we can help anyone. Once people know we don't have food, they just move on and we don't get much business."

"Isn't Cox Hospital just down the road?"

"Yeah, good luck with that. The last we heard, there were thousands of people surrounding the hospital—all waiting for care."

BETH WAS HAVING one of those moments she'd read about in one of her 'bodice buster' romance novels and one girlfriend had actually given her a true-life account. It was one of those instant palpitation, queasy feeling, nipple hardening and wet panty moments—and from what she'd just heard him tell her brother, he was married. *Sort of.* In her mind, she was already writing on the back of her Big Chief tablet, Beth Blaine, Beth Blaine —all in flowing cursive with little hearts over the 'i', just like in high school.

As they talked, she looked him over. He was tall and thin, and moved with a dancer's grace. Still young enough to hold a boyish charm, but the sadness in his eyes put age on him. She liked the way he looked right at someone when he spoke. No looking down, up in the clouds, or the worst, looking right past you like something more interesting was coming up from behind.

She was also afraid because this feeling hadn't hit her, *and hit her hard*, even with her ex-husband. It was nice in one way and scary in another. And it was bad, really bad timing.

Beth shook her head as her mind picked up the thread of conversation.

"I'm just moving around in this small area of the city, and don't see much beyond the end of my nose," Colt said. "What does it look like everywhere else? What's going on? Are things any better than the other day when we talked?"

Beth looked sideways at her brother, who shrugged at her, grinning at her discomfort.

"Go ahead," he said. "If you can speak."

Looking askance at her brother, she spoke to Colt. "As I'm sure you know, the gas shortage really hit the

Midwest hard. With no gas, transportation came to a standstill. With no trucks running, there's no food delivered. The city is breaking down. There are riots everywhere. The hospitals are jammed and there's no end in sight."

She grinned at him. "Does that make you ready to run away yet?"

"Not quite yet," Colt replied. "I may be stupid on a lot of levels, especially where my wife is concerned, but I'm not a coward."

She reached out and touched his arm for no other reason than she wanted to. "It sounds to me like you'd better look for greener pastures."

"Yeah, I think dummy is tattooed on my forehead. So," he continued, "is any help available from the government? National Guard? Locals?"

"Not a chance. And from what Arnie has heard, this situation is being repeated everywhere. It's the same situation all over the Midwest. I know a guy that's a ham radio operator. He runs the radio on a generator and windmill for power. According to him, it's like this all over the United States. That is why the government diverted all electricity and fuel to the East Coast. And..." She pointed north, over her shoulder. "See that big column of smoke? They're burning bodies, Colt. Thousands of bodies. That is the other shoe about to drop— sickness and disease. I'm afraid we're in for a really bad time."

"Wow," he said. "Can it get any worse than this?"

Beth looked at her brother, and Arnie said, "A thousand times worse, Colt. The last we heard, Homeland Security is stepping in. They didn't buy those millions of rounds of ammunition for nothing, and where they got the troops, I don't know, but they're definitely here."

"What do they think they can accomplish? What do they want?" Colt asked.

"Control," she said. "It's all about control and who can be the big dog."

Colt looked at her with compassion. He thought his problems were bad. "Why are you still trying? Do you still think you can make a difference?"

She shrugged. "I don't know. Probably not, but we have to try. That's kind of stupid, huh?"

"Well," he said. "I don't have any room to criticize, or call anyone stupid. My wife just hung horns on me for not taking care of her properly, and *left* with the big dog."

For some reason, he felt compelled to tell her the story. It didn't take long. When he was through, she gave him a sad smile. "I heard part of this when you were talking to Arnie. My quickie assessment is that you aren't at fault. In fact, I'd bet she's done this to you before. I don't know anything about your marriage, of course. But I'm thinking you value your wedding vows a lot more than she ever did, especially with her throwing you aside so quickly. That was really cold. You don't even know if this is the first time she and this Sam guy met.

"Isn't hindsight great." She chuckled and then turned serious again as if remembering something personal. "All the signs you miss when you're married and trusting like your spouse being a little too touchy feely, or standing so close to someone when they move they have to rub against her—just an innocent bumping...it seems so clear now, when it's too late."

She abruptly changed the subject. "I see you're carrying water bottles. Sterile, I hope?"

He nodded. "I boil all the water I drink or cook with. Read it in a book."

"Well," she said. "Keep reading. Where are you getting your water? I've heard of people being killed for a bottle of water."

Colt smiled. "It was the same article from a prepper website. For now, I find water in toilet tanks and hot water heaters. Most of the houses around me, and all of them on my street, are abandoned. I go on water raids with a bucket and a garden hose. And a pipe wrench."

"What about that commune where your children are? Did you see any of their sanitation efforts?"

"No, the guard wouldn't let me into the camp, but I'm betting they don't have any. I don't know what kind of rifle he had, but it had one of those long clips for ammo. You could get in easy, Beth. But I don't recommend the experience. You're just what they want, young and beautiful. Unfortunately, I think the sergeant or me would have to shoot our way in. It's kind of a closed camp, and I don't think your brother or I have the proper entry fee."

Arnie laughed. "I think you just got a compliment, Beth."

They talked a few more minutes, and then some women started showing up with children in tow, looking for help. The kids were bloody from cuts and abrasions. In one case, there was a broken arm.

Beth turned and spoke to him. "I'd like to talk to you again. Is there any chance of that?"

He gave her a long look. She was nice looking, and there was something about her...

"This is my first stop every morning, when I can make it. I'd like that, too."

Colt waved to Beth and her brother, and then hustled

on toward the rest of the mall, pushing through people who were just standing around and talking. He needed better shoes, and cargo shorts were on his shopping list. And maybe a ball cap or floppy bush hat to keep off the sun. As much as he disliked crowds, it was pushing toward May and warming up.

———————

COMING out of Kohl's Department Store, he squinted against the sun's brightness. It had been nearly dark in the store, and it took a moment for his eyes to adjust. He was surprised at how many people were in the store and that they were all silent. No one spoke a word. The only light came from flashlights or penlights. Luckily, he had one. All the jewelry counters were smashed. The whole area that kept watches, rings, and other valuable items was trashed. No one was hoarding clothes yet, that would come later, so he and the other shoppers could move about in peace. Once in a while he'd hear a scuffle and shouting in other parts of the store, but most of the time it was eerily quiet. As a true male shopper, he grabbed what he needed and left.

Outside, there were people everywhere, just shuffling around, not really doing anything or going anywhere. He thought it was creepy, and way past strange. Maybe the precursor to actual zombie-like behavior?

Three men weren't moving and the crowd of people went around them like water flowing around a large rock in a river. The men just stared at him and waited. He looked left and right, and then back at the three men. *What the hell?*

Out of all these people, he guessed over a thousand,

how did they find him? *Why* did they want to find him? Colt, his hands full, immediately cut left and tried to lose himself in the suddenly thinning crowd. People were developing an instinct for trouble because they were rapidly moving away from him.

They were right behind him, so he stopped and turned. He thought the men would look more at home as triplets in a muscle beach movie.

"Can I help you boys?" Colt asked.

The man in the middle stepped forward, away from the identical bookends. "We have a message from Sam."

Concerned and thinking of his kids, Colt stepped forward to meet him. "Why? Has something happened?"

The man swung at him, and Colt partially deflected the blow with the clothes he was holding in his hands.

All three men were on him quickly, and knocked him to the ground. He had that brassy taste in his mouth and knew he was bleeding. Colt got in a few punches, but they were ineffective. One satisfying punch caught a man in the throat and put him out of commission for a moment. Rolling and kicking, he felt his ribs give from a boot, and then a blow to the head left him groggy. One of the men on top of him discovered the knife.

"Well, lookie here." The man, breathing hard from the scuffle, held up the hunting knife for his friends to see. "This is a nice knife. Maybe we should cut him up a little with it. I don't think Sam would mind." He turned back to Colt, brandishing the knife. "If we please Sam enough, maybe he'll give us a turn at his new woman before she gets wore out."

Anger surged through Colt and he arched his back and kicked until the laughing man was off him. He reached into his pocket and pulled out the handgun.

The man backed away a few feet, no longer laughing, while Colt fumbled with the gun. Finally, he pointed it at the man who'd been on top of him. He didn't think about it, just pulled the trigger. Nothing happened.

"Aw, look. The wimp doesn't even know how to use his little popgun," the man said. "I always wanted one of those." Grinning, the three men advanced toward him again.

Colt remembered what Sergeant Wilson had shown him, thumbed down the safety, and fired. He just pointed, like pointing his finger, and the bullet hit the man in the center of his chest. The hole going in was innocent looking, but both men took blood spray from the exit wound. The wounded man slowly sank to his knees, holding his chest with blood seeping between his fingers.

He said weakly, "We were just gonna rough you up some. We weren't..."

Colt watched the lights go out, the man's expression relaxed and he was dead before his head hit the pavement.

He pointed the gun at the others, having no illusions at his marksmanship. He'd rather be lucky than good any day of the week, and he'd just been lucky.

Colt paused to spit out some blood from his cut lip. "You tell Sam, to come himself next time."

The men disappeared and he kneeled in his own blood. He shook his head trying to clear it, but that just made him dizzier. Colt groped around, looking for the clothes he got from the store.

A hand on his shoulder startled him. Looking up, he saw Beth.

"What happened to you?" she panted, holding her side. Clearly, she'd been running.

He sat on the pavement and wiped his bloody mouth with the back of his hand. "The brainiac over there, and his two friends, tried to beat the crap out of me. Then, they were having so much fun doing that, I think they decided to kill me."

"It looks like they were doing a bang-up job of it, too," she said as she looked him over.

He grimaced, and then replied defensively, "Yeah, well...there *were* three of them. One of them found my knife and tried to work himself up to cutting me. I finally got my hands on the pistol. The results are over there."

"We heard the shot. Are you all right? You don't look very good."

Colt struggled to his feet with her help. "Yeah, I'm just bruised up some." He winced. "They may have cracked a rib or two for me. Plus, I'm seeing two of you, but that's a good thing."

Sergeant Wilson came up with the truck. People immediately surrounded it. He shoved and pushed his way to the body, then came over to them. "So, it *was* you. We heard the shot, and that sister of mine took off like a bat out of hell, yelling, 'Colt.' You must have made quite an impression on her. She ran all the way here before I could get the truck going."

Beth started to turn red. "That's enough, Arnie. Is there enough fuel left in that truck to get this man back to his home?"

"Just barely, but we can do it."

"Forget it," Colt said, holding up his hand. "You need the fuel more than I do."

He stood a moment while Beth jumped into the truck

and came back with some bandages, gauze, and tape. He felt like a sideshow with the crowd just standing and staring at them.

"Take these," she said. "When you get a chance, clean up with boiled water." She put her hand on his side, and he winced. Keeping her hand there and probing gently, she looked up at him. "You have a nice body for a computer geek."

"Really? It's my new diet." Despite the pain he was in, he smiled at her.

She became flustered and took her hand away. "Sorry, I shouldn't have said that. I mean...being in shape probably kept you from being injured worse. I don't think anything is broken, but what the hell do I know? I just sell herbs."

"Beth, how long can you and Arnie hold out, trying to help people?"

She gave her brother a questioning look.

The sergeant said, "Beth and I are okay, at least for now. However, when command fell apart, the soldiers scattered. Most were National Guard anyway and had homes to protect, but our unit stayed together. For now, we have better guns than everyone else has and know how to use them. But that is changing fast. Most of the fighting is on the north side of town, for now. The armory has been overrun and weapons taken. The gangs and mobs on the street have the good stuff now. For us, personally, our big question is whether to go or stay."

"Where would you go?" Colt asked.

"Her farm is north of here, close to a little town called Everton. She really put a lot of work into it and is self-sustainable. Several small farms in the area formed a network. They trade work and goods, back and forth between them.

"The problem, at least for now," he continued, "is that everyone is trying to leave the city. A good number, and I mean thousands, are going north toward the lakes. They'll run right over her farm and anyone that is there."

Colt looked at her. "Do you have anyone waiting for you there?"

She looked at him, knowing what he meant. "Nope, it's just a one-woman operation. My husband ran off a few years ago. I think the work on a farm was too hard for him. Some gal swished her skirt at him, and poof...he was gone. No kids, thank God. I can't imagine the worry you must have about yours."

Colt was gathering up his gear. "Actually, it's Jen's running off that hurts. The kids have other children to play with, and for now, I think they're just as well off in the commune as they'd be with me."

Shaking her head, she said, "I hope you're right, but I don't think so."

Gunfire coming from the direction of the Walmart parking lot east of them interrupted any more conversation. There was a pause in the firing, and then the deep-throated sound of a machine gun started.

Arnie yelled, "That's our men on the .50 cal," and jumped into the truck. "Beth, are you staying or coming along?"

Beth lingered for just a moment, and Colt could see the indecision in her expression.

"I have to go with my brother. I wish..." She took a big breath. "You take care, Colt. Good luck and I hope to see you again." Her hand on his arm gripped him tightly.

She leaned into him and gave him a quick peck on the cheek, and then she followed her brother.

——————

IT TOOK him two hours to make the trip home. He stopped often to spit blood, or to pause and let the spasms in his side let up. His water bottles were empty by the time he was halfway home. Finally, getting toward dusk, he stumbled up to his house. The front door was hanging on one hinge.

Pulling the pistol from his pocket and making sure the safety was off, he set his possessions down and entered the house. It was a mess. Empty drawers were mute evidence of their search for anything useful. The kitchen was empty of any food and all his extra water bottles were gone.

Colt painfully eased himself into a straight-backed chair. He didn't think he could take the sofa. It was too soft. Sitting in it would be easy, but getting up would be nearly impossible.

Taking a deep breath, he looked around. This was not a random raid by foragers. Jen had to have told them about his food stash. Sam's men had taken everything he might use for survival. Considering the attack on him, he was surprised the house was still standing. Thinking about it, he figured if you burn one house, it starts another going, then the woods catch on fire, and then the tents go...and so on. He shook his head. It was time to go to the KISS method—keep it simple stupid. Otherwise, there were too many complications.

Too tired to do anything else, he finally went to the sofa, and used it as a crutch to help him kneel on the floor. He fished out a water bottle from his vest and then remembered they were all empty. Tomorrow he'd find water. Tomorrow he'd find food. Today, he placed the pistol on the cushion beside him, stretched out on the floor, and slept.

The next morning, he could hardly move. When he tried to sit up, the pain in his side was excruciating. Slowly, he rolled to his stomach, then using the couch as a crutch again, he was able to gain his feet. The pain in his side was not sharp and piercing, so he thought Beth's prediction of no broken ribs was probably correct, but this pain was bad enough. Walking gingerly, he moved into the house next door and ate one of the MREs he'd stashed there, along with a couple of water bottles. It hurt to breathe.

For three days, he took it easy and rested. He was grateful once again for the food Beth's brother had given him. Without that, he didn't know how he'd have made it. When he looked outside, no one was around. The heat in the house was stifling, but he ignored it. The pain in his ribs eased, and his lip healed. On the fourth day, Jen showed up at the house with the children.

SIX

AS HE WATCHED her come up the walk to the house, it occurred to him that someone had to be watching him. She didn't try to approach their old home, but came immediately to the one he'd moved into four days ago. And she turned up the sidewalk with no hesitation.

Jen was carrying Annie and holding Timmy by his hand. They were wearing the same clothes they had on when he left. She saw him standing at the open door and brought the kids to him. He kneeled and hugged them. One look told him they were sick. Their eyes were sunken and had dark circles around them. They were list-less and didn't seem to have any interest in anything around them. Neither of the children said a word.

According to Jen, Timmy and Annie had been like this for two days. What started as a mild cough had turned into full-blown wheezing. After sharing that little information, Jen just turned and left.

"Wait, Jen."

She stopped and turned toward him. "What?"

He couldn't believe how empty she looked. Obviously, her new life was taking a toll. Her hair was hanging loose, not in the usual ponytail, and it didn't look like she was using the communal bathing facilities. He could smell her, and there was no breeze.

"All these houses have been stripped, and our kids need medicine like cough syrup or decongestants. Are there any at the camp?"

Jen looked at him a long moment, her expression never changing. "Are you serious? Let's see...cough syrup is a good part alcohol, and they use decongestants to make meth. What do you think?"

"Why did you bring the kids here? I thought they were better off at the camp?"

He could see Jen was struggling to make her mind work. Finally... "There's a woman there who used to be a nurse. She said the kids just need rest and won't get it around the other children—they're always trying to play."

"I thought it was too dangerous to live here, that's why you went to the commune. Why bring them back now?"

After giving him a baleful stare, she turned and left.

The first thing he did was raise their shirts and put his ear to their chests. He could hear fluttering and wheezing. Remembering his parents used a vaporizer, charging the air with humidity when he was a child and had a bad cold, Colt got a tarp and draped it over the couch, making a tent. He carried heated water into the enclosure, hoping the steam would help clear their lungs and help them breathe. After watching and listening to them, he thought it gave them some relief, so he kept heating the same water repeatedly for steam and hot cloths to put on their chests. Carrying the water hurt his side, but he got used to it. When the water had cooled, he'd take it back to the grill and bring back the one that was boiling. He ran out of propane the first day.

He'd been awake with the kids for two days straight when Jen came back again. She stumbled through the door and saw the tent with the kids sleeping in it. Her eyes were bloodshot and watery. "What the hell's that thing? And, what's the matter with the kids?"

He just glanced at her, and then continued bathing them with a wet cloth. Since both had a fever, he thought the water would help cool them. "Not that you care, but they're sick. They're worse than when you brought them. The kids hardly move and won't take food, although Timmy seems to be a little stronger. I'm really worried about them, Jen."

She walked over and looked at them, then kneeled and held her hand to their foreheads. "No fever," she said as she stood.

Colt held up a thermometer showing a hundred and two degrees.

Jen ignored him. "Lots of kids are sick at the camp. They'll get over it."

"Have you returned for good from the camp? Or do you have more whoring to do?" Colt couldn't manage to put anger in his voice, he was just too tired.

He could see something close to pity in her expression as she looked at him. "The camp has a lot of visitors right now. There's a big meeting with Homeland Security types. Man, those people have everything. Anyway, it's been going on for a couple of days, and I'm worn out." She tossed something onto the sofa. "I brought bread."

"How many men did you have to service for that?"

She replied tiredly, "Go to hell, Colt. You're a broken record. I'll sleep upstairs."

––––––––––

THAT NIGHT the diarrhea and vomiting started. It was so violent he finally stripped them and put both of them in the tub so he could keep cleaning them up. When they were naked, they shivered from being cold. Once, he yelled for Jen to come and help, but she never woke. He finally just wrapped them in blankets. There were plenty of those. The cycle just never stopped, and he couldn't believe there was any fluid left in their bodies. The stench was terrible, and he was afraid. They were so weak and listless they couldn't stand.

At daybreak, he woke Jen up. "We have to take them to the hospital."

She sat up, groggy and disoriented. "What? Why? Why do you think there are doctors there?"

Colt snapped at her. "We have to try something. Just look at them. They're dying, Jen—our kids are dying, and I can't do anything for them."

She looked at him. "How do we get them there?"

"We walk, Jen. We walk, and we carry them. Now."

They wrapped their babies in light blankets and started walking. The viscous liquid from vomiting and diarrhea covered both adults before they walked a mile. Colt kept trying to get the kids to take water, but they wouldn't swallow. It was a blessing and a curse. He didn't think they were even awake.

They walked down the middle of James River Free-way, winding between stalled cars and trucks, to the turnoff for Cox South. There were people everywhere, and it was hot. He had the fleeting thought that he was not sweating enough but knew he'd had precious little water. All the roads and parking lots were full of people. It took them another hour of pushing and shoving to get close to the entrance to the hospital. It was jammed with people. The crowd was just standing as if waiting for something.

Exhaustion took its toll, and they sat down, resting on the grass median. They weren't even close to the door of the emergency room.

"Colt?"

After glancing at Jen and seeing she didn't speak, he looked up and saw Beth. She was hollow-eyed, her clothes covered in blood. He hoped it wasn't hers.

When he didn't respond, she seemed to take in the situation. "They're sick? Vomiting? Diarrhea?"

He looked at her in exhaustion. "Yeah, all of that. Beth, they're so weak. I can't wake them up."

Beth looked at Annie first. He saw her shoulders slump, and then she gently took her away from Jen, who was staring off into the distance, and laid Annie on the grass. She covered her up completely with her soiled blanket.

"She's gone, Colt. I'm so sorry."

Colt didn't know what to think or feel. Deep down he'd known it, but now he was just numb. Reaching over, he pulled the blanket from her face. At least she didn't look like she was in pain anymore. She looked asleep. Colt turned away and sobbed, and then pulled Timmy tighter to his chest.

"It's okay, Daddy."

Startled, he looked at his son. Colt hadn't heard

Timmy speak since Jen had brought him home. "What do you mean, son? How do you feel?"

He felt Timmy's hand on his face, wiping away tears. Timmy's voice was so weak Colt could barely hear him. "It's okay. We don't hurt anymore. Just let me go, Daddy. Annie is waiting for me. She said she loves you."

Timmy pointed. "She's right over there. Annie is waiting for me."

"Oh, no..." Colt choked out, shaking his head.

He glanced at Beth when he heard her sob. Tears were rolling freely down her face, and she held her fist to her mouth, shaking her head at him. "Hold him. Just love him and hold him tight."

"Daddy." Timmy's voice was weak. "I *have* to take care of her. You always told me that. Take care of my sister. Please, I have to go."

By the time Timmy had finished speaking, his voice was barely a whisper.

Colt looked around, desperate for some kind of help. They sat among thousands. Everyone had their own dead and dying to worry about. No one even looked at them. He held Timmy to his chest. "Oh, god. I'm so sorry."

Beth was openly crying now, just nodding to give him encouragement.

"It's okay, Timmy. Go to your sister and take care of her. You're the best son a man could ever have. This is all my fault. Your father failed you. Wait for me on the other side, Timmy. I'll be along."

He sobbed uncontrollably for what seemed like hours until he realized Timmy's body was limp. He was gone.

Beth took Timmy from his arms and laid him by his sister. She stood next to Colt for a moment.

He glanced up and noticed Jen standing there. *No*

tears. No expression. No life. "Jennifer, get the hell out of here. I don't want to see you again. Not ever. Go back and be Sam's whore."

Jen didn't say a word for a moment. Then after a couple of tries, she said, "I always loved you. The rest didn't matter."

"It mattered to me."

He watched her as she stood with her eyes tightly shut for a moment, and then she turned and walked away.

Colt got up and started after her, but Beth stopped him.

"She's already dead, Colt. Who knows what drugs they gave her, but she has to go back for it. She's gone, and she knows it. From what you've told me, she made her bed, and now she must sleep in it. You can't help her."

Numbly, Colt looked at his children lying wrapped in their blankets beside the road. Searching for the right words to say, he couldn't find them. He felt like crying, but no tears would come.

Oddly, Timmy's last words just before he died comforted him. He'd seen his sister standing just "over there" waiting for him.

"I wish I could have done better for you. I wish..." He stopped a moment and then drew strength from Beth's grip on his arm.

"Goodbye."

It was all he had left.

———

COLT WAS SITTING on the curb next to the bodies of his children. Beth was sitting next to him, leaning her head on his shoulder.

"I should bury them." His voice was hoarse, devoid of emotion. "Maybe have some kind of service?"

Beth sighed and then pointed up the road.

He could see men pulling handcarts, and they were collecting bodies as they came toward them. It reminded him of paintings and descriptions he'd seen of the black plague in the Dark Ages. As the men neared, he started to shake, reaching out to their bodies.

Then Beth's voice stopped him. "I wish I could sing."

It was such an off-the-wall comment that it caused him to stop, and he turned to her. "What? Why?"

She shrugged. "There's a beautiful poem that was made into a song. '*Do not stand at my grave and weep. I am not there. I do not sleep,*'" she quoted. "Remember Timmy saying he could see his sister and wanted to go to her?"

When Colt nodded, she continued. "These are just bodies here. Timmy and Annie are through with them and don't need them anymore. They don't mean anything. Just let them go."

He opened his mouth to speak, but she interrupted, placing a finger on his lips.

"Let them go."

Two men walked up to them, and one said, "I'm sorry, but we have to take these bodies."

Colt just waved them forward because he couldn't speak. In minutes, his children's bodies were gone, lying among the other victims of this mindless tragedy.

Coming out of his daze, he turned to Beth. "I'm sorry.

I've been lost in my own problems. Why are you here? Where's your brother?"

She shrugged and swallowed a couple of times before she could speak.

"Remember the gunfire we heard? It was Arnie's men, just as he thought. Some gang wanted the unit's weapons and food. When they didn't give them up, there was a firefight. They killed Arnie when he tried to help. They nearly caught me, but I took off running and got lost in the crowd. The strange thing was that there were men in black uniforms with the gangs. I think it was Homeland Security."

"That is weird. I'm sorry about Arnie. How did you get so bloody?"

"I went back after the gang left the parking lot and tried to help the guys. Some were still alive"—Colt reached out to her as she finished—"and torn up so bad. They didn't just shoot them. It was hand-to-hand, and the gangs used bayonets or something like that. Arnie..."

Beth took a deep breath. "I've been here since then just trying to help, five days of this hell. Sometimes I think I'm ready to die."

Colt pulled her to him and held her while she cried. Both had lost so much. Holding each other, they didn't notice the time until he realized it was almost dark.

The crowd around them had grown, and the moaning and crying from the sick and wounded sounded like wind through the trees at night. It was a Halloween nightmare come true.

Snatches of conversation came to him. "St. John's Mercy on fire. Fighting along I-44 interstate. Bloodbath. Army units from Fort Leonard Wood fleeing ahead of hordes of people from St. Louis."

It was full dark now, and holding Beth to him, he stood and faced the north. As if to put an exclamation point on the situation, the sky was lit up with explosions and flashes of light. In the past, Colt had seen news clips of night fighting in cities on the other side of the globe, and this looked just like it. It hardly seemed real until the breeze carried the acrid smell of burning buildings to them and the force of far-off explosions feeling like a gentle push against his face.

Beth finally confirmed what he'd suspected. "Look at those streaks of light. That is rocket fire, Colt. See, it's going from the air to the ground. Arnie said the National Guard had fallen apart, but those are gunships over there. I wonder who's flying them."

The only thing Colt could think of was where did they get the gas?

It seemed all the people around them had turned and was watching the battle, much as if they'd have watched a show on television or a video game.

She started tugging on his arm. "We gotta go, Colt. Let's go now, right now. People will be running from that fight. And if this is the only hospital left, they'll be running toward us."

He was still in a daze. "But there's no help here."

"They don't know that. All they know is they're hurt and scared. When people see the other hospitals are destroyed and they hear this one is still standing, they'll be coming, Colt. It will be like a cattle stampede because those people will be frightened out of their minds."

Beth continued softly. "And the Army will be coming."

"What?" He could barely see her in the gloom.

"If the Army or Homeland Security is firing on civilians now, they won't be able to tell the good guys from the bad. We're just ants, and in the way. Even worse, will be if Homeland Security is fighting everyone, *including* the guard units."

"But we haven't done anything wrong."

"It won't matter."

With just enough moonlight to see, they walked hand in hand so they wouldn't become separated, picking their way through the crowd and back down the on-ramp to James River Freeway. Colt knew there was no way they could get back to his neighborhood, especially in the dark. He took them off the road into the ditch. There was a space where a concrete drain cut into the embankment. He hoped it would offer shelter.

Using one of his barbecue propane lighters, he held it up and clicked it on. Several faces looked back at him. Frightened voices called out, "Turn that damned thing off. Turn it off."

"Sorry," Colt called, turning off the lighter. "We're friendly, just looking for a place to rest."

A voice whispered, "Shut up. We're hiding from the gangs. They're everywhere around here."

COLT SLEPT with Beth leaning on his shoulder. It was wet and muddy in the bottom of the culvert, and neither of them smelled the best, but at least they had some cover. The night was cool, and they cuddled together, sharing warmth.

It felt like he'd just closed his eyes when she elbowed him awake. At the other end of the culvert, he saw beams from flashlights waving in the air. The light came to rest on the people staring out from the concrete drain. Colt pushed Beth down on the concrete and into the mud. People were shouting at each other. He heard a man from outside yelling something about women.

Suddenly, the other end became a melee of fighting. A girl screamed as someone grabbed her, and Colt saw a man leap up to defend her. A rifle burst cut the would-be protector down. The bullets passed through the man and ricocheted through the tunnel, chipping concrete on the way out. More men poured into the tunnel from the other end, intent on capturing the women. The sounds of screaming, yelling, and an occasional gunshot rose to a crescendo, the noise intensified by the concrete tunnel.

Colt crawled toward the entrance closest to them, dragging a kicking Beth with him by the collar and part of her hair. She silently fought him as hard as she could. He got her outside and then pulled her into the darkness of the drainage ditch, finally having to pick her up and carry her. After they'd gone fifty yards or so, he stopped and put her down.

"You could have helped them," she hissed into his ear. "Those girls were being raped, Colt. Raped! Doesn't that mean anything to you?"

He whispered back, "We have our own set of problems, and I have my own woman to protect."

"But you have a pistol. You could have used it."

"You're right. I could have expended the few shots I have left and maybe chased off those guys with assault rifles, provided I could hit anything shooting in the dark, and provided I didn't hit the ones we wanted to protect, and providing their return fire didn't kill us." He grabbed her shoulders, locked his arms around her, and forcibly turned her around to face the other direction. "What about them?" He moved her again. "And those people over there?"

They could see several groups moving up and down the highway. They all seemed to have robbed every store in town of their high-beam flashlights and lanterns. The different groups made the sky look like a laser light show at a concert. Every time the gangs stopped, they could hear screaming and shouting. Gunshots usually followed, supplying more flashes of light. Looking across the road, they could see lights and hear screaming from the direction of the hospital. To Colt, it looked like wolves moving among sheep, picking and choosing their victims at their leisure. They heard a booming explosion, looked up and saw the helicopters were getting closer.

Colt was holding Beth tightly as they took all this in. Finally, she stopped struggling, relaxed, and leaned back against him. "I'm okay now. Really, I understand what you did."

He started to move his arms, but she tightened her grip on him.

"Just hold me," she said. "God, I'm so scared. I've never seen such a nightmare. Why are they attacking women?"

"I'm no expert, but I think it's because they can. Plus, they can keep them as captives for barter and their own use. I guess people can be as good or bad as they have the strength to be. There's no law now, and no one to stop them. It's like a mass hysteria that makes them want to inflict as much terror on people as they can before they have to face it themselves."

He could feel her chest rising and falling against his arms. Her breathing finally slowed to a normal level.

"Your woman, huh?" she continued. "You move fast."

Lowering his face into her hair, he said, "I didn't mean to presume..."

"It's alright. I understand our emotions are kind of suspect right now."

"No promises, Beth. Like an old country song says, there's no time for lengthy speeches."

She started to reply, but he squeezed her tightly with his hand over her mouth. This time she trusted him and didn't fight. In a moment, they could hear the shuffling of feet as several people snuck by them. He could hear muffled crying and whispering. In a couple of minutes, they were gone.

Beth continued, ignoring the interruption. "So, what do we do now?"

Colt shook his head and then realized she couldn't see him. "We hide until morning. Then, we try and get back to my neighborhood. If it looks safe there, we can resupply. I hid some food and supplies in different places. Maybe no one has found them. Then I need to see a man."

She picked up on his thoughts immediately. "Revenge? On this Sam character? Is it worth it?"

"I don't know," he said. "I'll have to try it and see how it feels."

He could vaguely see twin columns of limestone in front of them. Water runoff had cut the soil from between the stones to leave a small nook behind one of the rocks. Nearly in plain sight, but hidden. It would be good enough. It had to be.

The long night had begun.

SEVEN

THEY BOTH FLINCHED as thunder jolted them from a restless sleep. Colt stood and stretched as the first huge drops of rain started falling like soft hail. He pulled Beth to her feet. Groggily, she looked around and tried to brush off the dirt from her clothes.

"Next time, I pick the hotel," she grumbled.

Thunder rumbled again, and the rain came down in a solid sheet. Running water covered their feet. Colt looked up and pointed to the drainpipe that came off the hill above.

"That pipe must drain all those parking areas above us. We're going to be neck deep in water if we don't move soon."

They moved away from the small flash flood coming off the hill above them and moved toward the highway. Every tree, overpass, and building had people seeking shelter. Looking around, he realized all the people he could see were the sheep. The wolves had left, at least for now.

He could see people rushing toward cars and trucks for the protection they'd afford, and wished he'd thought of that last night. What he couldn't understand is why people didn't just go home. He must have vocalized that thought.

"They left home because there's no hope," Beth said.

"Like there's a lot of hope here?" Colt's voice was bitter as he looked around them.

They started walking back down the highway toward his house. "One good thing about all this rain," he said. "We won't have to wash our clothes."

The culvert they vacated the night before was starting to fill with water. As it did, the rushing water started pushing out bodies. Beth started cursing under her breath, and they kept walking.

The last bodies that washed out were three teenage girls. They were naked except for socks and torn underwear. Beth stopped and then leaned against Colt. He thought she was shivering from the cold rain and automatically put his arm around her. He pulled her tighter when he realized she was crying.

She spoke softly to him. "You know those old Western movies where the settlers are attacked? If all was lost, the women always saved a last bullet for themselves?" She pulled away and looked at him. "You do that for me, Colt."

"Beth..."

She shook his arm, her hand clenched painfully into the muscle, and said forcefully, "Promise me."

He nodded. Her gray-blue eyes stared up at him with an intensity he'd not often seen in anyone. Her clothes, plastered to her body, revealed curves he hadn't noticed before. Reaching out and smoothing her rain-slick hair back from her forehead, he said, "If I can."

———

THIS TIME he didn't enter his old neighborhood by walking boldly, and foolishly, down the street. He kept Beth behind him so she could warn him of impending trouble as he went house to house, making sure each place was empty before proceeding. They spent close to an hour doing this before arriving at his old home.

There were more signs of vandalism. He stood in the front room, hands on his hips as he looked around. Beth found a chair that was unbroken and sat down.

"What's the matter?" she asked quietly.

"Something isn't the same," he said.

"Yeah, this place has been trashed." She shook her head. "Somebody sure didn't want you to keep anything useful, which is stupid because I'm sure most houses have the same stuff."

Finally, he saw it. "Well, I'll be damned."

He stood looking at a shelf that miraculously still had framed pictures on it. One was missing. It was a picture of Timmy and Annie taken a few months ago, back when there was still ink and paper for the printer.

"I didn't think she cared," he said wonderingly.

Beth stood and came to him. "What is it?"

"Jen has been here. A picture of the kids is missing. It figures since it was the last one we took, and I wanted it."

"Your best pictures are in your mind, Colt. Your best memories are in your heart. That's where I keep Arnie."

He nodded. "I know, and you're right. But still..." His thoughts were on his children, hearing their voices, seeing their faces before they were sick. Willfully holding back tears, he shook from the effort. Somehow, Beth was holding him.

"Look, Colt. I know everything seems to be happening too fast to comprehend. At 'warp speed' to coin a phrase, but you have to let them go, and you have to let Jen go. You saw her, and you saw the way she was and know what she did and how she treated you."

"It's hard to do...to just turn your feelings off."

"Well, in Jen's case, I think you have to," she said softly. "From a woman's perspective, you know she's done it before. Being unfaithful, I mean. You don't just do what she did in a day or two, I don't care how scared you are. Did you see any women go rushing out to the gangs trying to trade favors last night? That's not a normal reaction, and for your information, it's beyond my comprehension, too. You don't throw away a marriage that quickly unless it's already gone. She's cheated on you before this, right?"

He thought of George and Amber, remembering how Jen had acted with both of them. When you ignore something bad long enough, you start believing your own lie, or in this case, your own denial.

Colt moved to a front window. He looked at her and nodded once. "Let's go."

"No discussion? Disagreement? Brilliant repartee?"

"No time. No words. Too tired."

She stood with her mouth open. "Wow. That's actually a pretty good comeback."

Ten minutes later, they were three houses down and across the street from his place. They quietly entered the split-level home and made their way toward the garage. Like all the homes, looters had ransacked this one. Not looters, he corrected himself. Foragers. He needed a new vocabulary, a new way of thinking. He led Beth into the darkened two-car garage. Twin beams of sunlight came in through the windows in the garage doors. He looked around a moment and then stood still. When he couldn't hear anything but Beth's breathing, he went to an old junker of a car that sat on blocks. He supposed the owner had been restoring the old car. *Back in better times.* He reached in through the open window and pulled the hood latch. Going around to the front, he tripped the safety catch and propped the lid open.

"See? Dinner is served." He'd stashed a half dozen MREs around the engine block. Colt gathered these and quietly put the hood down.

"Water?" she asked skeptically.

On a shelf was a coiled-up garden hose. It looked like it had been discarded, but one end went up into the attic. Colt took down the end with the valve on it.

He opened the valve and let the water run a moment, then took a drink. Handing it to her, he said, "Not great tasting, but clean."

"How did you do that?" Beth said after drinking her fill of water.

"This house has a hundred-gallon water heater in the attic. I put a hose on the drain and brought it down here. Just some insurance I thought we might need."

Colt smiled at her. "Of course, I didn't think the 'we' would be you and I."

Beth was tearing into one of the food packets. Pausing to look at him, she said, "Can you live with that change?"

"I'm getting there. It's called trading up."

They sat at a counter in the kitchen, eating their food.

Colt had already stuffed his pockets with the rest of the meals.

"We need to find bottles for water." He stood and started looking around the kitchen, then turned and looked at her. "And you need to change your clothes. More pockets."

"What we need are backpacks. We can carry more."

"I don't know," Colt said. "Then it will be obvious, and people will know we have something to steal."

Beth was wandering around. "You know, I like it here. Think about it, Colt. I don't think either one of us are survivalist types. No matter where we run to, unless we can get to my farm, we won't have all this stuff, like knives, pots and pans. Just tons of stuff we might need and can't take with us."

"What're you thinking, Beth? Like the book, *Alas Babylon*? Or, *On the Beach*? I've read those books, but I don't think they apply here. It's too soon, and the situation too violent."

"I don't mean long term. We need to get to my farm for that. I think we need to stay as long as we can stick it out. The big question is how long before the gangs come here, and how do we avoid them? Look, Arnie showed me something once." She rummaged around in a drawer and came up with a marking pencil. Sweeping everything off the counter with her arm, she started drawing.

Continuing, she said, "See? Here is Springfield. West is Joplin. North of us is Kansas City. St. Louis is up here. Southwest is the Little Rock, Fayetteville, Springdale corridor—and directly south of us, nothing bigger than Harrisonville."

"So, what's the point?" He was impatiently looking out the windows.

"You need to think of millions of people. Millions, Colt. What happened here when things went bad?"

Colt shook his head. "People flew out of here like a covey of quail. A lot of them must still be in the mobs running around the city."

"Right. And to some degree, that will happen everywhere. It's worse in the megacities. There are millions of people on the move." She started drawing concentric circles around each of the cities, wider and wider like ripples in a pool. "People from Springfield probably are going north and south. South to the hills, where they think there's game and water. They'll run to the north, toward farmland and lakes. It will be the same for all the cities. People are so desperate they just have to go. They need to try *something*."

"I know," he said. "When I've talked to people, everyone thinks they can survive by hunting game and fishing. Most don't realize how quickly an area can be hunted out."

"I thought you were a computer geek?"

Colt laughed. "I'm a computer geek who's been out of work for nearly a year and knows how to read. There's a ton of information out there. I just never thought I'd need to use it."

She took a big breath. "For now, I think we should stay. I don't want to join the crowds of people running everywhere, and I don't think we can avoid them if we're on the run. Sooner or later, we will be run over like roadkill."

Colt just stood looking at her expectantly.

Beth shrugged at him. "That's it. That's all I have."

Finally, he said, "Actually, that is what I was trying to do before Jen ran off and the kids got sick."

Sick. He still couldn't think of them being dead and because of that, still had a deep-down feeling that he should be going to them, finding them.

"I think we have as good a chance here as anywhere. It's a crap shoot, I know."

"Wow. You're back. For a moment there, you went away. So, do you want to try and stick it out here?"

"Why not? I don't have any better offers."

She slid easily into his arms and kissed him thoroughly for several minutes.

"What brought that on?" He leaned back from her, meeting her gaze.

She laughed softly. "I'm just checking to see if we might get along. I've wanted to do that since the first time we met."

Holding her, he took a deep breath. He felt relaxed and on edge for all the obvious reasons. "I'm going to guess we're compatible."

"Hell, I knew that when you walked up to the ambulance."

"How? Love at first sight?" he asked jokingly.

"Nope," she said. "I don't believe in that. Right now, I don't love you and you don't love me. What I do believe in are pheromones. And yours are kickin' my butt."

Guilt reared its ugly head once he started thinking. He tried to push her away. "We shouldn't be doing this."

She hugged him again. "I know it's too soon. I lost a brother and you lost two kids. Your wife self-destructed on you. I know. I get it."

Stepping back from him, she met his gaze. "I'm a little like your wife, Colt. I'm scared shitless. Sometimes I just need to be held."

"That I can do," he said. "And for the record, you aren't anything like my wife."

Her voice firmed up, knowing a decision was made. "So, we're staying for a while?"

"Beth, we're staying, but not right here. We need to find a place close to the outskirts of town so we have the option to go or stay. Right now, I think we are too close. We need to go farther out."

EIGHT

BEFORE THEY LEFT THE HOUSE, Beth and Colt took great care to erase any signs that they'd been there. They smudged out any tracks, erased crumbs from the table, and their meal wrappers were stuck in their pockets to use later.

When asked about all the precautions, Colt replied, "I don't know. It's just a gut feeling. The foragers will be checking all these houses repeatedly. I don't want anyone to know we exist."

Beth laughed softly. "Not likely. The foragers, as you call them, are running for their lives."

"So are we," he said. "Although it won't take long for the gangs to get more organized. They're hungry, too. And that's the real danger."

"Maybe we should just stay here and get dry. I'm not looking forward to running around in the rain again."

Colt looked at her and gave her an option that he didn't really want. "Do you want to stay by yourself? I'll come back for you."

"No, dammit, I don't want to stay by myself. I just

hope your stubbornness doesn't get us killed." She said the last very softly.

"I didn't catch that."

She smiled brightly. "I said that I'd love to get soaked to the bone again."

They left out the back door of the home and then cut through backyards and fences, heading toward the river and the commune camp. It was slow going.

Colt was glad it was still raining, off and on. The rain dulled all the sound of their passing. After a couple of sudden downpours, they were soaked to the skin.

Looking at her, he realized they needed better equipment to survive even a few nights. Although the temperatures were in the sixties, the rain was cold and Beth was shivering already. He could see her skin showing through the thin tee shirt she wore.

When she saw him looking her over, she ran her hands down the front of her shirt, effectively showing everything that was there.

She laughed at him. "Like what you see?"

He didn't know how she preened while they were walking, but she did it. "Are you flirting with me?"

"God, no." She gave a short laugh before continuing. "I'm launching a full-scale assault on you. I'm so far past flirting, I don't know what the word means."

She reached out and stopped him, turning him to face her. "Colt, I need to be honest. I'm already scared enough. I don't know what I'd do if you left me alone."

"So, like Jen, are you offering yourself to me for protection?"

His head rotated on his neck from the stinging slap. Then she stuck her finger in his face. "Don't you ever compare me to your wife in that way? So far, I haven't offered you anything but companionship, other than a damn good kiss. Anything else you have in mind, you'll be damned lucky to get."

"Look, I'm…"

He was talking to her retreating back as she stalked toward the last house in the addition. Rushing to catch up with her, he grabbed her and said, "Beth, I'm sorry. You didn't deserve that."

"No, I didn't." She folded her arms across her chest and wouldn't look at him.

Colt couldn't really explain it to himself, but this woman had reached him in just a few hours. He was beginning to think that he and Jen never had very much in the way of a relationship. It was a hell of a thing to find out now.

"Beth, I have a problem. Every once in a while I go brain dead—dumber than a box of rocks. I need you to help me and keep me grounded. I need you." He stuck his hand out. "Partners?"

Grudgingly, she studied him for a few moments. Then she shook his hand, pulled him toward her and kissed him softly on the lips. "Partners."

THEY WERE both lying on the same hill where the sentry had stopped Colt, seemingly a long time ago. The grass was sopping and mud seeped into their clothes. There was no sentry this time. In fact, they couldn't see anyone around. Some of the tents were there, and some were flapping in the breeze.

"What do you think?" Colt asked.

"I don't know," she said. "It looks like they pulled foot and left."

"Pulled foot?"

"I'm a country girl."

"Well, there's only one way to find out. C'mon, country."

They started down the hill. A few hundred feet from the bottom of the hill, they could hear a low hum, even over the noise of the rain. The sound was louder as they approached the first tent.

Colt ventured an opinion. "Bees?"

"No," Beth answered soberly. "Flies."

Like an exclamation point to her pronouncement, the wind shifted and the stench hit them. They backed away, coughing.

"What the...?"

"Bodies," Beth said. "Colt, we have to get out of here."

Colt was holding his nose. "Let's just take a quick walkthrough."

"You don't know why these people died. If we catch something, there's no medicine available. Think of the disease. Of the bodies we can see, I don't see any bullet holes in them, no wounds at all." She grabbed his arm when he'd have gone on. "Dammit, Colt, listen to me."

When he stopped, she continued. "We just said 'partners' a few minutes ago, right? Your words were 'keep you grounded.' If you start wandering through this camp and catch something"—she spaced her words out—"*you're going to give it to me.*"

"I want to look for..."

"Give her up," she abruptly yelled in his face.

Then softly, "Colt, you saw her. I saw her. Even if she's alive, she's dead."

He nodded reluctantly. Finally, in his mind, he was able to let her go. "Okay, you're right, as usual. I'm sorry to keep putting you through this. I guess I'm a head case myself."

She put her hand gently on his face. "We're all head-cases, Colt. The bright side is that we'll get over it."

By consent, they skirted upwind of the camp and approached the lake. This part of the lake was actually part of a river, and the water was moving briskly because of the rain. Every few feet, they'd see a flash of white as something turned over in the current.

"Oh, my god." Beth pointed downstream toward a bridge abutment where bodies were piling up against the concrete and starting to dam the flood.

"I wonder how long we'd have to boil *that* water to make it safe," Colt wondered. "That is a bigger disaster than anything we've seen. Maybe now we know why the people at the camp died."

He walked back toward the bodies in the camp but stopped short. Spending several minutes studying the camp, he finally said, "This camp has been stripped—no weapons, no cooking utensils, no nothing. If Sam's bunch didn't take all that with them, and I'm thinking they didn't, that means the gangs have been through here."

"If they have..." He looked at Beth bleakly. "They'll be spreading disease with them everywhere they go."

She just nodded.

"Okay," Colt said. "Let's get out of here."

"Hallelujah."

NINE

THE OVERCAST DAY began to darken even more as another line of thunderstorms started to move through the area. They stood under the canopy of a cottonwood tree to try to avoid most of the downpour. Colt hoped the lightning would avoid this particular tree.

He pointed up the hill to the west. "I wonder what's up there?"

"I think there are a couple of old estates. I remember the gates at the bottom of the hill. You can't see the houses because of the trees and undergrowth."

Colt pondered that a moment. It was still early in the game. At least, what he thought was the game. From the continuous sounds of gunfire to the north, the people in the city were killing each other off at a horrendous rate. No wonder people were fleeing the city.

In a macabre way, it made sense. There was a small amount of food, and too many people. Something had to give. It was just Mother Nature making an adjustment.

One of the websites he'd looked at predicted that if you could last the first thirty days after a collapse, you had a chance of survival. He knew they'd have to avoid conflict to make that happen.

Beth was waiting patiently for him to decide. "Alright, let's go see what's there. We'll check it out and make sure the gangs haven't left someone behind. Maybe we can find a place to spend the night out of this rain."

"We can't go back to your neighborhood?"

"Maybe," he said. "But we'll circle around and come into it tomorrow. From now on, we have to figure that even if a place is safe for the moment, it won't be safe when we come back."

They began their trek through the soggy underbrush. It was slow going up the hill, and steep enough they had to use small trees for handholds. About halfway up, they ran into a walking trail. The trail was cleared of brush but not paved. Making better time going up the hill, he stopped at the edge of the trees.

The house was not huge. In his mind, he thought a mansion would be. This one looked to be very old. The home had a two-car garage, and several outbuildings were scattered about the grounds.

It was nearing dark in the gloom of the woods, but Colt was reluctant to go forward. Between them and the back door, there was about fifty feet of grass. They watched for any signs of movement and didn't see any.

"Well," he said to Beth. "I guess we'll have to take a chance."

They separated from the tree line and walked slowly toward the back entrance, watching the windows closely. It was a three-story building, and from what he could see, every room had two or three windows. They watched the windows carefully.

Colt was encouraged the back door was intact.

Maybe no one had been here yet. The owners hadn't been very security conscious. The door was solid and heavy and fitted so tightly it would be hard to bypass the locks. Incongruously, it had windows in it. He could see the outline of security tape around the window glass, which would work great if they still had electricity.

He was pondering how to break out the windowpane closest to where the locks would be when Beth walked up with a brick and broke the window. As she reached through and felt for the deadbolt lock on the door, she smiled at him.

"You tend to overthink things. Sometimes simple is better."

The door swung inward and a musty odor rushed from the house. They stood for a moment, pondering their next move. In their new world, every action could end in a crapshoot.

"It doesn't smell dead, just old," Colt opined. "What do you think?"

"I think it's empty, but keep your gun handy." She gave him a pointed look.

Chagrined, he pulled the pistol out of his pocket. He hadn't even thought of it.

They stopped just inside the door in what appeared to be a mudroom. Their first great find came immediately. A half dozen hooded rain ponchos were hanging on hooks. In the gloom, their mottled green color made them hard to spot.

Colt quickly took two of them, rearranging the rest to try to cover up that they were missing. He tied knots in the arms and pulled the drawstrings together to make two big bags.

"Okay," he said. "Anything we want to take, we put in the bags."

"Why? Don't you think we can stay here?"

"If the gangs come, we'd be trapped. I don't want to stop anywhere we don't have several options to get away."

"Maybe they won't..."

"No," he said. "This is one thing we don't need to discuss. If we get pinned down and surrounded, we're done. We have to be able to move."

"Okay," she sighed. "What's first?"

"Go to the kitchen and look for any small bottles we can carry water in. Water is our biggest concern. If you find food, leave anything you can't put in the poncho bag. I'm going to see what else the house has to offer. There may be weapons. Also, we both need better clothes."

From the mudroom, there were three choices of direction. Left to the kitchen, straight down a hall to the garage, or right to a stairwell that went up the next floor or down to the basement. He went straight to the garage. There were no cars, so he made quick work of his search and found a drawer with a couple of small flashlights. Cupping the end to guard against showing light, he checked to make sure they worked and put them in his pocket. He made a mental note to look for a gardener's shed because there just wasn't much of use in this part of the house. Apparently, the owners were rich enough to have everything done for them.

Colt made a quick circuit through the ground-floor rooms, finding nothing to use in the short term. This part of the house looked more formal and, except for a den, he didn't think it was used. The basement consisted of a game room and exercise room. He was looking for a gunroom or anything like hunting paraphernalia, but didn't find it.

Beth yelled at him, and he flinched at the noise. "Colt, I'm going upstairs to look for clothes."

He followed on the carpeted stairs and they found every room had a full clothes closet. Colt found a good, heavy pair of jeans that fit and a pair of desert-style boots. The size was close enough. He quickly changed and added another shirt.

Taking a few extra clothes back downstairs, he found Beth had been very resourceful. She'd found water bottles and a couple of backpacks. She'd stuffed the packs full of Power Bars and canned sausages, and Spam. He was amazed at the food left in the house.

It was getting closer to dark outside, and shadows draped the inside of the house. He sprinted up the stairs and quickly went into the room he'd last seen Beth.

She was pulling off her T-shirt. Another blouse lay on the bed.

"Hey."

Beth let out a little shriek and then stood with her arms trapped by the shirt and her hands between her breasts, trying to catch her breath.

"Don't *do* that," she finally gasped. "Make a little noise, will ya?"

He stood for a moment, staring at her.

When he didn't say anything, she said, "Uh, hello? Earth to Colt?"

Snapping out of his stare, he said softly, "You need to hurry, Beth. It's getting dark and we need to get out of here."

Topless, she sat and bounced on the bed a couple of times. "We could make use of this nice, big four-poster bed, you know. Maybe spend the night?" She laid back and spread her arms toward the two posts at the head-board. "Were there any neckties where you found your clothes?"

He smiled at her. "As much as I'd like that...hell, you've no idea how much I'd really like that, but we can't stay here. It's not safe."

Staying well back from the upper floor windows that stretched nearly floor to ceiling, he watched outside while she grumbled quietly and dressed. Mostly. He noticed she didn't wear a bra.

"If we have to run, you're going to wish you'd worn a bra."

"Nothing here is even close to a fit," she said. "Who-ever lived here before probably provided milk for the entire neighborhood. I'll have to add that to another shopping list."

They went downstairs and unknotted the ponchos since the backpacks held everything.

"Dammit," he said. "I'll be right back."

He hustled back upstairs and retrieved their wet clothes since they'd have been a dead giveaway that someone had been here.

When he came back down, he paused at the bottom of the stairs and stared into the gloom of the stairwell that led to the basement. He thought he'd heard a noise. Glancing at Beth, he waved and got her attention, then held his finger to his lips. Her eyes got big, and she nodded.

The little pieces of information that had been tickling his subconscious suddenly came glaring to his mind. There was food here. Why weren't the people of the house at home? There was no reason to leave. Then the other pieces fell into place as he remembered the camouflaged ponchos, camo desert boots, and no sign of any kind of gun cabinets or any sporting paraphernalia.

Shit, how stupid was he?

Colt immediately sprinted toward Beth and tried to open the back door. When she didn't move with him, he glanced at her face, and then followed her gaze. There were several people behind them, and shadows of movement in the gloom. Now he could hear people moving around. A man spoke to them.

"You folks, just settle down a minute. We may let you go unharmed if you cooperate."

Hand on his pistol, Colt moved to place Beth behind him, hoping she'd open the door. "Look, we don't want any trouble. We just took enough stuff to help us through the next few days. That's all."

A female voice spoke. "Zeke, it looks like they're alone. We just checked the grounds, and it's clear out there."

The man he assumed was Zeke stepped closer, and Colt could see him better. He could also see the shotgun trained at them. At this range, it wouldn't matter if the man aimed the weapon.

"Alright," Zeke said. "Take your hands out of your pockets."

"And if I don't?"

Suddenly, the beams of two flashlights painted them. Now, he couldn't see anything but white dots in front of his eyes.

Behind him, Beth hissed at them, "Turn off that damned light. There are gangs out there that might see them."

The lights went off, and a woman chuckled. Colt

thought it was the first woman that had spoken. "See, Zeke. They're just like us. They don't want trouble."

"Yeah," Zeke said. "Maybe. Alright, here's what we're gonna do. I know you have a pistol in your pocket. You can keep it. We're going to lead you downstairs to a room with no windows. Then we'll turn on the lights and see what we've caught."

"If you don't mind, I'd rather leave," Colt said.

Laughter came from several people. "He's real polite, isn't he? Mister, you don't have any choice in the matter."

Zeke led them down the flight of stairs to the basement. Colt could hear a door open that sounded pneumatic. A bunker. He should have known. The same door closed, and then the lights came on. He'd been expecting it, so he'd closed his eyes.

Beth leaned her head into his back. "Shit, that's bright."

Slowly opening his eyes, he saw four men and two women in front of him. They were all dressed in army green, and two of the men were taking off what he guessed were night vision goggles. Their armament was an assortment of weapons, most of which were pointed in his general direction.

One of the men stepped forward. He looked to be in his forties, with salt and pepper hair and a square face. "I'm Zeke. You don't need to know any of the other names."

The woman whose voice he recognized spoke up. "Hey, I'm Mary, and he's a putz." She chuckled. "But he's my putz, so what can I do? So, what's your story?" she continued.

Since the woman seemed to be the talker, Beth took

the lead, moved forward and talked to her, filling her in on everything they'd done.

When she finished, Mary asked, "So, what's it like outside?"

"Chaos," Colt responded. "It's like the city is trying to self-destruct and mass hysteria has set in. People are fighting over everything. There's very little food or water. People left their relatively safe homes to stand around in the rain with thousands of other people. We heard the National Guard broke up and now fighting has started along the I-44 corridor."

"Who's doing that?" Zeke broke in.

"All we heard are rumors. Some said the Army from Fort Leonard Wood, running in front of people from St. Louis. More recently we heard it's Homeland Security trying to use up those millions of rounds of ammo they bought."

The people in the bunker all looked at each other.

"How long have you folks been down here?" Colt asked.

"We've been in a couple of weeks, only coming out at night. The house belongs to a relative of mine. She always told us to come here if things ever got bad. We're here and they aren't. They like to travel and had the money to do it, so I guess they got caught off guard and away from home."

"We saw some of the fireworks on the north side of town. It looks like we'll be here a while longer," Mary said.

Zeke turned and spoke directly to Colt. "We don't have enough food stored to let you join our group. I figure we'll need to stay here another month before we venture outside. I'm sorry, but you can't stay and I don't think we can let you go."

Colt was holding his pistol again. "Well, a month is a long time to be cooped up in here. Think about it. I know you can kill us, but these walls are concrete and look solid. I don't know how many bullets I have left in my gun, but if anything starts, you'll get all of them. When we all start firing, the ricochets may kill us all.

"Look," Colt continued. "We're not going to tell anyone where you are. That's not our style. We got food and clothes from you and for that, we're grateful. But we really need to go."

One of the nameless men stepped forward. "Zeke, kill him but not his woman. We're not exactly paired up in here, you know."

"You can't have me," Beth spoke up. "I already have a man. Before we're through with this circular firing squad, my body will stretch out right alongside his. Even if you did separate us, I'd kill you the first chance I got. That is a promise, mister."

After the two groups stared at each other a few moments, Mary stepped forward.

"Zeke, cool your jets. Let's just tone this down a bit." She turned her attention to Colt. "Do you have better weapons than that pistol? Did you leave anything stashed outside? You need more than that popgun you have." She turned and glared at the men in her group.

"Look, I appreciate the offer," Colt said. "I read an old science fiction novel that I got from a used bookstore. The story was almost like that movie *Hunger Games*. As a matter of fact, the movie was almost plagiarized from it."

"And the point is?" Zeke said.

"The point is that if you go into a situation like a lion,

armed to the teeth and looking for a fight, you'll find it and sooner or later be killed. If you go in like a rabbit and avoid conflict, you've a good chance of survival. I'm not good with guns anyway, so I don't need a lot of firepower."

Zeke shrugged. "Fair enough."

Mary glared at him.

———

THEY RETURNED Colt and Beth to the back door. Both he and Beth were now owners of two 1911 Colt .45s and two short-barreled shotguns on slings, along with enough ammo to make them sink to the bottom of any amount of water they tried to cross.

"Why are you doing this for us?" Colt asked as they got ready to leave.

"We've got a ton of weapons," said Mary. "And you two seem like good people. With all the dying going on, someone needs to live. I hope it's you."

Colt nodded, although he was sure no one could see. "Luck to you, then. And thanks. Try to keep your heads down."

As they eased outside into the darkness, Colt said, "Let's find a place close. I don't want to be stumbling around out here in the dark."

"We could use the flashlights and look around." Beth's voice was dubious as she peered into the darkness.

"And how far away could someone see that? It would give these people and us away. No, we'll have to chance daylight. If memory serves, there's a garden shed over next to the tree line. Maybe we can use that."

He and Beth stood for a moment in the darkness

watching the light show over Springfield. "You'd think everyone would run out of ammunition before long."

"Probably not in our lifetime," Beth said. "A year ago, who'd have thought people would be fighting for food and water? God, what a mess."

The shed they found had a sliding door, and the rusted rollers made a low grumble as the door opened. The little building was just large enough for a couple of riding mowers, with a bench on one side and shelves all around. He put the packs down, leaned their new shotguns against the wall, and spread their ponchos on the floor. He leaned against the wall and Beth sat between his legs and leaned back against him. She sighed as he hugged her to him.

"What do you think about the people in the bunker?" he asked. "Do you think they'll make it?"

He could feel her shake her head, her hair brushing his face. "Not a chance in hell."

"Why wouldn't they? That bunker seems pretty secure to me."

She chuckled softly and settled herself more comfortably against him. "Oh, the bunker is safe enough. That's not the problem. Think about it. There are four men and two women. And cooped up together for another month? They'd have to be really...uh—"

"Tolerant?"

"—not the word I was looking for. More like polyandrous. And Zeke didn't impress me as being into sharing."

Colt squeezed her tightly and yawned. "Well, I'm glad you aren't either. I appreciated what you said back there."

He felt her shrug. "I guess it would depend on the circumstances. Some people make it work, I even know of a few. But it can't be forced. Everyone has to agree and have an equal say in it. Am I shocking you?"

"Not really," he said. "Flabbergasted is more like it."

She wrapped his arms tighter around her. "Don't worry about it. When I'm tired, my mouth tends to run. What's going to happen, Colt? I mean, tomorrow. Next week? We're not ready for this. Being a survivalist isn't in my skill set. I'm a nester, not a fighter."

"We learn to survive. Any way we can. We may not be hardcore survivalists, but we aren't stupid either."

"I don't know, Colt. There are a lot of smart people with IQs off the charts dying out there."

"Okay, then. How about being lucky?"

Beth sighed. "Lucky, I can live with."

"Then that is how we do it. Survive every day. We just have to start stringing the days together."

TEN

COLT AWAKENED the next morning to sunlight streaming through the cracks in the door. The rain had moved out during the night and left the morning smelling fresh and new.

He gently moved Beth to the side. Sometime during the night, she'd turned and drooled on his shirt. *Cute.* He left her sleeping and stood up. Or he tried. His back was in such a cramp that he had to use the garden tractor and workbench as crutches to get up. Finally, he was able to move to the door.

The grumbling of the door opening brought Beth awake with a start. "Wha...?"

Holding his hand up to quiet her, he eased his head out the door and looked around. It appeared to be a fresh spring morning. All he heard were birds and squirrels barking in the trees. The morning sun was heating up, providing a fog in the lush foliage around them. He was amazed that he could hear no sounds of fighting. After looking and listening for about five minutes, he said, "All I hear are birds, and it looks pretty tame to me."

She groaned as she stood up. "God, I hurt all over."

"Yeah, me, too."

Looking closely at him, she said, "What's on your shirt?"

He grinned at her. "You drooled on me last night."

"I did not."

"Did."

Beth held his gaze a moment and then sternly spaced her words out. "It never happened. I do not drool."

Switching gears adroitly, she reached into a pack and brought out a chocolate-covered Power Bar and bottle of water. "We can share this for breakfast."

They each sat on the seats of the riding mowers. Out of curiosity, Colt unscrewed the gas cap on his saddle tank. It was full. "The gas Nazis didn't get this far up the hill, I guess."

"Can we use that for anything?"

"Well," he said, cutting a glance at her. "Maybe we could escape on the mowers. Anyone gets in our way, we just mow them down."

All he got from his comedy act was a raised eyebrow and another stern look. Returning to breakfast, he made short work of his half of the bar.

Beth licked her fingers. "If we really conserve, we might stretch this food into two weeks. We could be at the farm by then."

"We'll try. The only trouble is the bars are salty, and that makes us drink more. Maybe we'll get lucky and be able to replenish somewhere. In the meantime, we'd better get going."

When he started to gather their gear, she said, "Uh, Colt, before we get our packs and stuff on, I'm about to bust my bladder."

He looked around. "Inside would be safer."

She looked around. "Okay, but no looking. We're not even going steady yet. Opposite corners?"

He finished and could still hear her going. "Beth, you must store more water than a camel."

She giggled. "Does this mean we're going steady?"

"I'd like to think we're closer than that. Who knows, maybe engaged. Of course, I'd have to break into a jewelry store and steal a ring."

Beth sighed. "Great. I'm squatting in a corner over a giant puddle, and my man may have, sort of, proposed to me." She stood and looked steadily at him. "And I don't need a ring."

———

MOVING INTO THE TREES, he stopped when they were undercover. Unslinging the shotgun, he asked, "Are you comfortable with this thing?"

"I guess," she said. "I've used them before." She pushed a button and pulled back the slide at the same time. "See? This lets you see if there's a shell in the chamber." She slid it back up and pointed to another button. "This is the safety. All you do is push it in with your thumb and pull the trigger. Pump and pull. Pump and pull."

"What about the pistols?" He tapped his .45 in its clip-on holster.

"They work just like the nine-millimeter pistol my brother gave you. With the four clips each, we should be okay. If we need more than that all at once, we're probably dead anyway."

Carefully, they made their way through the trees and

down the hill. Once in a while, they'd hear people coming and step behind trees to hide. There were a lot of couples, and some groups that looked like whole families working their way south through the woods. When they were almost to the edge of the woods, they heard running footsteps coming directly toward them.

From behind a dense stand of brush, they saw a young girl running right at them. Her clothes were ripped and muddy. Trying to hold up her jean shorts as she ran, she was crying and looking behind her. Every time she looked behind, she'd stumble and lose ground.

A few yards behind the girl, a man sprinted after her. They heard him panting and laughing at the same time. "I got ya. I got ya."

She stumbled past them, and they could hear her sobbing. The man was close behind.

Colt took the shotgun off his shoulder, and when the man drew even with them, he stepped out from behind the tree and buried the barrel into the man's gut. The loud whoosh of the man's breath expelled from his body caused the young girl to stop and turn. The crunch as Colt slammed the butt end of the shotgun into the man's forehead caused her to hold her hand over her mouth. The man twitched a couple of times and then didn't move.

Beth came around the tree and kneeled to check the man's pulse. "He's dead, Colt." She looked up at him. "I'm going to have to reevaluate your skill set. Remind me to never piss you off."

He just shrugged, amazed that he was giving the dead man no thought at all. Nodding toward the young girl, he said, "What about her?" He was surprised the girl hadn't kept on running.

Beth walked past him to the girl. "Are you okay?"

When the girl nodded, Beth said, "Are you alone? Do you have family you're trying to get to?"

The girl just looked at the ground, still breathing heavily. "No, no one. My family is dead."

"What happened?" Beth asked.

The girl shrugged and then gestured to the dead man. "We were trying to get out of town. God, it was awful. They caught us last night. The gangs are everywhere. Dad went down fighting them...he never had a chance. My dad didn't believe in guns. Mom was next after they..."

The girl took a deep breath and continued. "When they were through with her, they just killed her. It was like throwing out the garbage." They watched as the girl fought back tears. Then, she said vehemently, "I fought them. I fought hard. *I did*. But it didn't do much good. They all went to sleep, and I finally got away this morning and ran. Thank you for what you did." She looked around her. "I just don't know what I'm going to do now."

Putting her hand on the girl's shoulder, Beth said, "You're going to survive any way you can, girl. Be strong. Look, at the top of this hill is a house. You can't miss it, it's an old mansion. Go in the back door and just sit there. It may be a day or so, but someone will find you and help."

Colt looked at her sharply, thinking of their discussion about the mismatch of sexes in the bunker, and she caught the unspoken message. "Okay, here's the deal. We were just up there and checked it out. When someone comes to help you, there will be more men than women. If they let you stay with them, you may be required to 'help out,' so to speak. Wait," she corrected herself.

"That's stupid, especially after what's happened to you so far. I'm talking about sex. Do you understand what I'm saying? There are other women up there, and I think they're good folks. But still...this time, it will be your decision."

The young girl looked at Beth and suddenly seemed to be a lot older. "I understand, ma'am. I need to pay my way with what I have." She looked at the dead man. "Hell, it can't be any worse than what I've already been through."

The girl suddenly hugged Beth. "Thank you again. Regardless of what happens up the hill, thank you."

With a quick, frightened look around at her surroundings, she went bounding up the hill toward the house.

"I bet she won't thank you if she sees you again," Colt said.

"What?" Beth said, smiling. "You thought we'd take Miss Perky Tits with us? Then we'd be in the same fix as the people in the bunker."

He held up both hands in surrender, a difficult feat while holding a shotgun. "That never entered my mind. And thanks for the glowing accolades of my gender."

Beth replied seriously, "Well, I'm not sure your gender deserves a lot right now."

Kneeling by the man he'd just killed, Colt went through his pockets. The only weapon he found was a deadly looking switchblade knife. Colt wondered just where the man had come from. He looked at the knife a moment and then tossed it on the body.

"Why did you do that?"

"I had one of those once when I was a kid. It was always going off in my pocket."

She smirked as she went past him. "No lasting damage, I hope."

Stopping, she gathered up the knife, examined it a minute, and then stuck it in her pack. "It will make good trading material."

———

THEY SKIRTED the camp at the bottom of the hill. While they didn't hear the flies from their vantage point, what they did hear was worse. Dogs. Growling and fighting with each other. Colt slumped for a moment. He hadn't thought of dogs. How could they hope to survive if he didn't think of something obvious like that?

"I'm thinking Mary was smart after all, giving us the shotguns even after I told her I didn't want them."

"Why?"

Colt nodded back toward the camp. "Fido."

Beth shuddered and didn't look back. "That could be bad. I didn't think about dogs."

"I didn't either," he said. "And I should have." His voice turned so serious Beth turned to look at him. "I've got to get ahead of the curve. If I don't, I'm going to get us killed."

"We," Beth replied. "Partners, remember?"

From their vantage point, they couldn't see the houses of the old neighborhood. Skirting the empty homes at the bottom of the hill, they climbed a rocky point where the highway department had cut through the limestone rock to make an exit for the highway.

"Dammit," Colt cursed, looking at the housing addition. "All that food and water is gone."

"Now what do we do?"

They could see several dozen people going from house to house. All were armed and seemed to be acting as a unit. As some would pause at the door, others would stand guard as the first members went in. Just like they used to see on TV with all the police and SWAT shows. Only these men had no uniforms, just red headbands or armbands.

"Gangs. They've finally moved south."

"Thank you, Mr. Obvious," Beth said.

"Someone finally got smart and started organizing them. Look what they're carrying."

At nearly every house, men and women would carry out buckets of water. On the street, there was a large container on a wagon with gang members filling it. It was two or three times larger than a hundred-gallon water heater, and it was nearly full. The tanks were on wagons, and waiting to move it were men and women kept under guard. Human horsepower. Slaves. It had come to that.

"Well, I guess they figured out your water heater method of getting water. Too bad," Beth quipped.

"Water is the main problem for everyone right now. We've been concentrating on food, but we need about a half-gallon of water each day. That is going to be hard to find. I know water is heavy, and we can't carry enough water to last more than a few days. How many bottles did you pack?"

"I found a case of twelve, so we've six apiece. By your figures, we need four a day." She sounded worried. "That's not going to last long for us."

Back in the other world, before the breakdown, one of the things that made Colt good at his job was his ability to compartmentalize a job, break it down to its finer points, and find a solution. He tried to concentrate on that skill now.

"C'mon," Beth said, pulling at him. "We gotta' go."

"Hang on, I'm thinking about something."

She gave a very unladylike snort. "We got our asses hanging out, sitting on top of a flat rock with armed gangs heading our direction, and you want to stop and think about something?"

"Got it," he said, ignoring her. "We have to make another raid on a house somewhere."

"Colt, I think anything with water in it's already been stolen. We've enough supplies for a few days. I don't think we should take the risk. Let's get out of here."

"Well, Suzy Homemaker, we need a bottle of bleach and an eyedropper. If I remember correctly, the rate is two drops to a quart of water."

He helped her off the rocky point, and still holding her hand, started back west. "Look, Republic Road goes straight west from here. We'll roughly follow it to get out of town."

"No, that is a bad idea." She gripped his hand tighter. "You set the precedent, so let's take a moment to figure this out and not make a snap judgment.

"I figure we have two choices. One: we go south," she said. "By crossing that bridge that we really, really don't want to cross, we'll be in farm country within a couple of miles. It's still dangerous, but I don't think the gangs will venture out into the country yet. It's just not in their comfort zone. Once we hit the less populated area, we can strike west for a few miles. If we make it that far, then we can try going north toward my farm.

"The second choice is trying to skirt the city by going north along Highway 65. It would be the quickest way, but it would put us going through part of the city. What do you think?"

During their conversation, they'd found cover in the brush between the on and off-ramps to the freeway. Colt thought for a moment, and looked west, thinking of all the neighborhoods they had to cross, not counting having to go back toward the hospital and then back at where he knew the gangs were.

"I don't think number two will work, Beth. From the smoke I can see, I think there are some major battles going on between here and I-44. Every water tower has a fight going on."

Beth interrupted. "I thought all the water had been drained from them a long time ago."

"Maybe so, but most towers have a well. If they can get those going someway, whoever wins that fight owns the city. The second big battle is at Springfield Underground. I'm betting hundreds of people took refuge there because of the tons of supplies housed in the caves. Somebody will be fighting for that."

He thought momentarily, shaking his head. "That's what all the fighting is about. I'm betting Homeland Security is trying to secure both of those locations, and I don't think we could ever get around them."

"I agree. Arnie was afraid of them more than anything. He always said that Homeland Security was out of control even *before* all this started."

"Okay, then. I think south is our best bet, and then take the long way around. That's a lot better than my idea. Okay, General. Let's beat feet out of here. We need to get across that bridge before someone decides to make it a toll road."

ELEVEN

COLT AND BETH crossed the road going south. He glanced behind and saw several men and women of the gang they'd been watching start advancing toward them. He hoped they were more intent on finding houses with water than chasing a couple of refugees. When he looked again, they were already slowing down.

Making it to the bottom of the hill, they struck east through the nature preserve toward the bridge across Lake Springfield. On this side of the road, the brush and trees came up close to the four-lane highway. They were about to cross the ditch and start across the bridge when they heard people coming. Colt pulled them back to the tree line to see what was going on.

"Wow," Beth said. "There are hundreds of people."

The road was a solid wall of people coming toward the bridge. The mass of people stretched as far as they could see.

"Maybe we can just mingle with them and cross. What do you think?"

Colt shook his head. "We'll wait."

The mass of people was halfway across the bridge when the firing started. The front line of people crumpled. A few had guns and fired back at the other end of the bridge. The rest tried to stop, but were pushed forward by the press of people behind them. Some began using bodies as shields against the hail of bullets.

Beth pointed at a bluff next to the other end of the bridge. They could see drifting smoke from a placement about halfway up the rocky face. Men in black uniforms were using machine guns. From their vantage point, it was like shooting ducks in a barrel.

"Well, that answers that question," Colt said.

Beth couldn't believe it. "They don't want us to leave town, do they?"

"Nope," Colt said. "They don't care if we die, probably prefer it, but they need us to stay bottled up." He slapped her on the shoulder. "We gotta go. Now."

They started running back the way they came, following along the shore of the lake. "We need to find a spot to break out of town before they get it sealed off. We're lucky to be south of the James River Freeway. I'm betting that is their containment line."

"But why?" Beth panted.

Colt looked behind at her. She was having a hard time with the heavy shotgun and the pack. He stopped, took the shotgun, and slung it over his shoulder. Now, at least she balanced.

He started jogging west again. "I don't know why," he finally answered. "I'd guess it's all about control. Maybe it's a hold-over from old orders, before the breakdown, of not wanting to spread disease into the countryside. Who knows?"

"Look." She pointed breathlessly up the hill. "Isn't that where the old mansion was?"

Black smoke billowed from the top of the hill. They could hear heavy firing and then an explosion that rocked them off their feet. Colt grabbed Beth and pulled her under an overhang as rocks and wood rained around them. The shooting stopped.

"My god," Beth said. "They blew themselves up."

He pulled her to her feet, and they stood brushing themselves off. Colt picked a few splinters out of her hair. Standing close and holding her, he asked, "You okay?"

"Why do you always get personal when we don't have time to do anything about it?" she asked. "And, yes. I'm alright."

They were past the hill now, making good time. "I still can't believe they did that."

"I'm betting they didn't."

"What?"

"Think about it. No castle is without a bolt hole, an escape route. Those people prepared for all this right down to the finest detail. They probably set a timer and beat feet out of there."

"You think so? How'd you get so smart?"

"I read a lot of stuff."

Colt stopped. To the north was the hospital, Cox Health Center and the sprawling medical complex. Most of it was burning. He turned and went straight south. This was now mostly residential, with no main roads.

"Okay," he said. "This should get us out of town."

They walked down the middle of a street. Once in a while they could see people in the homes. Some would come out and stare as the couple walked by. Most of the homes looked deserted.

They came to the edge of the addition, and he could see pasture and a couple of farmhouses beyond. "Here," he said as he handed her the shotgun back. "Keep this handy and take the safety off. Please don't shoot me."

"Funny."

COLT TURNED and walked toward one of the last houses on the block. "Now that we know the way is open and we can get out of here if need be, let's go shopping."

The house was a ranch-style, stretched out and flat. With only a single level, he thought it would be easy to see if anyone was inside, a safer choice than the split-levels or even three-story houses that lined the street. There were flowerbeds in the front waiting for plants and mulch, and toys littered the yard.

Moving to the door, he found it unlocked.

"Beth, please watch the street." As he said this, he went into the foyer, leading with the barrel of the shotgun. He went slowly, trying to make sure all the shadows were only that, and not someone hiding. Turning left, he went through a family room and toward the kitchen and heard Beth coming behind him, closing the door.

On this end of the house, there was the kitchen and dining area, plus an office and bedroom with a half bath. The final space was a utility room with a washer and dryer, hot water heater, and central air. As far as he could tell, only the utility room and bathroom weren't carpeted. Clearing these rooms, he went back to the kitchen and started looking through the cabinets. Most were empty, with everything edible missing.

Mentally slapping himself, he went back to the utility

room and looked in the built-in above the washing machine and dryer. What a surprise. Bleach. Carrying this back to the kitchen, he set his pack on the granite countertop and dug out a water bottle. Drinking all the water, he called out, "Beth, look in the bathroom for an eyedropper. I have the bleach."

He could hear her rummaging around and then heard a sharp intake of breath. Not hearing anything else, he called.

"Beth?"

"Uh, Colt. You'd better come here."

Leaving the bottles on the counter, he moved quickly down a long hall to the other end of the house. She was standing in a large bathroom. A door was open, which was a large walk-in closet that connected the bathroom with a bedroom. Coming up behind her and looking over her shoulder, he saw a woman and three kids crouching under the clothes hanging on a rack. The woman was holding the children against her, and the smallest child was whimpering.

"Please," the woman said, shivering in fear. "Please, don't hurt us."

Colt looked at her for a moment. "Beth, take them into the bedroom and see what you can do to convince them we're not going to hurt them. I'll make sure no one else is home."

When nobody moved, he said to the woman, "Look, we won't hurt you, okay?"

He turned and went through the rest of the house and didn't find anyone. Returning to the bedroom, he found the woman and her children sitting on the bed. She and Beth were in a deep conversation.

He looked at the kids and, thinking of his own loss, it

broke his heart to see how skinny they were. "Are you hungry?"

The older two nodded, so he went back out and retrieved his bag. He stopped, thinking he'd heard something, and went to the sliding patio doors to look outside. Not seeing anything, he then went back to Beth. He took three Power Bars from the pack with a bottle of water and gave it to them.

"Share the water," he said.

Beth was already doing the same for the mother.

"Thank you," the woman said, not meeting his gaze. "We haven't eaten in a couple of days. Not since the men came."

Turning to him, Beth said softly, "She's been raped, Colt. Repeatedly. When they left, the men said they wouldn't kill her kids as long as they could come back and see her again. They promised them food."

She looked at him and said vehemently, "God, I hate this new world we have."

"Ma'am," Colt said to the woman. "You need to take your kids and get out of here. They may not let you live when they come again."

"I can't," she said. "We've no food or water. The men stripped everything from the house."

"Well, hell." He dug into the pack and took out a box of Power Bars and some beef jerky and then handed it to her. "There's enough to last you a few days. Just get away and hide. It's the best you can do. You can't stay here."

The woman started crying. As she hugged the woman to her, Beth said to him, "Softie."

The noise came again from the kitchen, and Colt leveled the shotgun toward the door. "Beth, someone's here."

When he looked out of the bedroom door, there wasn't anyone in the hall or where he could see. As he quickly advanced toward the kitchen, someone standing in the foyer wrenched the shotgun from his grasp, firing it into the ceiling in the process. He was quickly grappling with two men. As they shoved him against the wall, he could hear screaming in the bedroom along with another shotgun blast. Colt tried to pull the .45 from his waistband, but a kick to the stomach doubled him over. He fought with everything he had. A grinning face in front of him took a hit with his elbow, and then he threw a punch at someone else and missed. A blow to the back of his head knocked him off his feet. He rolled and desperately dove into someone's legs, kicking and hitting. The fight lasted a couple of minutes, and he was getting tired. He got one man against the wall and kneed him in the groin. Drawing back his arm for another hit, he heard a loud noise and felt a blow to his head at the same time. He could feel himself fading but couldn't do anything about it. Trying to finish his swing at the man, he felt his arms fall to his sides. The last he remembered was the floor coming up fast.

WHEN COLT WARNED HER, Beth leaped up from the bed and reached for the shotgun she'd leaned against the dresser. She heard a shot from the kitchen and whimpered, "Colt?"

The woman on the bed screamed as the doorway suddenly filled with bodies. Beth shot the first man coming through the door and then was overwhelmed with bodies before she could pump another shell into the chamber. They took the shotgun from her, threw her on the bed, and found the .45 and the switchblade. The woman and her kids were trying to get out of a window and screaming at her to run. Beth tried to get up, and they tossed her back on the bed. They slapped the other woman until she stopped screaming. Someone took the kids and put them in the bathroom. The kids were screaming and then silenced by gunfire.

Suddenly, it was deathly quiet. As she looked in horror toward the bathroom, all she could hear was herself panting for breath and the other woman's racking sobs, saying, "No...no..."

Two more men came in the door and joined them; one was bent over at the waist, and the other had a bloody nose. The man pointing the shotgun laughed at them and said, "What happened to you?"

"Hey," one replied. "For an amateur, that man could fight. He was like trying to bag up a box of cats."

"Damn you," Beth yelled. "What did you do to Colt?"

Bloody nose replied, "You mean that peckerwood out there? I shot his sorry ass. He won't be bothering us any. You'll just have to find yourself a new man."

"You son of a bitch," she yelled as she came up off the bed.

The man with the shotgun caught her with one arm and threw her back on the bed. "Don't be in such a hurry. We've got plans for you."

Beth scrambled backward, glancing at the other woman. She was just sitting there as if she'd gone into a catatonic state. As Beth backpedaled on the bed, looking for anything to fight with, one of the men started to unbuckle his belt.

She locked her gaze on the man. "I'll find a way to kill you."

"Lady," he said, grinning, "all you're goin' to do is learn to like it."

Once again, the room suddenly filled with gunfire. Beth grabbed the other woman and rolled to the floor. It was over in moments, and then the silence was deafening, except for the ringing in her ears. She was holding her breath and shaking all over.

"Ladies," a woman said. "You're safe now, so come on out."

Recognizing the voice, Beth crawled weakly up the bed and then stood. The woman beside her didn't move.

"Well, I'll be damned."

Looking past the four men lying dead on the bedroom carpet and the blood splatter on the walls, she saw Mary standing just inside the door with Zeke peeking over her shoulder.

"I thought you guys died in your bunker," Beth said. "But Colt said you weren't that dumb, that you'd have a way out."

"Your man was right," Mary said.

Beth started toward the door. "I need to see Colt."

Zeke shook his head, blocking the door. "It's too late for that."

"No," Beth cried vehemently and then tried to go to the closet door to get to the bathroom. They blocked her way again.

Mary shook her head, tears in her eyes. "Not that way either. The bastards killed the kids."

Beth stood a moment and then collapsed on the bed with deep racking sobs. "It's just not fair."

Zeke came into the room and looked at the woman on the floor and then kneeled beside her.

Puzzled, he looked at Mary. "She's dead. And not a mark on her," he said wondrously. "That is seriously weird."

Finally getting control of her crying, Beth said, "She'd already been raped by these guys, or at least I think it was them, and then they killed her babies. Before you came in and saved us, she looked like she was in a trance. I think she just turned off." She looked around at them with tears in her eyes. "I wish I could."

One of the men she remembered from the bunker poked his head into the room. "Guys, we gotta make tracks outta here. We've been here too long and made too much noise."

Zeke started gathering up her pack and handed her the .45 and pistol belt. "I'll keep the scattergun for now."

They led her in a daze down the hall toward the front door. She stopped when she saw Colt crumpled in a corner and lying in a pool of blood. When she reached for him, they tried to stop her, and she fell to her knees. Racked with sobs, they picked her up and forcibly hustled her out the door.

One of the men said, "What's with the bleach on the counter, next to an open backpack? It looks like someone was going to fill a bottle with it. Was he making a bomb?"

Beth mumbled, "We were going to treat water with it to make it safe to drink."

"Yeech," he said.

"Hey, it works," Zeke said. "Fill a bottle with it. That man struck me as being pretty damned smart. And bring that backpack."

Beth said, "Colt was incredibly smart. He was just out

of his element. But he was so damned lucky. I thought he'd make it."

"Huh," said Mary. "We're all out of our element. Zeke worked construction, and I'm an insurance adjuster. Boy, do we have the claims now."

———

AS THEY CROSSED a pasture and entered a wooded area, the group stopped for a moment.

"Well," Zeke said. "We're out of town and safe for the moment. Any suggestions, boss?" He looked at Mary.

When she didn't reply, Beth said softly, "I have a farm."

They all turned to look at her. Three men and their women all decked out like an Army patrol. They were just like her brother, Arnie, and the antithesis of Colt. She missed them both. The young girl they'd sent to the mansion looked like she'd settled in nicely. Thank God for that. Beth couldn't bear the thought of what she'd sent the young girl to do.

"Where's your fourth man? Or should I ask?"

Zeke looked at her with a level stare. "He stayed. The batteries for the timer didn't work."

"I'm sorry about that. That took some serious balls. So, north of town. I raised organic vegetables. It's really out in the sticks and hard to find. Colt and I were going to try to make it there. I have food stashed away and water. I think there's enough for us to get on our feet and maybe survive the coming winter. That is if we can get there."

The couples just looked at each other and smiled.

"Well, Beth," Zeke said. "Unless we get molested by a

couple of helicopter gunships or armored vehicles, we'll get you there. Can you guide us?"

Beth stood, looking back toward the house that contained Colt's body and thinking of what might have been. She didn't know Zeke and Mary's story but knew that, in a way, all their stories would be the same. They'd all lost somebody. The young girl had lost her whole family. She lost her brother and Colt. It was almost too much to bear. But what had Colt told her? *No time for lengthy speeches.* And she added to herself, *No time for regrets. Gotta boogie.*

She took a deep breath and squared her shoulders. "Let's do it."

They walked single file, with Beth in the lead. The women followed her, and the last man guarded the rear.

Beth looked around. "Where's Zeke?"

Mary just smiled. "He's around. And don't worry about losing him. He's scouting around because he dearly hates surprises."

"He must have really hated it when he had to blow up his bunker."

"Oh, you've no idea."

TWELVE

COLT HEARD SOMEONE GROAN. Trying to open his eyes, he could only get a partial view. The groan came again, and he realized it was his own. Slowly, he brought a hand up and wiped his face. He rubbed his eyes enough to open them and see that he was lying in a pool of blood. It didn't take much imagination to realize it was his. Everything he tried to move hurt beyond belief. Getting his hands under him, he slipped in the blood as he tried to get up. Blinding pain erupted in his head, and he crumpled back to the floor.

Okay. Maybe later. He was so tired.

Voices faded in and out. "Hey, man. They all dead in here."

Another voice. "You surprised? Sounded like a war going on."

Farther away. "Jeez, buncha kids in the bathroom. Shot to rag dolls."

He felt something prod him in the back.

"This dude gone, too. If he ain't dead, he will be soon. Musta bled a gallon."

Later, he heard, "Let's get out of here. Nuthin' worth saving."

When Colt woke again, it was dark, and he was thirsty. Cautiously, remembering the pain in his head, he rolled to his side and leaned against the wall. Looking around, he could see vague shapes in the darkness. Despite the pain, he was starting to lose the fog he was in earlier. His head was a dull throbbing ache, and it seemed every inch of his body hurt. Remembering the fight, he was amazed he was still alive.

Beth. He lunged away from the wall and then slumped against it again, nearly fainting from the pain in his head. *Dammit.* He couldn't help her now. He'd have to wait until morning. He'd have to...somewhere in his jumbled thoughts for Beth, he faded away.

―――――

HIS EYES HURT. Colt sat up from where he'd slid down the wall. He was dizzy for a moment, then that cleared and he realized it was daylight. Crawling to a kitchen chair and using it as a crutch, he carefully stood and leaned against the counter. One eye still had fuzzy vision, but he could see well enough. He had to know about Beth.

Walking like an arthritic old man, he slowly made his way down the hall. He glanced into the bathroom and saw the three kids. Memories of his own children flooded his senses. For a moment, he gagged and thought he'd vomit but fought it off. He carefully moved the feet of a little boy so he could close the door.

He made it to the bedroom in a few steps. There were bodies everywhere, but no Beth. A woman's body lay on the floor by the bed, and he immediately recognized her as the mother of the children. He looked around carefully. There were no weapons, but when he searched the bodies, he found the switchblade knife that Beth had carried. He put that in his back pocket but didn't find anything else useful.

It took a few minutes, but he slowly searched the whole house and looked out the windows. Beth was gone. The packs were gone. Maybe she got away, and he prayed that was so. When he thought about her, he felt loss and regret that he'd pushed her away. Even though disaster and impending death accelerated feelings and actions to push people together, it was just too soon for him. Losing his children and the way he'd lost Jen simply turned that part of him off. Now, he wished he'd taken what Beth offered. The chance may never come again, and she was a beautiful woman.

Thirst overrode every sense he had. After closing the bedroom door, hopefully to keep the smell from the rest of the house, he made his way to the utility room and checked the water heater, praying the foragers had missed it. Turning the spigot at the bottom, a trickle of water came out. He palmed the water, brought it to his mouth, and kept doing that until his thirst was slaked. Brackish and tasting of the limestone deposits in the bottom of the tank, it was still a lifesaver. He went back into the kitchen, rummaged around under the counter and found a shallow pan. Without a hose, that was the only thing that would fit under the spigot.

Back at the water heater, he was thankful the piping was plastic and not copper. He grabbed it and pulled until both lines broke. As soon as he broke them, he heard a gurgle, and water was pouring out of the bottom into the pan. Almost crying in relief, he kneeled and drank from the pan as it filled. Once he had his fill, he let the pan fill and then turned off the valve.

Taking the pan, he went to the little half bath and looked in the mirror. He didn't recognize the image in the mirror. No wonder they thought he was dead. Blood matted his hair and covered his head, and dried over his eyes. He stoppered the sink and poured in part of the water.

Searching around, he found a washrag, soaked it, and started cleaning off the blood. With his eyes clear of dried blood, now he could see just how lucky he was. It looked like a bullet had glanced off his skull. It was probably small caliber because it had followed the contour of his skull and left about a three-inch-long gash.

He got more water from the tank and filled the sink. Looking in the medicine cabinet, he found a bottle of peroxide and poured part of it into the water. With that, he kept washing his head, finally just submerging his head in the sink and working the wound until he was reasonably sure that it was clean. He gasped for breath at the throbbing pain in his head. When he finally straightened, dizziness overtook him, and he leaned against the wall until the nausea passed.

After he dried his head with a towel, he found a tube of antibiotic cream and applied it to his head wound. He still found it amazing how every home he'd been into was fully stocked except for food and water, and wondered how long that would last.

Finally, he sat at the kitchen table and took stock. Beth was gone, and he didn't know if she was alive or dead, if she was captured or by herself and running. He certainly didn't know where to look for her. If she did get away, he was sure she'd head for her farm.

He was glad to have water but hadn't looked for any containers to carry it in. There was no food. He doubted if any of the neighbors that were still around would share. If the foragers from the gangs had hit this place twice, he was sure every other place fared the same. For now, he was too weak to go very far and didn't want to leave his water source. He'd just have to tighten his belt for a few days.

Once his headache passed for the moment, he stood and went to the end of the house he failed to look at before. He wouldn't make that mistake again. All his mistakes were costing the lives of people he cared for. He didn't know if he was lucky or cursed.

Colt opened the door and stepped down into a two-car garage. The big, double door was down and closed, but the door opening to the backyard was open. He closed it and turned to the benches lining the walls. Since both vehicles were gone, if they ever had two, he assumed the residents had tried to flee the city. This far out on the edge of town, they might have made it. He hoped so.

Finding nothing of use for his immediate survival, he went back into the house. Going through the cupboards and drawers in the kitchen, he saw that someone had taken any small containers that might hold water. If they thought that far ahead, why didn't they think of the water heater tank? Maybe they had water at the time.

He did find freezer bags. It would mean carrying all of them in another bag, like a shopping bag, but it was doable. He filled bags until it was too dark to see, piling them up on the kitchen counter. On one bag, he used a marking pen to mark it for the purifier. He poured that bag full from the container of bleach he'd left on the counter. The rate of two drops per quart for purifying water was not very much, so he thought the bag would last.

With this done, he collapsed on the couch. He didn't want to go to the bedrooms at the end of the house where the bodies were. Exhausted, he slept where he sat, his night full of tortured dreams.

———

THE NEXT MORNING Colt awoke to pain and hunger. He was getting tired of that. His head was not pounding like before, but his muscles were stiff and sore. Going to the counter, he drank a bag of water and then stepped out to the back patio to urinate. *Water in, water out.*

While he was outside, he stood and listened. Just barely daylight, the surrounding area seemed quiet and peaceful. He was learning lessons quickly though, and didn't trust the silence.

Back inside, he went to all the windows and looked outside. Especially up and down the front street. He didn't see anything, but before the ambush, he hadn't seen anything either. Moving around, he realized a lot of his soreness was leaving, and he didn't have a headache. It was time to leave.

He'd found a heavy shopping bag the day before, so he filled it with the water bags. Sliding his arms through the handles, he had a makeshift backpack.

Turning back to the counter, he found a couple of sharp steak knives. On second thought, he put them back. He couldn't carry them in the pack because of the plastic bags, and they were too long for his belt. Guess the switchblade would have to do.

Opening the front door, he walked out on the step. He caught movement to his right, looked, and didn't see anything. When he started to look the other way, he felt the cold steel of a gun barrel against his head.

Well, shit.

"You gotta choice," a voice said. "Live or die."

Colt slowly raised his hands to shoulder level. Movement started around him as men came out from the side of the house and surrounding houses. He started to look around and received a nudge from the gun.

"I didn't tell you to move. Now, drop the...whatever the hell that is on your back."

He complied, and a man came up behind him from inside the house, and picked it up.

"Just water," he heard. "No food or weapons."

"Check him."

They searched him, roughly pushing him around, and found the switchblade. "I always wanted one of these," said the man searching him.

"So, keep it."

The gun moved away. "Alright, shithead, turn around."

Colt turned and saw a man facing him, holding a short-barreled rifle. Around him, he saw about twenty men with weapons. He also saw a couple of closely guarded groups coming down the street. His eyes searched the group of women, but he didn't see anyone he recognized.

A man in a black uniform came walking through the crowd, and it was clear he was in charge. The captives and gang members parted in front of him as if he were Moses going through the Red Sea. Looking at him, Colt knew this was Homeland Security that Beth's brother was so worried about. The man looked more like the pictures of the Gestapo than any soldier he'd seen.

The newcomer stopped and looked Colt up and down, then grabbed him by the hair and pulled his head down to look at the wound. When Colt resisted, the man let his head go. Colt could feel a trickle of blood on his cheek from the newly opened wound.

"Well, you've got a little spirit anyway. Don't worry, you'll lose it. My name is Colonel Tyler. Actually it used to be captain, but I gave myself a promotion, and..."

Behind them, they heard a distinct 'snick,' and the man who'd put the switchblade in his pocket gave a small squeal. Colt didn't turn but couldn't keep a small smile off his face.

Tyler looked at him with what might have been grudging respect. "You knew that was going to happen, didn't you?"

"The safety doesn't work on it. Your man needs to be more careful around sharp objects," Colt said softly.

Someone kicked him in the back, and he sprawled on the grass, narrowly missing Tyler.

"Listen closely," said Tyler as he leaned over Colt. "You're now a captive and will live or die at our discretion. You do what we say or die. It's that simple. We control most of the city. Homeland Security has control of the food and water."

"Then, you must have won the battle for the Underground and at least one of the wells," Colt interrupted.

When one of the men started to hit Colt with his rifle butt, Tyler held up his hand. "That's very astute of you.

Are you military, or do you fancy yourself as some sort of urban tactician? Or are you just a natural troublemaker?"

Colt shrugged. "It's just logic. A plus B equals C. For you to do all this." He waved at the men around him. "You must provide what they need to live, otherwise they revolt and become more bodies on the street."

Standing, he caught himself a moment until the dizziness passed. "Also, you've recruited the gangs..."

"Some gangs," Tyler interrupted with a cold smile.

"So you must have lost a lot of your own men. Obviously, enough of your men survived to secure your position. Whatever the reason, you need the gangs to do your dirty work."

The sound of distant firing interrupted him as Tyler paused to listen.

One of the men was picking up the bags of water. "What's this one marked with a 'P'?"

He turned and saw the man was one of Colonel Tyler's, wearing a black uniform. "It stands for pure."

As the man started to open the bag, Tyler said, "I wouldn't drink that if I were you."

Opening the bag, the man smelled it. "That's bleach!"

"My bad," Colt said, then chuckled as the man dumped all the bags out.

Tyler laughed. "I think we'll keep you alive for a while just to see what you do. There's little enough entertainment anymore."

They pushed him toward the group of male captives.

"Hey, what's your name, smartass?" Tyler called.

"Colt Blaine."

"You seem to have all this figured out. There's one thing you've forgotten, Blaine. What's your role in all this?" Tyler looked at him expectantly.

Colt looked at the captives and listened again to the gunfire in the distance before he answered.

"Cannon fodder."

Looking around him, his only thought was, what did it matter? His wife and children were gone. Beth was gone, although he prayed she survived. He didn't know what type of relationship he had with her. All he knew was they needed each other. He'd read something once about wartime romances being sudden, and surprisingly, lasting.

But all this? Tyler said captive, but it looked more like conscription. It looked like they were being shanghaied, like old England with His Majesty's Navy. It was an old English form of the draft but seemed to be effective.

Pushing and shoving, the Homeland Security soldiers got them all started back toward Springfield. Moving to keep up, he knew one death was as good as another—it just didn't matter. Not anymore.

THIRTEEN

THE CONSCRIPTS WERE HERDED through town. Walking north on Glenstone Avenue, Colt couldn't believe how much damage had been done in just a few days' time. Many buildings smoldered or still burned. Fires were burning in the residential sections behind the retail strips and bodies littered the parking lots. Each block they passed added more people to the group. During the trip, none of the conscripts spoke or looked at each other. It seemed to Colt that their will to live was gone. When he stumbled and fell a couple of times, no one helped him up. One of the gang members would just wait for him. To stay on the ground was to die.

Even though he'd been in the area just a few days before, the trip was surreal. Each block they passed was a testament to destruction. Every building along the street appeared burned, gutted, or reduced to rubble. Very few people were seen, and those that were soon disappeared. After a couple of miles, they passed a water tower on the east side of the road. Black-suited troops surrounded the buildings adjacent to the tower. Stumbling forward with the rest of the conscripts, Colt wondered how the fight for the other towers was going.

They put the women in the university football stadium, and a few blocks later, they pushed the men into the stadium for the local baseball team. Once inside, they gave them water and an MRE. Colt wolfed down some kind of desiccated mystery meat and drank all the water. Men started throwing all the bottles in an empty trash barrel. Colt couldn't remember ever not needing a water container. He stuck his bottle into his back pocket, and was startled when the turf in front of him blew up and the echo of a shot reverberated around the walls of the stadium.

"That's your only warning, Mr. Blaine." The sound came from a bullhorn.

Turning, he could see a group of men lining the upper deck guardrails. He couldn't recognize him from the distance but supposed one of the men was Tyler. Colt walked casually over to the trashcan and lifted the plastic bottle high, then dropped it into the can. Being the curious sort, the only question he had was how did they power that loudspeaker? Was it battery-powered? There must be some limited electricity. Listening intently, he couldn't hear the hum of generators. *Strange.*

He went toward the wall and slumped down with his back to it. Remembering vaguely that if you have a concussion, you should stay awake, sleep found him immediately.

———

MORNING CAME with the sound of men bringing in water and food, and his life as a conscript began.

A man sitting a few feet from him said, "We must be going to fight today. That's the only time they feed us in the morning."

The man continued, "My name's Joel, by the way."

"I'm Colt. Do they just feed us once a day?" Colt asked as he glanced over at the man.

Joel nodded. "Like I said, mornings if we fight or afternoon if we don't."

"So, what's the pecking order around here?" Thinking of a prison, he said, "Who runs the yard?"

With a low chuckle, he said, "No one lives long enough to worry about that."

"How long have you been at this?" Colt asked.

"I guess longer than most." Joel looked curiously at him. "Why?"

"It's just an idea kickin' around in my head. I'm curious about something. We're here at Hammond's Field, and the women are at the university football field. Are there children being held somewhere?"

Looking at Colt with haunted eyes, the man shook his head slightly and said, "Kids aren't brought in." The man walked away.

They killed the children or left them to die. That was insane. Colt thought he'd gone through every emotion possible since the loss of his own children. In the forefront was anger and despair. Lately, since meeting Beth, he had hope—which now evolved into hopelessness. Looking at the men guarding them from the walls and at the conscripts around him, he added a new one. Hate.

His despair and depression ended at that moment. Now, even though it was unformulated for the moment, he had purpose. Now he had a reason to live.

The battles started that day. In the early morning,

guards brought them food and water. After the meal, they went to a huge pile of weapons lying on the cement in front of the stadium. They could pick their weapon. All the guns were loaded, but with no extra ammunition, so most of the men chose the rifles that had the banana clips or held the most ammunition. Colt simply picked up a .45, since he was familiar with it, plus a shotgun and hunting knife. He was about to ask someone what kept the captives from turning on the guards when gunfire erupted. He could see someone running away and then go sprawling on the cement. The guards didn't look at the fallen man again, except one went to retrieve the weapons.

Colt realized that answered the question. The conscripts might revolt and get a few of the gang members but would die in the process. The only option for escape was in the field. Gang members who guarded them were only slightly less expendable as the conscripts. So, Homeland Security was running the show using their own gang members to corral the conscripts, which kept them insulated and out of danger.

It was madness but smart. He kept that thought in the back of his mind. If things got any worse, he might use that as an option. But he couldn't think how the situation could get any worse. A frog sitting in warm water, slowly brought to a boil, will never try to jump from the pot. The conscripts were frogs. There was always just enough hope to try to live another day—hope of escape, of a steady supply of food and water. All they had to do in return was kill people and obey.

They attacked the downtown square at noon and had to clear out all the surrounding buildings. Since he wasn't exactly a warrior, Colt stayed back to see how things were done. It was simple and devastating for both sides. There was no guile or finesse, just rush the building and fight until one side gives up or runs away. Today, the conscripts were losing.

Colt looked around and found Joel near him, squatting behind a marble statue with another man. He ran to join them.

"You both have rifles," Colt said.

"Yeah, so?" the man with Joel said.

"So, our people are getting cut to pieces by their snipers." He pointed to three locations in the second-floor buildings facing them. "Take them out."

The man looked at Joel and then shrugged. "Sounds like a plan."

With Colt directing fire, they killed the snipers before they realized there was a new tactic directed at them. Then they started concentrating fire upon the opposition's people that were better armed. In minutes, it was over, and the conscripts were walking around killing the wounded.

Colt was standing with his new friends when Tyler, with his ever-present guard of Blackboots arrived.

Joel and the other man stood looking at the ground. Colt stared at Tyler.

"That was a good job, taking out their shooters," Tyler said.

"You could have done that yourself from your position," Colt said. "Why all the useless slaughter?"

Tyler laughed, looking around at his guard. "That's why I like this guy." He brought his attention back to Colt. "It's simple, really. It amuses me. Look at it this way. The only thing these gangs running around the city are doing is killing people and stealing food. That's all they're good for."

"It looks like most are just people trying to survive. You are the aggressor, not them."

Tyler shrugged. "All they need to do is give up, and we will take care of them. Look around you, Blaine. We wiped them out and still have plenty of people left. I can always get more people to fight. And like vermin infecting a food crop, these gangs have to go."

The next day at the weapons pile, Colt noticed Tyler standing close by.

"Hey, Tyler. Where are we going today?"

Tyler looked at him a moment and then shrugged. "You're going back to the square. A gang took over the Heer's building. If they hold that building, they have high ground and can pick us off from a half mile away. We need them out of there."

When Joel and the other man picked up rifles, Colt shook his head. "Those will be too hard to use in close-in work." He picked his .45, a short-barreled shotgun, and hunting knife. After watching him a moment, the two other men did the same. He saw Joel talking to a few other men, and they all chose the same weapons.

The Heer's building was a multistory high-rise with a restaurant on the ground floor, then offices and residential apartments above. It was a brutal fight, and at the end, when both sides ran out of ammo, hand-to-hand combat.

Colt let the crazies go in first. He recognized the first day that part of the conscripts were just a mindless horde that would run screaming and yelling into each fight as if they had a death wish. Maybe they did.

After they breached the front door, Colt followed with

his men. He'd been amazed when they arrived at the building and found ten men waiting for direction from him. Joel seemed to be their leader.

"What's with the men, Joel?"

The man shrugged. "You saved lives yesterday. We're hoping you'll do that today. Not everyone wants to die around here."

Colt looked at the men. "Alright. It's your funeral." A few of the men chuckled at that. *Talk about the blind leading the blind.*

They fought their way to the top floor using the stairwells. Colt still had eight men with him. He heard screaming from one of the rooms that sounded like children and rushed to the door. Huddled against the far wall were a few women and about a dozen children. None of them were armed. Out of ammunition, the crazies had pulled bloody knives and were advancing toward them.

"Stop them." Colt's men immediately jumped the crazies from behind and killed them. It was short and brutal work.

Standing in front of the women and kids, he asked Joel, "Is this normal? Have they been killing the women and children?"

Joel couldn't meet his eyes. The other men didn't even try. Finally, Joel said, "The women we can turn over to the Blackboots. But the others?" He shrugged his shoulders.

"Do Tyler or his men ever come into a building after we clear it?"

"Shit, no," one of the men answered. "They're scared to."

Colt sighed, looking at the men behind him. "This ends now. These people aren't a threat to anyone. They deserve a chance to survive." Some of the men were lifting their eyes, starting to show a little pride. This one small action gave them a little control back.

"Tyler will kill us if he finds out," Joel said.

"So, we use our new slogan. We're dead anyway."

Suddenly one of Tyler's gang members pushed in through the door.

"Nits make lice, shithead. Kill them now, or I'll report it."

Colt calmly raised his .45 and shot him in the head. The man went down like a puppet with the strings cut.

"Sorry," he said when he saw one of his men wiping blood and brains off his cheek.

"Are there any objections?" When he didn't hear any, he said, "Good. We stick together on this. If Tyler's gang members object, or even if you just suspect they might turn us in—you know what to do."

Turning back to the women, he asked, "Do you have someplace to go? Can you get away?"

One of the women stood up. For a moment, he thought she was going to curtsy. He put his hand on her arm to stop her. "Will you be okay?"

"Okay?" She shook her head. "We'll never be okay. But, thanks to you, we'll survive a while longer. The kids will survive."

"Good," he said. "Do all you can to make sure that happens. Wait until tonight, and then clear out. If you stay here, keep your heads down so nobody sees you." He paused, thinking for a moment. "If you hook up with other people, tell them to stop fighting and get out—there isn't anything here worth fighting for. Once there is no one else to fight, this madness will stop."

Her expression was so fierce he took a step back.

"This is our home! Those were our men you killed. We'll never stop fighting."

With a sad expression, he said, "And now, what do you have because of that stance? Get your babies to safety. Maybe I'll see you again."

———

THE CONSCRIPTS FOUGHT every day for two weeks straight. Colt and a few others survived by learning to fight dirtier than their opponents and being a little smarter. Coming back to the stadium one evening, he tiredly dropped his weapons on the pile.

"Blaine," he heard someone call.

He turned to find Tyler standing a short distance away. Colt smiled, knowing Tyler surrounded himself with guards, but still didn't trust anyone. Not that he should.

"I see you're still alive, Blaine."

Colt shrugged. "I'd rather be lucky than good any day of the week."

"Maybe," Tyler said. "But I think you're a real fast learner. I'm surprised you haven't escaped. It would be easy enough for a smart man."

"Are you trying to tempt me, Tyler?" Colt shrugged. "I'm just like everyone else here. One death is as good as another. I managed to lose all my reasons to care. It just doesn't matter anymore."

"I've noticed you seem to have a small cadre of followers, Blaine. Whatever you're planning won't work, you know."

"We're just some guys helping each other survive."

"One more question, Blaine. Some of my civilian

friends seem to be dying. Do you know anything about that?"

"By civilian friends, you mean gang members that just happen to be on your side? I don't know a thing, Tyler. I can't get past you thinking you have friends."

Tyler smiled. "Point taken. I'm not doing this to win friends. Well, good luck to you."

As the man turned away, Blaine called, "Tyler."

When the man paused, Colt said, "You do realize your conscripts could fight harder if you fed us twice a day? Even galley slaves would get that."

"That's true," Tyler replied. "But those of you that come back don't need the strength to fight me."

Surprisingly, they gave the conscripts an extra ration that evening. Looking around, he saw there was hardly anyone left from when he first arrived. Joel had become his right hand and a few of his men still survived. The faces kept changing. That was good news and bad news. He didn't trust some of the new faces.

As they were eating some kind of mystery stew ladled from a huge cook pot in the center of the arena, Colt said to Joel, "I heard someone fell into the latrine pit again."

Joel didn't look at him. "It was just another one of Tyler's spies. He was asking why there doesn't seem to be any women prisoners brought back with us."

He thought about it a minute. Tyler seemed determined to find out if Colt was planning an insurrection. Once an inkling of that idea got back to Tyler, their death would soon follow.

"Tell the men to keep their eyes open and their mouths shut."

"You got it, boss."

Boss? Who'd a thought that.

FOURTEEN

COLT HUGGED the west wall of the stadium, trying to stay in the shade. He tried to stay away from people if possible, not liking his own unwashed stench, let alone theirs. The thermometer on the infield wall registered a hundred-ten degrees, and all the men were sitting around panting like lizards.

According to his brand-new stolen watch, today was the first day of July. They'd been fighting for over two months. Their last battle had been two days ago, and their last loss of life had been a week ago. Everyone left in the cadre of conscripts was hardened and battle ready. As their numbers grew, Colt thought more of escape. They were reaching a tipping point where the risk versus reward might just dictate a revolt.

One of the men sitting close to him spoke softly. "Heads up, here comes a Blackboot."

Glancing up from beneath the bill of his ball cap, Colt saw a man in a Homeland Security black uniform walking toward him.

"Thanks, Chris. Look at him. He's got to be cooking in that black uniform," Colt said.

"Yeah, I hope he fries."

It was significant that they didn't use the loudspeaker to call for him. Things must be worse and whatever batteries or electricity they'd used before are gone now.

"Stand up."

Colt stood and leaned his hands against the wall as the man searched him.

"Alright," the guard said to him. "Come with me." The man turned his back and marched off toward the door.

As Colt strode after the guard, Chris deftly tossed him a small knife. Colt stuck it in his pocket. He didn't know what this was about, but didn't think it would be good since he had never been summoned before.

They walked toward the convention center just down the street. Outside the stadium, two guards had fallen in behind Colt for the trip. He was amazed every time they left the confines of the stadium at how everything had fallen into ruin in a few short months. He was used to the smell, but it still registered as an affront to his senses. There were huge columns of smoke from different locations around town, and he was thankful for not having cleanup duty. Homeland Security burned bodies every day.

After a battle or skirmish, people would come in and haul away the dead. Amazingly, no one from either side would bother the so-called ghoul squad, even during a fight. Everyone knew that the dead bodies would spread disease. Fighting continued every day. Warring factions left in the city couldn't agree on who'd control what. Every group of people had their own stash of food, which

Colt knew had to be dwindling fast. Of course, Homeland Security wanted to control it all.

Entering the convention center, they crossed through the large open auditorium and went through the double doors to the front of the center. Colt immediately saw Tyler standing with a group of Blackboots, as the conscripts called them. He wondered if anyone realized how much that rhymed with jackboots of Gestapo and Nazi fame. Hell, thinking back to the state of the education system, most had probably never heard of them.

The buzz of conversation stopped when they brought him in, then the volume picked up again as they ignored him. Tyler came over to his small group.

"Search him."

"Sir," one of the guards said. "We already…"

Tyler spoke coldly. "Again."

Once again, Colt was turned and spread-eagled against the wall. Their quick search found the small knife he'd put in his pocket.

Confronting the guard, Tyler said, "If he'd killed you, it would have been well deserved. You don't bring a lion in among the sheep without pulling its claws."

Colt was standing normally again. "Hardly a lion," he said mildly.

Tyler gave him a small smile and said, "You haven't looked in a mirror lately."

The group of Blackboots came over and joined Tyler. "This is the man I was talking to you about. His name is Blaine, and he seems to have a knack."

One of the men spoke. "He doesn't look like much."

Tyler interrupted Colt's reply.

"What did you do, Colt? Before all this dust-up started, I mean."

Colt answered tersely, not liking the direction the conversation was going. "Computers."

"Computers." Tyler shook his head and then turned to the rest of the Blackboots. "After the first couple of fights this man was involved in, he started making suggestions to his fellow combatants. Of course, it is a given that we always succeed, it's just a matter of numbers. But our attrition rate started coming down. More men started following his directions and still more lives were saved. Of course the result is, now we have more mouths to feed."

Tyler laughed. "It kind of reminds me of the movie *Gladiator* when Maximus took charge. Now, I seem to have a well-organized group of men in the stadium that are fiercely loyal to Blaine. I have to put extra men on the walls for guard duty. And it kind of leaves me with a problem."

One of the men spoke up again. "Just kill them. All of them."

"So, Fred," Tyler spoke to the man. "Do you want to lead the next charge?"

Fred's gaze found the floor.

"I thought not," Tyler said. "Okay, you men are dismissed. This is my decision, and I'll let you know what to do."

He turned to Colt. "Let's take a walk."

They walked down the foyer toward a smaller auditorium. There was a guard at the door. When the guard moved and pulled the door open, Colt knew there were conscripts inside before he saw them. He could smell them. The open door let in the only light to illuminate the room.

"Bring them out," Tyler told the guard.

He didn't count, but there must have been at least thirty women brought out and pushed against the wall in the bright sunlight. The bright light blinded them, and they held their hands over their eyes. They were dressed mostly in tee shirts and shorts. Some had shoes, most didn't. Colt thought that odd, since there were enough shoes left in the stores to outfit thousands.

The women slid down until they were sitting with their backs against the wall. Tyler looked them over. "Is that all of them?"

"Just the special prisoners left," the guard said.

"Oh, they're in here? Bring them out."

The guard brought two women out in chains. The first was tall, and despite a lack of food for everyone, looked very strong. She challenged everyone with her gaze, and that look was full of hatred. She had hacked her hair short, and her clothes had ripped from fighting. There was blood on her arms from small cuts and a larger cut on her side that still trickled a little blood. While the other women sat, she stood and leaned against the wall. The stance highlighted muscular thighs and arms. *A fighter*. There was a clear difference in the attitudes between the women slumped to the floor and this one. Sadly, Colt knew the answer. She hadn't been given to the troops yet.

Colt thought that this woman didn't come easy and wondered how they captured her. Maybe, just like him. You never think it can happen, that you'll die fighting or always get away. Then, one day, you wake up with a boot on your neck. When she looked at him, he gave her a small smile.

The other woman was smaller and blonde. She was

dirty and disheveled, but not nearly as bad as the fighter looked. Dejected looking, she slumped to the floor.

"So," Tyler said, drawing his attention from the women. "Here's my proposition. Thanks to you, and some other groups like yours, we pretty much have control of the city. There's one last stronghold, and it will be a hard nut to crack. Can you guess where it is?"

"It should be the airport," Colt said without hesitation.

"Right," Tyler said. "The airport—how did you know that?"

"Hell, we've been everywhere else, Tyler. It's not rocket science."

"No, I suppose not. I keep forgetting you actually think. Anyway, I'd like for you to lead that little campaign for me."

"Like I have a choice? Since when do we have choices? What kind of weaponry do they have?"

Tyler laughed. "That is what I like, straight to the point. The answer, we don't know for sure. We do know they have some heavy machine guns, maybe left over from the helicopter unit stationed there. Hell, they may still have diesel for the chopper gunships for all we know. As you may or may not know, the Army destroyed anything bigger than a machine gun before they went under. So, it's going to be tough. And, for your information, the assault will include all of us. I'll naturally be in charge. However, I want you to lead it—as one of us, of course."

Tyler laughed as he continued. "I'm going to promote you from slave to captain."

None of this made any kind of sense, but Colt decided

to play along. Hell, he thought. *It's not as if I have anything else to do.*

"If I should take your deal, are there perks to go with my promotion?"

"You mean, other than being a member of Homeland Security? Well, there's food when you want it, you might actually get fat, and water when you want it. Look around you. Have you noticed our men are actually clean? Our water supply is almost unlimited, especially with the small number of people using it now."

Inadvertently, Tyler had given him an insight into his twisted thinking. *If you have a finite supply of food and water, then you must adjust the number of people using that resource. You kill the extras.*

"Now, for your men," Tyler continued. "We're going to combine forces and send all these women to your men in the stadium. Later, they'll fight alongside you. You, personally, will have your pick of them before they leave this building. How's that for a perk?" Tyler wrinkled his nose. "I have to tell you, a bath for you would be welcome."

"I suppose I could use a little sprucing up," Colt said, looking at the women. This was like a used car salesman trying to sell him a gem of a deal off the back of the lot.

"Go ahead. Look them over. Most are very pretty." *Meaning ugly girls were not brought in?*

As Colt walked over to the women, he noticed their beaten-down look. None would look up at him. They were dressed in rags and tattered clothes, and lifeless. "I suppose these women have already served your troops and the gangs?"

Tyler laughed. "Well, let's say none of them are virgins."

Colt controlled his anger, turned, and pinned Tyler with his gaze. "Then why give them up?"

Tyler dropped his gaze and turned slightly away. In the old world where body language was part of every negotiation, he flunked every sign. Something was wrong. "Their usefulness is over for us. We'll get new women and pass these along to your men."

"Why?" Colt asked, relying on this man's need to talk —to be superior.

"It's none of your business, but I'll tell you anyway. It's just a simple reward system to keep your men in line. Clever, don't you think?"

He stopped at one girl, kneeled, and pulled her chin up. "What's your name?"

The young girl cleared her throat. "Marcie."

"How old are you, Marcie?"

"Fifteen."

When she started to look down again, he said, "Look at me."

When she finally met his gaze, he whispered, "Don't give up."

Colt stood and moved on down the line of women. Finally, he came to the chained woman on the floor. Her hair was down in front of her face, so he couldn't see her. *Something...*

He turned and pointed at the tall woman leaning on the wall. "What about this one?" He nudged the woman with his foot and she hissed angrily at him.

"Not possible," Tyler said. "She was just captured on the west side of town today. We've been trying to get her for weeks. This one hasn't been broken in by the troops yet, but we'll remedy that today. Actually, she's kind of like you, Colt. She's a fighter—misguided, of course."

"So, why ruin her and kill her? Just conscript her like you did the rest of us. What's the big deal?"

"Last week, she set an ambush and killed twenty of my men. Not conscripts, as you call yourselves, or our gang members. Homeland Security, my men. She's going to pay for that. It's a matter of honor."

He glanced incredulously at Tyler. "Honor? You'll have to show me an example of that sometime."

Colt looked at the woman with a grudging respect. The woman stood tall, probably about six feet. Her dark hair was cropped short as if she'd done it herself with not too much care for how it looked. She stared relentlessly over his shoulder at Tyler, and he had no doubt that if she wasn't chained, she would have launched an attack regardless of the cost. Stepping closer, he whispered, "Bravo."

The woman brought her gaze back to him, pinned him with dark brown eyes. Then she smiled at him, and he felt the tug of desire for the first time in months.

Colt moved back to the other woman. She seemed familiar. "What's your name, girl?"

When she didn't answer, he asked, "Move your hair back so I can see you."

When she didn't, he reached down and moved her hair away from her face. She looked at him with a tear slowly leaving a dirty streak down her face. *Jen!* It was all he could do to keep from confirming he knew her. Steeling his emotions, he turned back to Tyler.

"I want both of them."

"I said no, Blaine. They aren't part of the deal. You may pick as many of the others as you wish if you have that much energy. But these two stay."

Colt stood and shook his head. "Maybe we need to rethink the deal."

Tyler shoved him against the wall with a thump that rattled his teeth. Guards started moving toward them. "Don't forget who you are."

Looking calmly at him, Colt said, "I know exactly who I am and what I am. You know that I'm the one who can bring you to the airport with the least amount of casualties to your own precious men. And since you already know most of us won't survive that little onslaught, you might as well kill us now and get some fresh recruits to do your dirty work. I'm tired and don't feel like running all over the place just so your men don't have to fight."

Tyler backed away from him, shook his head, and then glanced at the women. "They have to pay. Look at them. The tall one looks beaten, but it took four men just to hold her down and chain her up. She's a lot stronger than she looks, and she fights dirty."

Colt snorted and grinned. "Is there another way to fight? I like a woman with spirit. If I can convince her, she'd be a help to me if what you say about her is true. You need fighters. And I want the smaller one, too."

"You're really trying to deny our fun, Blaine. What I had in mind was having the troops use them for a day or so, then take them out and cut their throats. They need to suffer for what they've done so we can make an example of them." Tyler paused for a moment as if thinking. "However, you do have a point."

He could tell Tyler didn't like it. They must really want that airport.

"The tall one only did what any soldier would have done, so I guess a chance to die on the battlefield, so to speak, would be sufficient. But Blaine, she must die. And the other woman? I need to do something to punish her. My men would revolt if I didn't. She was sneaky. The woman would lure my men into a building and then kill them."

Colt played the man's ego. "Your men will do what you tell them to do. Of course, you know if you send her with us, she'll be condemned to death anyway. Cannon fodder, remember?"

Tyler looked at him quizzically. "I feel like you're making an argument based on something other than wanting these women. You know her, don't you?"

Colt saw something in the other man's eyes that he didn't like. This was a test, and it was life or death for all of them. If Tyler got an inkling that he knew this woman, it would be over. Any leverage or advantage would be gone.

"Never saw her before," he said. "She looked familiar at first, but no. The woman I knew is dead. So," he continued, "how do you want to punish her? If she's a fighter, she's no use to me all busted up."

Tyler was still looking between him and the girl like he was trying to figure something out.

"Hey," Colt said, watching him calmly. "You came to me, remember? You're still the master. At the end of the day, I'm still just a conscript. You have all the power here."

All the women had their heads up looking at them, sensing the power play. The guards were inching closer, not sure what was going on but feeling the tension in the air.

Finally... Tyler stepped away from him.

"Alright, Mr. Blaine, they're yours. You'll see to it that

they don't survive the battle, even if you have to shoot them yourself. It's regrettable that you won't become one of our elite members of Homeland Security. But for now, I'm just not sure you can be trusted. Instead of directing the attack from safety, you'll lead the charge. If you survive, maybe then we can think about your position with us."

"I wouldn't have it any other way," said Colt. "Until we launch the attack, I'd like to request food and water, plus the shower facilities at the stadium. You can call it a last supper kind of thing."

Tyler wore a small smile. "You're always trying to get a little more, aren't you? No facilities, but I'll have water brought in for bathing. You can have a regular feast before you die, plus the benefit of female companions. See? You can't deny that I'm not benevolent toward my subjects."

"Subjects? We're slaves, Tyler." Colt shrugged. "Like the gladiators said in the old stories, 'we who are about to die, salute you.' Now, if you please, would you take the chains off these women? I'd like to see what I just bought with my life."

"Sure," Tyler said. "But this one must be punished first." Tyler pulled a small conference table up to them. "Blaine, you seem to be trying very hard to convince me that you don't know this woman. As an object lesson on who's in charge here, I'm going to take your woman first. If you don't know her, it won't matter to you, will it?"

Tyler laughed. "This way, there will be a little something of me present, even at your reunion. And you, my friend, will help me make this happen."

He snapped his fingers, and the guards came forward and pointed their rifles at Colt.

Colt started to object and then caught himself. *You sick son of a bitch.* It was still life or death, and he was sure this was just a game to Tyler. What game, he didn't know.

The guards pulled Jen to her feet by her chained wrists and then pushed her face down over the table facing Colt.

"Grab her wrists by the chains, Blaine. Hold her tight, now," the grinning Tyler said as he was staring at Colt.

He looked at Jen, and she locked her gaze on his eyes.

Shaking her head, she said, "No."

Tyler would think she was protesting her treatment, but she never took her eyes from Colt. He knew what she was telling him. *Don't do anything.* An evaluation would be made of his every action and expression. Colt abruptly grabbed her chained wrists and roughly pulled her toward him, stretching her torso over the table, her feet barely touching the floor. He held her there as Tyler got behind her, kicked her feet apart, and pulled her pants down.

It lasted about a minute. Other than a wince of pain at entry, Jen was expressionless during the ordeal. She just stared at Colt, and he looked back at her. All he could hear was the slapping sound of Tyler grunting in exertion, shaking the table, and a couple of the women crying. He could feel the hungry stares from the Blackboots watching the rape. This was normal and expected for them.

Panting, Tyler finally backed away. Immediately, another guard stepped up, starting to unbuckle his belt.

"That's not the deal, Tyler. I'll kill the next one or die trying. Then you'll be on your own for your last glorious battle."

Tyler stared at him a moment and then motioned for the soldier to get away. Taking a key from his pocket, he tossed it to Colt. "I keep my bargains. See that you do the same."

Motioning for a couple of the women to get up and come to him, he gave one the key. "Get both of these women unchained, and then take care of them." Colt looked for any objection from Tyler but didn't get any.

The group of women started to file out the door, and Colt stopped and called to the fighter, still playing to the audience.

"Hey. You got a name?"

"Lila," she said softly. If a whisper could be menacing, she had it down.

"Alright, Lila. The Blackboots say you're a fighter. I'm putting you in charge of these women. When you get to the stadium, keep them in the foyer and away from the men until I get there. Understand?"

She stared at him a long moment, then gave a short nod.

As the guards herded the women out the door, Colt turned to Tyler. *Let the games begin.* "Well, is our little pissing contest over?"

The other man laughed. "I still think you and the blonde know each other. Sometimes I wonder just who's in charge here."

"You shouldn't wonder. If I were in charge, all this wouldn't be here."

Tyler shook his head. "Can you not concede that, at least in this corner of the city, I've secured water and food for those of us that are left?"

Colt grudgingly gave a nod. "I just don't like your

methods. So, when do you want to do this little exercise at the airport?"

"Soon." Tyler's grin was feral.

He nodded, lost in thought a moment. He couldn't help it. No matter the circumstance, his mind kept churning away. "What's so important at the airport that we have to die trying to storm that particular castle?"

"Not your concern, Blaine."

"Okay." Colt shrugged. "Let's say the day after tomorrow so we have another full day of rest. We'll move out before dawn."

"That'll be a Wednesday," Tyler said. "And we'll move out in the daylight, not before dawn. I don't want you disappearing on me in the dark. See? I'm always a step ahead of you."

Colt replied, "I don't care what day it is. Days don't mean much anymore. I'll tell the guards when we're ready."

FIFTEEN

COLT WALKED BACK to the baseball stadium with his guards in a loose trail behind him. If there wasn't so much destruction and death around him, he could have enjoyed the walk. It was hot with a cloudless sky, and the humidity had to be approaching ninety percent. Seeing the haziness in the west, he thought that in a couple of days, the weather might be perfect. Rain and low visibility would make things a lot easier.

As he walked into the stadium, he could see the men had already heard about the arrival of the women. They grouped about fifty strong on this side of the field.

As he headed out to meet them, Jen stepped out in front of him.

"Wait," she said. "Can I talk to you?"

"Shut up." Hands on hips, he glanced around them.

She stopped talking, startled. He could see an angry flush start on her face.

"The walls have ears, and we're watched constantly. If we're going to talk, it will be later. For now, I have one question." He stood looking over the group of women. Strangely, Lila came to stand beside them.

"Will these women fight, or has the life been beaten out of them?"

Jen just shrugged.

"Lila? What do you think?"

He could see her staring at Jen. Shrugging, she said, "I guess it depends on the woman. For the most part, I'd say yes. Given a chance, they'll fight. The question is who?"

Jen interrupted, "Do you know who you're fighting?"

Colt looked at her. The woman that walked out on him was gone. While only months ago, it seemed like years. The old Jen would never have thought of that question. It was a relief that he could look at her critically now and keep emotion out of it.

She returned his gaze calmly. "What? I'm not the same little selfish and insecure yuppie girl that left you."

Looking him up and down, she said, "You're different, too, you know. I thought I knew you, but right now, you scare the shit out of me."

"It's been rough...for both of us." He looked around them and at the people watching them expectantly. "Just remember that, at least for now, things aren't always as they seem. Will you trust me? Will you help me?"

"Asked and answered," she said flatly.

"Can I trust you?"

He watched her eyes drop from his, her gaze sliding to the floor, then back to his. "Yes, of course." *Body language.*

Off to the side, he could tell Lila was watching both of them. He looked at Jen a moment longer until he saw her eyes soften. "I can tell you're cooking up something. We haven't been that long apart. Whatever it is, live or die, I'll help you. Just tell me ahead of time what you're doing so that I know my part. Is that clear enough?"

At that moment, he knew she was a plant. Her words were too sincere. He also remembered Jen telling him once there was a big meeting between Sammy Boy and Homeland Security. Was Tyler so afraid of an insurrection that he'd go to these lengths to find out what it was? He shook his head. Was he overthinking the situation again? Beth would have told him yes. One fact was solid. Tyler was bat-shit crazy.

Although he kept his game face on, inside, he was a swirling mess. The shock of finding Jen, knowing that she didn't die, and then realizing he still couldn't trust her, was about to cause a brain lock.

Jen gave him a push. "You'd better get to work."

Nodding to her, he walked on through the group of women and out into the sunlight. Looking behind him at the skyboxes, and could see shadows moving around in the covered spaces. They were always watching, but there might be a way. *In the meantime...*

"Alright," he said. "Gather around up here."

He didn't understand the hold he had over these men. Most everything he did was for his own self-preservation as well as theirs. When push came to shove, they all traded food and water against a chance of death. But, somewhere along the line, he started feeling responsible for the survivors. New conscripts were apt to charge a building, or wall, just to take a bullet and end it all. They were the crazies. All the rest were just trying to hang on until something changed, trying not to be the last frog in the slowly boiling pot.

Colt looked at the men in front of him and glanced at

the women behind. The Blackboots were desperate and anxious for some unknown reason, so Tyler and his cohorts were vulnerable for the moment. The men, at least a solid core of them, were as battle-hardened as they could be. It was time to roll the dice. If Tyler wanted a revolt, maybe it was time to give it to him.

He waited until everyone could hear him and then continued. "We're going to have to fight again, and it will be a tough one this time. The Blackboots are sending us to the airport. Now, Tyler is waiting for me to come up with some grand scheme to take down the terminal, but there is only one way to do it. There aren't enough of us to get sneaky and creative, and apparently, we can't wait them out, so it will probably have to be a frontal assault. My guess is—not many of us will survive."

Turning slightly, he could see the women edging closer to listen. "Until then, we have the rest of today and all tomorrow to rest. The Blackboots want us to have all our strength for this one. Food will be coming, and I'm sure it will be a gourmet meal." He paused as the men chuckled. "There will be water provided for bathing. I insisted on this because anyone we go against can smell us coming from a block away." More laughter.

"Now," he continued, "you see the women behind me, and for the most part, they're scared to death. These women are *conscripts* just like you. Slaves. They've been beaten and used repeatedly since their capture. Think of your wives and daughters you may have had. These are your sisters in this slavery that has been put upon us."

He paused to look around at the men. Feeling something brush his arm, he saw Jennifer standing at his side, and strangely...Lila, watching Jen.

"Hear me," he said. "These women will *not* be forced. I haven't counted, but I'm sure there are more of you than there are of them. I don't care how you pair up, or what you do between yourselves. I have one warning. These women have been through hell. If they say no, it means no and I'll kill any man who breaks that rule. Is this understood?" The men shuffled around for a moment. Finally, a few of the men stepped forward— men he knew could be trusted.

Joel stepped forward. "We'll make sure it happens, Colt. You can count on it."

———

THE SUN HAD SET and the only light in the stadium came from several campfires. The Blackboots had delivered water as promised but allowed no privacy so they could watch the women bathe. Colt had his men stand between the soldiers and the women to afford at least a small amount of privacy. After the women had dressed, he had the men strip and do the same. After exposing themselves to the guards, the Blackboots left them alone. He guessed the peepshow wasn't as good.

Now, everyone seemed paired up as Colt and Jen walked around checking. Colt had been serious about not forcing the women, and there were still a few of them sitting by themselves against the wall. The tall, dark-haired fighter was one of them.

As he was about to go sit down, he heard a commotion close by in a darker portion of the enclosure. He quickly strode over to find a couple of the new conscripts holding down one of the women as she struggled to get away. Starting to grab them, Joel and a couple of his men shouldered past him. They dragged the men off the girl and brought them to Colt. Glancing around, he could see most of the men and women were standing and watching them. It had been a silent encounter up to this point.

Addressing the two men, he asked softly, "Did you hear me earlier about not forcing the women?"

One of the men tried to bluster his way out of it. "These are just whores."

"Kill him."

One of the men with Joel leaped forward and produced a small knife. He grabbed the man by the hair and cut his throat. The whole action took about three seconds.

"What about the other one?" Joel asked.

Colt shrugged. The point had been made. "Let him go. Just make sure he sleeps alone."

Lila came up, took the girl by the shoulders, and led her away.

Colt turned abruptly and spoke to the rest of the men surrounding them. "I *will* be obeyed."

———

HE AND JEN found a place in a dark corner, away from the other people. Colt finally groaned and slid down with his back to the outfield wall. Jen sat between his legs, using Colt for a backstop. She took his arms and wrapped them around herself, leaned forward, and cried. They stayed that way for nearly an hour before she finally stirred.

"Why did you ask for me?" she asked softly. "I was

ready to die. I knew that was what they had planned for me. They did it to another woman. After the men were through, they didn't have to kill her. She just laid there and died.

"But," she continued. "Then you were there, and I didn't want to die anymore. What happened with you?"

"When this whole thing started, with Tyler using conscripts to do his fighting for him, I figured I had a choice. I could die trying to get away from Tyler or die fighting for him. When it came down to it, I just didn't care. Then, things got a little better. Instead of just dying, like everyone else, I made myself useful to him. I learned to kill in ways you wouldn't imagine."

"I doubt it."

"Yeah, well, anyway, you probably heard what he offered to me. He suspects we know each other, but if he knew for sure you meant something to me, I think we'd both be dead. I just wish I knew what was so important at the airport."

"I can answer that one. Food," she said. "There's a huge stockpile. The people there aren't gangs. A bunch of preppers took it over when they couldn't get out of town. It's mostly men and women, and something you don't see much of around town anymore. Children."

"Kids?"

"Yes. And that is who I've been helping for the last few weeks. I figured if we cut down the numbers of Homeland Security, or Blackboots as you call them, the families there would have a better chance of survival. That's what I've been doing."

"Beth said you were an addict and would die."

"I don't blame you for thinking that. Whatever drugs

Sam gave to the women made us more pliant but didn't seem too addictive. This may seem hard to believe, but with what was going on it just seemed easier to take the drugs. Then there were no worries."

"Shit," Colt said. "What a mess we made of our lives."

"We're alive, and we still have something to talk about, Colt."

"I'm sorry for the way things turned out, Jen, but—"

She interrupted him, "Jennifer. The old Jen is dead."

"Alright. Jennifer. But I think we do need to rest."

"No burning questions? No more 'why in the hell did you do that' kind of questions?"

"Not really," he said. "It just doesn't matter anymore. Our world was blown apart. I blame you for leaving me, but now I just don't care. You were afraid, and I didn't offer any solutions. It was as if this bomb was sitting there, and I didn't see the fuse burning. I blame myself for that. I should have grabbed you and the kids and headed for the hills. I'll forever blame myself for that. My kids died, and my wife turned into a whore because I didn't have a plan."

Jennifer turned and sat on his lap and hugged him to her. "Damn you, Colt, no matter what happens from now on, don't ever blame yourself for what happened. I was a damned stupid bitch and let my fear control my mind. It cost me everything."

She was starting to nuzzle his neck and grind herself into him.

"What're you doing?"

"I thought we could make love one more time before you go and do whatever plan you've cooked up. Even if you don't love me anymore," she pleaded. "Please do it for me."

He pushed her away, alarm bells going off in his head. It was just too pat, too scripted. Things that he'd shoved into his subconscious were working their way forward. He realized that she wasn't skinny or starved-looking. She was dirty enough but not filthy like the rest. And the most telling of all? It had finally hit him. She smelled good. And he knew she hadn't bathed with the other women.

"Sorry, Jen. Someone told me penicillin is really hard to come by nowadays."

He didn't hear what she hissed at him when she stalked away. It was probably a good thing.

———

AS SUNLIGHT PEEKED over the top of the stadium, Colt woke in a fog. He didn't know how much sleep he got, but it was not much. Looking around, hardly any of the prisoners were stirring. The guards were moving around the walls and seating areas. He walked to the center of the field and helped himself to water from the tank, and then went to the corner they used as a latrine. When he got back, Jen was waiting for him.

He handed her a container of water.

She stood. "Where do we...?"

Colt pointed toward the latrine dug at the far corner from them. She slowly made her way toward it.

When she came back, she said, "Colt, we need to talk."

"No, we don't. I can't think of anything we'd need to discuss."

"Okay, I guess I deserve that, but we need to plan."

Colt had been thinking about that. The Blackboots would be expecting some sort of plan from him, and he was curious about her plan, thinking it would be Tyler's plan also. So far, without having seen the airport for a long time, he had no plan at all.

Her plan was simple. "You remember that I told you I've been helping the people at the airport? I can't attack them, Colt. There are too many families there. So, what we'll do is go straight at them. At the last moment, their middle will give and the conscripts will pass through. Kind of like that movie *Braveheart* that we saw. You know, when the two factions charged each other, then wound up shaking hands?"

"When did you get to be such a field general?"

"Necessity is the mother of invention. Right? Hopefully, we'll catch the Blackboots by surprise. Your people and my people will combine and attack them in force. We should be able to wipe them out once and for all."

"Your people and my people?" He snorted. "That's well and good, but how will the airport folks know the game plan? It's not like we can call them up, and I'm fresh out of carrier pigeons."

She looked at him for a moment. "I'll tell them."

When he didn't respond, she said, "I'll talk to some of the women. They'll distract the guards and I'll just waltz out of here."

"If it's that easy, why don't we both go? Or we can all go."

She shook her head. "One person can hide and get away undetected. If we all escape, they'll know and kill us. For some reason, Tyler watches you all the time. He thinks you're up to something. If you'd tell me what that is, we could make sure our plans don't interfere with each other."

She looked at him expectantly. When he didn't say anything, she continued. "Who'll lead the attack if you escape? Colt, we need to suck Tyler into this. Otherwise, he'll just find another way. You may not feel the same way about it, but I don't want to leave you, now that I've found you again. But I just don't see another way."

Colt stood looking at her, thinking about the plan. Just simple enough, it might sound good to someone who didn't already have their suspicions up. And Jen. She'd betrayed him once. *Once a cheater...and how does she know about Tyler watching him? This was nuts.*

"I don't like this." Colt's voice was a dry rasp. "What if I don't cooperate?"

"Then I'll get away and help defend the terminal building as best I can. We'll be waiting for you. I don't want to think about that. Help us."

"You're using the words 'we' and 'us.' Who's that? Someone special?"

She didn't explode in anger like he expected. He watched sadness cover her face and her eyes welled up with unshed tears. *God, what an actress.*

"You still don't trust me." She stood slump-shouldered, looking defeated. "Will I have to pay forever?" She raised her chin and looked at Colt. "There's no one else. Period. The people at the airport helped me. In return, I want to help them. It's that simple. The decision is yours."

She was right. He didn't trust her. But they were going to have to attack the terminal anyway. Otherwise, they'd die right here at the hands of the Blackboots. They were damned either way.

Finally... "Alright, I'll do what I can. Hell, I don't have a better plan. But I still don't like it. One thing, though. You need to leave right now. As soon as we start getting weapons together, they'll double and triple the guards."

THEY SPENT THE DAY APART. He was rousting the men and making sure they went to the covered walkway to pick whatever weapons they wanted to carry. Jennifer was talking with the women. The next time he looked, she was by the weapons pile. When he looked again, she was gone.

He noticed Lila and thought about her a moment. If she was the fighter Tyler said, he needed her. She certainly looked the part. He'd also noticed that she was one of the women that sat by the wall and didn't mingle with the troops. He grinned to himself. Hell, they were probably afraid to approach her. She looked like she could take any two men he had.

She turned to him as he approached.

"How's it going, Lila?"

Her voice was soft and rough at the same time. Back in the day, he'd heard singers like that. A whiskey voice.

"Peachy," she said.

"Did Jennifer trust you, Lila?"

The woman's eyes never stopped scanning the walls. She was neither pretty nor plain, and her brown eyes looked at him directly when she was not checking out her surroundings.

With something between a snort and a sigh, she replied, "Trust is probably a word that you should scrub from your vocabulary. Nobody trusts anyone. You know that."

"Alright." He smiled. "I can live with that. Let me ask this another way. Was Jen already there and chained up when they brought you in?"

"You, too, huh? No, she wasn't. And that's a curious thing. They brought her in just before you and dickhead arrived. The funny thing was that she just walked in all by herself. I had an honor guard of four men with me. Two to hold me and two to make sure all my female parts were still there."

He shook his head. It was an awful circumstance, but he couldn't help but grin at her. "Is that normal?"

"Normal? Hell, I don't know. I've never been captured before. What I do know is I'll never let that happen again."

"Can I trust—" he caught himself and changed his wording, "count on you long enough to tell you how we may or may not be killed tomorrow? Someone needs to spread the word to the women. We don't have much choice in the matter."

She gave him a half-smile. "Do you remember an old comedian named Jerry Clower? One of his routines had two guys coon hunting one night. They shot at one and thought it was wounded and had climbed up a tree. So one of the dummies—alcohol was involved—climbed the tree to kick it out. Next thing you know, the guy on the ground hears an awful growling and screeching, and his buddy was screaming in pain. Then the guy in the tree was yelling, 'Shoot it. Shoot it.' Seems they'd cornered a bobcat in that tree, and it was not happy.

"The hunter on the ground yells back, 'I can't see it. I might hit you.'

"And then the guy in the tree yells back, 'Well, shoot on up here among us. One of us has got to have some relief.'"

The corner of Colt's mouth twitched, but he controlled himself.

"I think we're kind of in that situation right now." She paused and looked at him skeptically. "You're not a country boy, are you?"

"Nope. City boy. Computer geek." He relaxed under her easy voice and manner.

"God. How'd you get to be such a stone-cold killer? I mean, that deal last night was..."

He sighed and shrugged. "I guess the same way as anyone. Practice. And lots of it."

She stayed by him, and he could tell she wanted to ask something. "What, Lila? Spit it out."

"I don't understand," she said. "Why are you still here? Doing this? Couldn't you get away?"

Colt looked at her for a moment. "What did you do back in the real world?"

"I was a small-town cop and not a very smart one." She shook her head. "We could see things were falling apart, so myself and a few cops from neighboring towns came to the big city to help. Lord, what fools. The Black- boots disarmed us immediately. Some of the guys put up a fight and were killed. In the confusion, I got away and hid. I thought about trying to get back to my town, but then thought of the people I knew—men that I respected —that they killed. It pissed me off, and I've been killing Blackboots ever since."

"All the guys you see out there?" Colt said. "We're all pretty much the same. You get to the point that you're too tired to go on, and mentally just beat down. Then someone like Tyler shows up. He has the keys to the food locker and has the power to make things better for you. You think you're dead either way, so you adapt. When it comes down to it, most people would rather be the hammer than the nail. So, you go along and do what they tell you. Some of us learned too well. Now, we'll pay for it."

"It's even worse for women. We're usually the punch board."

He couldn't help but laugh. "You have a nice sense of humor."

"Gallows humor."

She put a hand on his arm. "I noticed you didn't do anything with that woman last night." When he looked at her, she said, "So, I'm a voyeur. And I'm kind of curious. I took a stroll around last night after she left you. She wasn't in the compound at all. I wonder where she spent the night?"

"Weren't you afraid of losing your virtue out there?"

Her laugh was low and melodious. "Lord, Colt. After you had that man killed, I'm not sure a case of Viagra would have helped some of those men. Believe me, there was no problem."

She continued, "I don't trust her for a lot of reasons. Call it what you want, a cop's instinct, or whatever. She just doesn't ring true. And because you like her."

Colt looked at her. "She's my wife, and I don't like her at all."

"Shit," Lila breathed. "Now, there *has* to be a really, really long story to go with that."

Colt was surprised at how long they'd been talking and just how easy it was to continue. "So, what're your plans for tonight?"

Lila looked at him sternly and then barked a short laugh. "Protecting my assets."

"Well," Colt said. "You might as well keep me company. We can tell long stories, and I promise not to bother you. Hell, it's been so long, I'd probably just embarrass myself anyway."

SIXTEEN

IT WAS JUST BREAKING DAYLIGHT, and Colt had the men and women ready to go with weapons and ammunition. Each had a small bottle of water and a piece of pan-fried bread and mystery meat. He didn't know what the meat was but knew he hadn't seen a dog in forever.

He worked his way through the group. The men and women seemed to have paired up the same as the first night. Maybe lovemaking and fighting were the same. He'd check a weapon, fix a strap on a pack, anything to look busy. For each one, he looked them in their eyes and asked, "Do you understand?" They all did. This was a one-way trip. No coming back.

"Blaine."

He turned to find Tyler marching toward him with his guard in tow.

"So, what's the plan, Blaine? How are we going to take down that building?"

He shrugged and said, "The same way castles were breached in medieval times. They'd find a weak point, and send in the foot shoulders as the tip of the spear. The ground pounders would weaken the door and make the defenders expend their weapons on them. Once that was accomplished, then the knights in their protective armor, that's you guys, under cover from their archers, would breach the castle."

Tyler rolled his eyes. "And that applies to us…how?"

"We're the serfs and the knights are Homeland Security," Colt explained patiently. "The weak point at the terminal building is the front door. It's made of glass and not made to be a defense point. The defenders will be outside of it, and inside."

"How do you get the defenders to all come to that spot?"

"Simple. They'll have to," Colt said. "That's the only place we will attack. And they'll need everyone there to defend."

He could see Tyler thinking about it and knew the question that was coming.

"How about we come in behind the building while you distract them in the front?"

He shook his head. "The defenders would see you coming a mile away, across the tarmac. Then we will have expended many lives for nothing. Dividing our forces will just weaken us.

"Look," Colt said. "Once we get close enough to shoot out all the glass in the doors and walls, then we breach at that point. From there, we fan outward and take them down from the inside out. We'll have the defenders breaking out windows trying to escape."

Tyler finally nodded. "I like it. It might just work." He looked around at the conscripts. "Where's that Jennifer woman?"

"Who knows?" Colt replied. "I heard last night that one of the women died and they threw her into the pit. Maybe you should check there."

"You're lying, Blaine. I could tell you were sweet on that woman. If you let her go..."

"I found something better." Colt turned and called, "Lila."

She came strolling over, reminding him of a big cat. He knew she'd been listening and suppressed a smile. "Are you my woman now?"

Playing her tough girl persona, Colt knew if she chewed tobacco, she'd have spit at their feet. Lila looked between the two men, then replied, "Whatever you say, sweet cheeks."

They could see Tyler turning it over in his mind. "Did you spend the night with Blaine?"

Turning to walk away, she said, "I'll be bow legged for a week if I live that long."

"So, you and the other woman weren't together last night?"

"Nope. I kind of figured you were keeping tabs on her. When she wasn't around, I thought maybe you had her."

The man stared at him a moment and then left.

Tyler was smiling as he left, and Colt just shook his head. He wasn't up to Tyler's games and none of this made any sense. If he was alive tomorrow, he might worry about it.

————

AN HOUR LATER, they were at the parking lot fronting the terminal building, unloading from the two trucks that brought them. Where Tyler found the diesel fuel, he couldn't guess. They lost two men and a woman on the way. Apparently, the gangs or anyone else with a rifle considered them a target-rich environment.

Just before they assaulted the front of the building, he pulled Tyler aside. "Look, change of plan. You need to split your men into two forces. Once we engage the defenders, you act as if you're attacking on two more points. That will spread the defenders out just for a moment and will help us make the breach. At the last minute, both your groups will sweep in behind us and take the building."

"How will I know we can make it inside?"

"Well," Colt said, "if you can't, we'll all be lying on the parking lot dead, and the defenders will be mooning you from the door."

"Funny. Okay," he said. "But I want you to stay to the back of the attack. You'll go in with us."

"I go with my people."

"That was not a request, Blaine. You do as you're told."

Tyler looked around at the conscripts and the Homeland Security soldiers guarding them. Even though the prisoners were armed, weapons remained holstered or pointed at the sky. If a barrel of a rifle so much as dropped or a pistol started to come out of a holster, the guards killed them. It had happened often lately.

"You're working something, Blaine," Tyler continued. "I don't know what you're planning, but it won't work. What you think of as your plan was already in the works...by me. When you assault the front of the terminal, you'll have a column of my troops on each side of you. Their guns will be trained on you, not the building."

"It doesn't matter," Colt said, trying not to show his anger. "We're screwed anyway."

When Tyler didn't reply, he continued. "Give me about ten minutes for a weapons check, and then we'll begin."

Tyler walked away and left him to his thoughts. The old depression was setting in. Tired, hungry, and thirsty —sometimes it didn't seem worth the effort.

"Buck it up, boss." He turned to find Lila approaching him. "You look like this is your last day on earth. With the plan you guys came up with, I'm hoping it's our first day of freedom."

"Lila, I wanted you to lead the assault." His abrupt response startled her. "Now, I don't."

"What? Why?"

He grinned at her. "The Blackboots have ordered me to stay at the rear of the pack, so they can watch me. I think that is a pretty good indication this is a trap."

They stared at each other a long moment before she said, "Maybe I'd rather stay with you."

He glanced around to make sure no one was close enough to hear. "I don't trust them. Look, there aren't a lot of good choices left to make. If things go as planned, as soon as they see our people going in unscathed, they're going to attack the back of our column. I'm sure that is their plan, no matter what happens. The Blackboots are getting to be more afraid of us than they are of the gangs. If you stay with me, they'll kill you or take you prisoner again. You know what they do to women who cross them and I wouldn't wish that on my worst enemy."

"What happens if your woman didn't get through to the terminal with the plan?"

He looked at her. "Then we're dead either way." When

she tried to interrupt, he said, "No, Lila. You stay in the middle of the pack. The first people will be either the safest or the first to die. In the middle, you'll have a buffer from either direction. That is your best chance. You don't know any of these conscripts, or owe them any loyalty. And Lila," he paused to make sure he had her full attention. "If you make it through the front, just keep going. Right out the back and don't stop. Don't wait for anyone.

"Look," he continued. "This is it for us. Today, we live or die. Don't think of the group; think of yourself and survival."

"Alright, I'll do as you say. But the same goes for you. God, arguing with you is like trying to piss up a rope in a windstorm." She reached out and touched his arm, and then kissed his cheek. "Look, if you come through this... well, I'd still like to try that 'bow legged' thing. Promise?"

He was so surprised he couldn't speak for a moment. "You'll be at the top of my list."

———

JUST AS THE ATTACK STARTED, Colt felt the cold steel of a rifle barrel against his back. He stiffened and turned to find Tyler and four of his henchmen behind him. And...Jen. He just stared at her. Part of him wanted to be surprised, but he wasn't. She wasn't a captive, never had been. All he felt was sadness.

"Yeah," Tyler said with a malicious grin. "We kind of fooled you on that one. It's all part of the plan—my plan, not yours."

Increased gunfire made Colt whirl to look back at the

assault for a moment. "Why?" he asked. "Why do all this...charade?"

"Simple," Tyler said. "Food and water. There are enough supplies stored there in the terminal to last us years. Providing, of course, we cut down on the number of people we have to feed. So, we'll let everyone eliminate each other, and then we'll walk in and take it all.

"And, you might ask why *you*? That is the interesting part," Tyler continued. "Someone has to control these wolves you call men. Without you, they wouldn't mind so well. It's simple insurance. Now, since you've become my greatest threat, I'll rid myself of you and your men. Plus, I'll have all the food and water I need for a very long time. And the icing on the cake? I have your woman, Blaine. Damn. It looks like I'm the winner, all the way around."

Colt was shaking his head. "I still don't understand why. We'd have had to attack the terminal anyway."

"Man, you're simple," Tyler said. "The story we gave you, and you so kindly spread to your men, gave them hope, Blaine. Anyone fights better if there's some hope of survival. We just had to supply the carrot on the stick."

Jen stepped toward him then, with her hand out. Tears coursed down her cheeks, but he couldn't tell if they were real or fake. He just didn't know her anymore and doubted if he ever did.

"Stop," he told her. "Don't come near me. So, you went from Sammy Boy to Tyler. Does betrayal come so easy for you, Jen? When does it end? Do you feel safe yet?"

Colt continued speaking. "You asked what I thought. I'm thinking it's easier to forgive an enemy than forgive a friend. It's a simple matter of trust. And you don't even have the decency to be ashamed."

Jen was backing away from him wide-eyed and looked as if he finally got through to her.

Tyler laughed. "Well, too bad you won't get a headstone on your grave. We could inscribe that on it. Oh, this Sam, or Sammy Boy, as you call him? I took her away from him. It was easy for a *real* man. He's working for me now, and I have him out north of town looking for a farm we heard was set up for long-term survival. It's supposed to be quite a place and will add nicely to our supplies.

"So, you see?" Tyler continued. "I'm always a step ahead of you."

The guards stepped up and stripped Colt of his pack, rifle, and handgun. Then they pushed him forward. He was surprised. They hadn't found his boot knife.

Tyler pushed him forward a few steps. "We'll just watch from here to see how well our little plan works."

Colt watched as the attacking force approached the front of the building. The first sign of betrayal came when heavy fire centered on the women leading the charge. He flinched because he knew Lila would be at the head of the force, no matter what she promised him. And they were falling in waves while the men pressed forward from behind. From where he stood, he could tell his men were already running short of ammunition. They didn't have enough for a long battle.

The two groups of Blackboots began firing at the terminal from their outside positions. The return fire was devastating, and a couple of heavy machine guns opened up. Since there was no cover, the Blackboots began to retreat. They had no stomach for this kind of fighting.

"Hey, Tyler," Colt said. "Your elite fighting men are

running the wrong way. The fight is in front of them." The blow to his head was worth it.

Amazingly, Colt's original plan worked the way he thought it would. He'd learned that if you were willing to accept major casualties and concentrate on one point, the assault would be successful. His men breached the doors and started flowing inside. A strange pride hit him because they'd succeeded, and at the same time he felt sorry for the loss of life. He could hear screams of fear and anger from inside the terminal. Instantly, the Blackboots halted their retreat and, within minutes, started pouring in behind the attacking force. Just as Colt had predicted, once they were inside, the defenders could do little but fight like cornered rats.

Then, the one thing happened that surprised them all.

The main floor of the building erupted in a blinding explosion, sending shards of glass and metal flying across all the parking lots. Even from their safe vantage point, the force of the explosion knocked them backward. Colt stood, looking at the building. His expression settled into a grim mask. All those people. His men. Lila. He couldn't care less about the Blackboots. *All gone.*

The rest of the guards surrounding him scrambled to their feet. He turned and looked accusingly at Jen. "Didn't you say that building was full of children? Did you know they wired it? Don't you ever think about what your betrayals do to people?"

She just stared in horror at the destruction and didn't speak.

"The food?" Tyler asked her. Finally, he shook her arm to get her attention. "What about the food?"

She finally came out of her stupor. "It's in a basement storage room. It should be fine," she mumbled.

"Alright," Tyler said briskly. "Jennifer, you come with me. We'll go back, gather some more men and come dig it out. Actually, this has worked out just fine." He pointed at the guards. "You men go over and see if any of our troops survived that."

"What about survivors?" one of the guards asked.

"If they aren't ours," Tyler said harshly, "kill them." He then pointed at Colt. "And kill this one, too, after you get some work out of him. I'm tired of looking at him."

After they left, the men stood staring at each other. One of the guards went with Tyler, so that left three men. He could hear the truck slowly leave the parking lot.

Unless they decided to shoot him on the spot, he knew there was a chance. There was always a chance. He waited for someone to make a mistake. Finally, the guard pointing his rifle at him made it. Colt bent over at the waist, with his hands on his knees, pretending to be sick. When the man poked him with the barrel of the rifle, Colt's arm swept it aside, and his other hand came up with the hunting knife. It was a beautiful knife, bone handled with a stainless-steel blade. It was sharp as a razor and the blade parted the guard's stomach like butter and came to rest under his sternum. Pulling the knife free from the falling guard, he lunged at the two remaining men. One got off a round that passed through Colt's shirt before he was on them. It was over in seconds. These men had always watched the fighting as guards and failed their first lesson.

Colt stood looking in the direction Tyler and Jen had gone, his shoulders slumped, shaking his head. *Never again.*

Quickly, he stripped the guards of everything useful. Approaching the building, he carefully picked his way through the debris. Most of the people he came to were dead, but there were survivors. He was amazed at how many and could see a few dazed men and women walking away. From what he could see, some had wounds that would lead to their deaths, just later and more painfully. He could do little to help them.

After working his way through the debris and bodies, he finally came to Lila. For some inordinate reason, he was proud that she'd gone down facing the enemy. Stupid, he knew. He didn't know her except for their brief time last night. But to him, it showed character. Most of the Blackboots that were wounded or dead had their wounds on their backs.

Her back was covered in blood, and he kneeled by her, brushing her hair away from her face. Looking more closely, he saw only the one exit wound, high up on her right shoulder. He gently turned her over to her back. Just the one wound and a small cut and lump on her forehead. Her eyes were looking at him, and he was thinking how his first assessment that she was plain looking was off the mark. He brushed hair from her forehead.

She blinked. It took him a moment to realize what he'd seen and that she was alive.

He spoke softly. "Do that again."

When she gave him a small smile, he smiled back. With him supporting her, she sat up, and then gasped when she looked at him. He looked down and realized how bloody he was.

Shaking his head at her, he said, "It's not mine."

Trying to talk, she was just making sounds. "Dizzy."

He put his finger to her lips to quiet her. Quickly looking around, he took a pack off one of the dead men and began filling it with water and food from others scattered around them. He quickly grabbed another rifle and pistol. She still had hers.

Colt didn't think he could use up any more time scavenging, and was turning back to Lila when he heard someone faintly call his name. He looked around a second before he found the source. Taking the packs back to Lila, he returned to Joel. The man lay amid a jumbled pile of bodies, and he was using a dead woman for a pillow. Both of his bloody hands were fighting a losing battle to keep his intestines in his abdomen. A large caliber bullet, probably from the machine gun, had passed through his abdomen side to side, blowing him open like a burst melon.

"Colt," his voice rasped. "I've been trying to make myself die but just can't do it. I need help. I'm sorry, man, but the dogs'll get me before I die from this."

He knew it was true and put his hand on Joel's shoulder. "I'm sorry, but I don't know if I can. I'll leave you a pistol."

Joel held up a bloody, slippery hand, and it was shaking like a leaf. "Do you think I can hold a gun? I'm begging you, Colt. The pain is getting bad, real bad."

Colt took a big breath and stood, looking down at Joel. He was not really a friend, just someone who had his back when needed. They'd never talked about anything. He didn't know his last name. *Shit.*

"Please, Colt."

Finally... "To better times, Joel."

"Better times—"

The sound of the shot echoed around the debris field for a moment and then was gone. Colt stood, looking off into the distance, and for a moment, his mind went away.

The only thing going through his mind was an old song that the singer Johnny Cash made popular called "Hurt." In his mind's eye, he could see Johnny banging one note incessantly on a piano, building in crescendo. The line 'what have I become' kept going through his mind.

What have I become? Dammit! He would give anything for a do-over.

The sound of a motor snapped him back to the present. They were coming back with reinforcements. Part of him wanted to stay. He wanted nothing more than to have Tyler and Jen in the sight picture of his rifle. Better yet, up close and personal with a blade to end it right here. But another twenty men? It was too many. He could wait.

He ran to Lila and pulled her to her feet, and she could barely stand. As she stumbled, she said, "I can't walk yet. Just leave me, or do me like your friend. It's okay. Just get out of here, Colt."

Slinging her rifle next to his, he then dipped and caught her up in a fireman's carry. His knees nearly buckled under the weight. She was a big girl and no lightweight. Heading northwest toward the nearest stand of trees, he didn't know how far he'd be able to carry her. If they made the trees and got out of sight, they had a chance. It was a small one, but a chance.

SEVENTEEN

"PUT... ME...DOWN." Her words came out with the same cadence as his lumbering steps.

After getting away from the blown-up terminal building, he'd grabbed Lila and headed north into the trees. It was over a mile before he came to any adequate cover. About a hundred yards into the dense growth, he was finally ready to fold up.

"Dammit, Colt! Put me down."

He pushed his way into a stand of evergreens and fell to his knees. Lila landed on her butt with a grunt, and he stretched out by her, trying to catch his breath. His lungs were burning, and his legs felt like rubber.

"Don't you ever, ever pick me up that way again. If I'm so bad you think I need to be carried over your shoulder like that, just shoot me." She sat rubbing her belly. "Did we get away clean? Did anyone see us?"

"I don't think any Blackboots saw us," he gasped. "Not sure, though."

"God, you've got bony shoulders." She gave a strangled laugh. "See how easy it was, Colt? All you had to do was walk away."

The start of a smile died on his face. "Yeah, and watch over a hundred people die."

"I'm sorry about your friend." She put a hand on his shoulder. "You did the right thing."

She continued, "Hey, we cheated death again. I wonder how many more times we can do that."

He got up and helped her take off the backpack. She winced at the pain in her shoulder. "Do you think they'll follow us?"

"Doubt it. It will take them a while to dig out the basement. When they find the door, it should be all over."

He was unbuttoning her shirt. Her hands came up quickly and held his wrists. "What do you mean, it will all be over?"

Pulling the shirt away from her shoulder, he tried to look at the wound. When she tried to stop him, he said crossly, "I have to look at that wound, Lila."

She tried again. "What do you mean, it will all be over."

Almost like it was a choreographed play, the explosion came on cue and was large enough to rattle the tree limbs around them.

Jen. Tyler. A fitting end. He hoped that they'd be happy in whatever corner of hell they landed in. Maybe they'd land in several pieces.

"How did you...?"

He reached out gently, hooked his finger under her chin, and closed her mouth. "Can you imagine someone who felt so strongly about not letting their families fall into the hands of the Blackboots that they'd blow themselves up to prevent it...can you imagine them not booby trapping the food storage basement?"

Lila sat staring at him and then shook her head wonderingly. "I don't think I'd have that kind of courage."

"Sure you would. You already have." He held up both hands, palms upward. "You have death on either hand. The outcome is the same. And yet, you chose the one you thought you had some control over."

"But," she said softly. "The children. How could they kill the children?"

He tried to sidetrack her train of thought. "You'd think someone brave enough to charge the particular hell you did today would let me see her shoulder."

She smirked at him and then grimaced in pain. "That's a whole 'nother kettle of fish, buster. You're not gettin' to my sweet and girlies without a fight."

He shook his head. "Well, the wound doesn't seem to be bleeding too much. If you're feisty enough to argue with me, you can walk. We need to go find a house." Looking at the sky, he figured it was past noon. "It would be nice to find it before dark."

Already getting to her feet, she asked, "Because?"

"Pots, pans, boiling water, cleaning wounds, and trying to make sure you don't die of infection. Getting you cleaned up is a big priority. And, changing our diet away from dried dog meat."

"Dog?"

"Fido."

"I never thought of that. If I weren't so hungry, I think I'd throw up. I may do it anyway."

Colt grinned at her. "Or, cat. I hear it all tastes like chicken."

Holding her stomach, she said, "If I ever get my strength back, I'm going to seriously hurt you."

Walking slowly to the north, she said, "Okay, all of this sounds simple enough. We have escaped from the Blackboots, and you've rescued the damsel in distress."

"Damsel?"

"Hey, give a girl her fantasies. So, that should take care of today. What're we going to do with the rest of our lives?"

"I'm really interested in that farm Tyler was talking about. The farm set up for survival. I think that is probably where Beth is."

She stopped and then scrambled to catch up with him. "Beth? Who's Beth? I swear, Colt. You've got more women than a pimp in Kansas City."

They were walking on a blacktop road, ready to jump the ditch and go into the trees at the first sign of trouble.

"Are you sure we should be out in the open like this?"

"I don't like it. But do you want to start plodding through all the pasture and plowed ground around here? We're already tired and worn out. This is quicker."

"Actually, you mean I'd be worn out, don't you? I'm slowing you down."

He ignored her. A few minutes later, they saw a large housing addition off to their left. When they were close enough, they stopped to look for any signs of life. While they watched, they saw an armed man go from one house to another. Looking closely, they saw a couple of men on top of one of the houses, looking toward the airport. Undoubtedly, they were looking at the smoke cloud rising from the terminal building.

Without speaking, they both got up and continued

north. It was late afternoon when they saw an isolated farmhouse set back from the road.

Colt pulled Lila along with him. She was exhausted from blood loss, the blow to the head, and malnutrition in general. He knew she was operating on sheer gumption and will but figured that particular tank was about empty.

He checked the outbuildings first while she sat under a small tree guarding against any other surprises. Then, while she stood guard outside, he entered the house. It just felt empty, but remembering the mansion in town, he checked it from top to bottom, every closet, and even under the beds. He took special care to ensure there was no basement. The house was clear.

Helping her inside, he made her lie down on the first bed he came to. He went to the kitchen and rummaged around for a pot to boil water in. Turning on the gas kitchen stove, he was shocked to smell propane coming from the burner. Quickly turning it off, he put the pot on the burner and started to empty a water bottle into it.

Just for giggles, he tried the water faucet. Nothing. A quick flip told him there was no magical electricity for lights. The propane was a minor miracle in itself. There had been several miracles today. A working well would be asking too much.

Feeling a strange sense of normalcy, he dug out a lighter and started the burner. While waiting for the water to boil, he went to the bathroom and raided the medicine cabinet for antibiotic cream. There was no water in the stool tank. Huh.

He went back to the kitchen and found clean towels in a drawer. After the water boiled for a few minutes, he gathered everything and headed back to the bedroom.

Time for Miss Grumpy.

She was sound asleep, arms out wide and her legs half on the bed. Gently pulling her up, he took off the backpack and then unbuckled the belt for her handgun. He laid her back on a pillow and washed her forehead and the bump on her head. It was turning a nice shade of blue but was not a huge goose egg. It worried him a little. The blow to her head was enough to knock her out, so she may have a concussion.

When he started unbuttoning her shirt, it was déjà vu all over again. Her eyes popped open. He couldn't fathom what kind of internal alarm system it took to make that happen.

Her voice was sleepy. "You're at it again?"

"I need to clean that wound, Lila. Help me out here."

She took her hands away and her arms listlessly flopped back on the bed as she closed her eyes. "Fine. Have your way with me. I'm too tired to resist, anyway." Slightly raising her head, she said, "Just leave the bra on."

"The strap is in the way. It's coming off."

Her last word before she went to sleep was, "Shit."

He hurried to get everything done while she was out. He got the shirt off easier than he thought. There was still some seepage from the wound, so the shirt hadn't stuck to the dried blood. The wound was from a small caliber bullet, maybe a .22. The size of the entry wound precluded any of the military weapons, or even a .223. The huge amount of powder behind those slugs made the bullet tumble, and it made a terrible wound. Her wound was on the meaty part of her shoulder, above the collarbone. It would be painful, but hopefully not too serious. He washed both sides of the wound and didn't see any bits of cloth in it. Finally, packing both sides with the antibiotic cream, he put a bandage on both sides and taped it up.

There was still enough light for him to go to the closet and try to find a shirt for her. There was underwear in a drawer. He couldn't decide if they'd fit and didn't want to risk opening the wound again trying them on her, so he decided to wait until morning. They needed the rest, anyway. Covering Lila with a light blanket, he left her to sleep.

Wandering around the house, he checked the hot water heater and found it had some water in it. He found out the man of the house only wore bib overalls, but at least he could change his shirt and socks. With another wet cloth, he cleaned himself as best he could and changed clothes. He did another circuit outside, then came in and made sure he locked the doors. Then, smelling of freshly applied underarm deodorant, he sat on the couch by the front door and immediately went to sleep. He was up at daylight, going from window to window and checking outside. As far as he could tell, there was no one around. It was as if he'd stepped into a different world. In the city, there was always someone around. But they were still within a couple of miles of the airport, and that was too close for comfort.

After checking on Lila, he made a more leisurely check of the house. Everything was well-kept and neat. It was obvious to him that an older couple had lived here. The television was not the newer flat screen, and he didn't see a computer anywhere—odd for even an older couple. He could almost picture them, knowing someone was coming to take them away, cleaning up the house. His grandmother had always said she didn't want to leave and come home to a dirty house.

There was no food anywhere, so someone had thought of that. Every food item was gone from the cabinets. It wasn't ransacked, just gone. Probably, their children or grandchildren had come to get them. He hoped they were in a safe place.

Above the door in the pantry, an old shotgun rested on a couple of nails driven into the jam. He took it down, moved the slide back and saw it was loaded with birdshot. Squinting to see the engraving, he saw it was an old Winchester Pump, Model 1897. Still well-oiled and ready to go. If he sawed off the barrel, it might be useful. What he liked was the actual hammer on the gun. With a hammer, you don't have to wonder if the safety is on. But he couldn't take the time now. Gingerly, he leaned it against the wall. There was no need to keep the gun away from kids, at least not now. Maybe not for a long time.

In the silent house, sound carried easily. He heard a sharply indrawn breath, followed by a soft groan, and knew Lila was awake. He found her sitting on the side of the bed, fingering the bandages on her shoulder.

"Leave those alone."

Surprised at his appearance, she clutched the blanket against her breasts. "You could have put my shirt back on."

"It was all messed up." Looking under the front pad covering the wound, he said, "The edges aren't even red, that's good. It may be early, but at least there's no infection yet."

"Look, I'm sorry. Thank you for dressing the wound. If you're wondering, my shoulder is sore but I can use it." She looked around for her shirt. "Do you intend for me to walk around topless?"

When he started to smile, she emphasized, "No. Way."

He relented by saying, "There are clothes in that closet."

"Why didn't you find something for me to wear?"

Colt laughed. "I learned a long time ago never to make fashion decisions for a female. Even my young daughter wouldn't allow it."

She paused on her way to the closet, the blanket still clutched to her chest. "You had children?"

He was immediately sobered. "Had is the operative word."

Lila understood immediately. "I'm so sorry. It's turned into a shitty world." She hugged him, forgetting about the closet. "I'm so very sorry, Colt. At least I never had that particular hell to face."

He shrugged. "I know, and thanks. You're the second person to tell me that. Mostly, I've put that away. Sometimes it comes creeping back. But memories of them are good except for the last days."

"So, that Jennifer bitch was their mother?"

When he nodded, she stepped back and realized the blanket had dropped and she was naked from the waist up. Blushing, she started to cover up and then dropped her arms. With a little laugh, she said, "I guess it's a little late for modesty."

Colt smiled back at her. "It was too late last night, Lila. Meet me in the kitchen when you're dressed. We need to come up with a plan." He ruefully shook his head. "Not that the last one turned out so good."

"She really did a number on you, didn't she? Or was it this Beth chick you're so hot to find?"

"What do you mean?"

"Look at me," she said. When he didn't, she yelled at him, "No, don't turn away. Look at me."

He turned and met her gaze, then took in her body. Other than the gauze patch on her shoulder, she was beautiful and looked whipcord tough. There were a few smudges of blood that he hadn't cleaned up. Bruises covered her upper body, old and new. A newly healed cut on her side was still pink, and numerous scratches had scabbed over. But it only added to her Amazon status. His breath quickened as he forced himself to look at her as a woman. Her arms were muscled and toned, and she sported a six-pack of abs that supported her conical, puffy nippled breasts.

"Okay," he said as his breath caught in his throat. "I'm looking at a beautiful and desirable woman who seems to be in pristine condition except for a wound in her shoulder and various cuts and bruises. And I can plainly see why you wanted to protect your assets the other night." He smiled at her. "They are very...generous and desirable."

Instead of laughing with him, her eyes filled with unshed tears. "Am I so ugly you can't stand to touch me? My god, are you blind? I know you were married, and I know you want to hook up with this Beth woman again. But I don't think you're a practicing monk or celibate. Are you gay? I'm prancing around half-naked in front of you and..."

Colt reached his hand around the back of her neck, then upward to grip her hair in his fist and brought her to him. He could feel her breath on his lips as he looked into her eyes a moment before he kissed her. At first it was tentative, with him withdrawing slightly to look at her, and then their passion grew until they finally broke apart and were both panting as if they'd run a mile. Her eyes were closed when he finally stopped—her mouth was open and wet, and he rubbed her lips with his thumb.

"Okay," she finally breathed. "So you're not gay."

He brought her to him again, crushing her chest against his. "I wish my shirt was off. This would feel a lot better."

"So, make it happen," she panted. "I told you what I wanted to do the first chance we got."

"Lila, I want you so bad it hurts." She had his shirt unbuttoned and was rubbing herself against him. "But it has been a while, and now isn't the time. If I start with you, it's going to be all day and all night. We're only a couple of miles from the airport. We need to keep watch."

His shirt was off by then as she ground against him. "There are still a lot of bad people around."

"You don't understand, do you? I want you right now. I've wanted you ever since you came strolling in with Tyler and didn't back down with him. I don't want to wait. We may be dead tomorrow." She stepped back from him and never lost eye contact. Then she hooked her thumbs in her pants and started that sinuous side-to-side movement that left them pooled at her feet.

"You're going to break that wound open."

She ignored him. "Did you check around outside?"

His voice was hoarse when he could finally get a word out. "Yes."

"Was it all clear? Did it look safe?" Her cat-like gaze never left his.

"Yeah, but..."

"This won't take that long."

All the emotion of Jen's betrayal, Beth's constant teasing and promise, months of celibacy, and Lila's pure animal vitality burst to the surface as they came together with a forceful slap of skin like two wrestlers trying to overpower the other.

———

WHEN THEY LEFT THE FARMHOUSE, the sun was high, and he knew she possessed the knowledge that he didn't do anything in a hurry, especially in bed. They had to re-bandage her shoulder, but to her credit, she didn't complain.

Colt hated to leave a home full of things people used to take for granted, and the house had proved to be a treasure trove of items they needed. He'd taken a tactical vest from one of the dead Blackboots, and he traded that in for a hunting vest that was lighter and had more pockets. Hiking boots replaced his tennis shoes, and they fit reasonably well. He even found a lightweight sleeping bag that attached to the back of the vest by straps.

Lila didn't fare quite so well with clothing, but had gathered up some utensils they'd need, especially for boiling water. When he mentioned about bleach, she filled one bottle with that and found an eyedropper. She'd also found several long-barreled propane lighters.

He tried to put extra padding on her shoulder, but the weight of the pack still caused some discomfort, so he transferred more items from her pack to his own. As he worked on her pack, their eyes met and she started a small smile as she watched him.

The weapons added extra weight, but not knowing what was ahead, he was afraid to leave anything. They each had a .45 pistol, and thanks to robbing the bodies of the Blackboots at the terminal, plenty of ammunition. He was carrying three rifles on slings, plus a sidearm and pack, when they stepped out.

"How much does all that weigh?"

Colt grunted as he shifted his load. "Feels about like carrying you, only not as squirmy."

They kept to the paved farm-to-market road heading west. Before they left, they'd looked over a map spread out on the kitchen table. From what little he'd learned from Beth about her farm, he knew they needed to go west and then north. The plan was simple. They needed to go across country to the west until they intersected with the T highway. That would take them north and west to F highway going north through Ash Grove. After that, it was anybody's guess.

"What if we don't find this farm?" Lila had asked.

"Then we go on to Stockton Lake. If that land isn't hunted out, there will be game, and hopefully, the water is okay. For now, it's the best idea I have."

As they were walking, Lila said, "You do realize this is my old stomping grounds, don't you? I told you I was a cop in a small town north of Springfield."

He stopped and looked at her. "Well, damn me for an idiot. I'd forgotten all about that. Then why did you...?"

She laughed. "I just like to see you get all bossy and stuff. It's cute. Just follow me, sweet cheeks. I have a real good idea how to find this farm."

After a mile or so, Colt said, "Sorry. I should have asked."

Lila chuckled. "Well, you did have a lot on your mind."

"That was rape back there, you know."

"Only the first time."

EIGHTEEN

TWO DAYS later found them just south of Ash Grove. They were hunkered down in a stand of trees while they watched a group of men and women walking south on the blacktop road. Dirty and emaciated, the group looked like they were just wandering aimlessly. They would stop and look around or just stand there and then move on. Some carried packs, but most didn't appear to have anything but the clothes on their backs.

"They look like they're starving," Colt whispered to Lila.

"Yeah, poor bastards," she replied. "If it were one or two, we could share. But that group looks like thirty or forty people. If we wave a granola bar in front of them, they'd just stampede right over us. We might get a few of them, but not enough. You'd think that, as long as it has been since the world went to pot, they'd have found a source of food—or died."

"More likely, their source dried up. You might notice we're still living on manufactured food. Eventually, that is all going to go away."

After the people were gone a few minutes, they stood and regained the road. About a mile before the town, she abruptly turned west along a path wedged between two fences.

Colt was holding his rifle at the ready. "Where are we going?"

"Trader Jack's. There's a guy out here that used to run kind of a trading post. It's way off the road, and most town folk don't know about it. He's a survivalist and deals in about anything you could want, legal or not. It used to be a hangout for outdoorsmen and hunters, especially during deer and turkey season, and most of them weren't real picky about seasons. It used to be a nice setup if you were into living simple. It can be somewhat rough, but you're used to that. It's one place the conservation agents didn't go to. If you've read Western novels, they'd say the people that hang out there are rougher than a cob, in fact, they are so rough they wear out their clothes from the inside out." She looked at him and didn't get the response she wanted. "If you were a country boy, you'd have thought that was funny."

Ignoring her, he said, "And yet, you hung out there? I suppose you were doing undercover police work?"

"Yes, I did hang out there. And no, I never got under the covers with anybody." She paused to see if her second try at a joke hit home, shook her head, and continued. "Sometimes it was business, but usually just for fun. I guess when I was younger, I was attracted to bad boys."

"You still are."

She gave him a cool look. "Maybe, but to get back on track, if Jack's still there, and I'm betting he is, we can get more supplies and maybe get a handle on your Beth's farm."

"She's not my Beth."

After an hour on the dirt track, they came to a densely wooded area bordering a high bluff that looked like it ran for about a mile in either direction. They stopped just short of the trees. Lila looked around and then called out.

"Jack Hammer."

Colt laughed. "His name is Jackhammer?" He thought he saw movement behind them and turned to face that way.

A voice came from the trees. "Not many folks know Trader Jack's last name. Who are you, and what do you want?"

"Tell him I used to bust him about once a month," she called out. "Tell him it's Lila."

"Alright, come on in. I remember you, and I'm bettin' you don't have a warrant this time." The man cackled at his own humor, and then the voice turned serious. "And you tell your man to shoulder that rifle. We might think he's unfriendly if he doesn't."

Lila turned to him. "Shoulder it, Colt. Be cool, now. These aren't gangbangers in baggy pants."

Three armed men met them at the edge of the trees. Their rifles weren't pointed right at them. Well, not exactly.

Colt nodded his head back toward the trail. "I saw some movement back there."

He noted that this was a careful bunch of people, because one of the men immediately broke off and went to check. They waited silently until he returned.

"Just movers," he said. "I encouraged them to keep moving."

The men ushered them toward a log cabin built into

the bluff. It was set about ten feet above a spring that came out of the rocks below it. Trees surrounded the cabin and the front was barely visible until you were right on top of it.

The man who led them there held up his hand. "The woman can come inside by herself. You wait here."

Colt already had his pistol half out of its belly holster when a voice from inside said, "Bring them both in, Adam. If this gent is with Lila, then he's all right with me."

Adam shrugged at them, grinning insolently, and took them inside.

A huge man was sitting on a bench next to a window. He was dressed in bib overalls and T-shirt. His ball cap didn't look like it had any hair under it, and his face sported a full beard. If he'd seen a picture of a mountain man, he didn't suppose it would look any different.

Colt could feel a cool breeze coming from the back of the store and held his hand up to test the breeze.

Lila answered his unspoken question. "The cabin was built in front of a cave. That's where the cool air comes from. Limestone caves are always about sixty degrees, winter or summer."

She went forward and held out her hand. "How's it, Jack?"

"Officer Bentley," he responded, shaking her hand and holding it longer than Colt thought necessary. "Nice to see you're still alive."

"Yeah, well, meet the reason I'm alive. Jack, this is Colt...uh?"

"Blaine, Miss Bentley." He stepped up and shook Jack's hand. "Colt Blaine."

"Nice to meet you," he said. "What brings you to our neck of the woods?"

At a nod from Colt, Lila took the lead.

"We've been runnin' for our lives, Jack."

She brought him up to date on everything she knew about Springfield and the Homeland Security Blackboots.

"Anyway," she finished. "We finally got shut of that nightmare, and started looking for a farm owned by a friend of Colt's."

"What's the name of this friend?" Jack asked.

Colt replied, "Beth Wilson. She said to come by if I got a chance. I actually don't know if she's still alive or made it back to her farm."

"She had a brother." Jack was watching him closely.

"Arnie was trying to keep his National Guard unit together. He was killed by one of the gangs."

"Well," Jack said. "I guess you did know her. You two seem to have had quite a time. What do you need from me?"

Lila thought for a moment. "Some supplies if you have them to spare. And directions to the farm if it's as good as they say."

Jack looked at them with hooded eyes. Colt didn't like his expression.

"How're you going to pay for these supplies?"

"We don't have money or whatever you're using for currency," Colt said as his hand unconsciously caressed the butt of the .45 at his waist.

Adam spoke up from behind them. "You've got a woman. A couple of turns with her would get a lot of supplies."

Colt just looked at Jack and spoke quickly as he saw

Lila start to unsling her rifle. "Lila is off limits. How about a food cache?"

He told them why Tyler was there and about the second explosion.

"One question," Jack asked. "Do you think that cache would've survived the explosion?"

Colt shrugged. "No way to tell. I'm sure the door was wired, and I'd bet the explosion was shaped to go out. It just depends on the configuration of the room and what kind of containers the food is in."

"That makes sense." He turned to his men. "Adam, why don't you get some of the boys together and check this out before anyone else gets to it? It might be a real find. And use the pickup. It'll be worth using up gas."

"Alright." His eyes were on Lila. "First thing tomorrow."

Jack pinned the man with his gaze. "Today would be real good."

Adam lost the staring contest, mumbled something, and turned to go. At the door, he stopped. "Jack, we're all supposed to be equal here. Do you mind if I take this woman with me?"

Jack stood up, and Lila started to say something, but Colt had spent the last couple of months with some insanely tough men and had learned the lesson of how even the perception of weakness can get you killed. He beat them to the punch.

"What's the matter, Adam? Run out of little boys to play with?" Colt said.

If the other men in the room hadn't tried to stifle a laugh, Adam might have let the barb go by. His expression turned to an ugly snarl as he started to lift his rifle.

Colt was on him in two steps. His pistol jammed up under Adam's chin.

"Now, you think long and hard about what you're going to do in the next few seconds." Colt stared at him a moment, saw what he was looking for in the man's expression, and knew he would have to watch his back with this one. "Now, you lean that rifle against the wall, real gentle like, and then drop your belt gun."

After a quick glance at his men, Adam slowly complied, and Colt holstered his pistol.

"You watched too many cartoons and movies when you were a kid," Colt said.

"What?"

Colt continued. "What were you going to do? Were you going to start shooting at me in a room full of people? You realize I'd have been moving. Did it enter your head that you'd have shot Jack and the woman you want, just to try to get me? Dumb shit."

"I suppose you want my knife, too?"

"Nope," said Colt. "A knife would be just between you and me. Personal. If you feel lucky, then try me on. We'll dance until we drop. Otherwise, leave. Your friends can bring your weapons to you."

Adam tried to bluster. "This ain't over, mister."

"Oh, it's over. Otherwise you're a dead man."

When he couldn't think of a reply that wouldn't get him killed, Adam left and Colt turned to find Lila and Jack in conversation like nothing was going on.

Jack looked up, unconcerned. "You're quick with that belly gun. I never saw anyone carry a pistol like that."

Colt shrugged. "I read it in a Western novel." He glanced at Lila. "Yeah, I've read Westerns."

"He reads a lot," Lila said, smiling. "You're developing a temper, sweetie. We need to work on that."

Jack gave them a supply of MREs and dried beef jerky still in the package. When Colt pulled out the dried meat they already had, Jack took it and threw it outside.

"The dogs will eat it," he said. "It looks like roadkill." A black and tan hound ran up and sniffed the jerky, looked soulfully at them, and shuffled away.

"Or, maybe not," Jack said.

Soon, they were ready to go. Lila got directions to Wilson Farm, which wasn't too far away, along with a warning.

"Those folks are living on borrowed time," Jack said. "It's like they don't think there are any bad folks out there. A raid will happen, eventually. It won't be pretty."

At Colt's questioning look, he continued. "Adam and a couple of others have been visiting. There are some women there that"—he glanced at Lila—"well, they're friendly. Working girls, you know?"

He shook his head and then continued. "Is there anything else I can do for you?"

"There are two things, Jack," Colt said after thinking a minute. "I need something better than bleach to purify water."

"Yuck." Jack immediately reached under a counter and came up with two boxes of tablets. "These actually use something similar, but they don't taste as bad. You might be separated, so there's one for each of you. You can fill your bottles in the spring outside. It's clean and pure. We make sure it stays that way. And what's the second thing?"

Colt looked at Lila. "I want to trade in a couple of these rifles for something more useful."

"What?" Lila cried.

"Look at it," Colt said. "We don't need a lot of fire-power. For sure, we don't need three rifles. You can carry the little M-4 if you want. Besides, if we run into something that we need automatic weapons for, we need to run away. Fighting will just get us killed."

"What do you need?" Jack asked.

"The first thing we need is a field first aid kit. I have a suspicion you might have some of those. I'd also like a sawed-off shotgun, something light that we can carry, not that Chinese knock-off, along with ammo for it. I'd also like a 10/22 with a large clip." Lila started to argue again, and he held up his hand. "I know, it's not a mankiller, but we can carry a ton of ammo for it, and the long rifle shells will kill about anything we need to eat. Plus, the sound doesn't carry as far. If we get surprised, we still have the .45s and the shotgun for close-in work."

"Lila," Jack said. "You hang on to this man. He uses his head for something besides a hat rack." He turned back to Colt. "Why don't you like the automatic rifles, M-4s, M-16s and the like? I'm curious."

"I'd some experience with those. And we just saw a good example with your man Adam. You don't know how many times I saw a man expend his whole clip in about ten seconds, then stand and get shot because he was out of ammunition. A single-shot carbine would have done him better. The auto does provide a lot of noise and flash, but not much bang for your buck."

"Well," Jack said, "I can't disagree with you, although there are some that would."

Colt stared outside a moment. "Jack, you talked about it being just a matter of time until that farm is attacked. On the way here, we saw maybe forty or fifty people just wandering down the road. All our experience has been in the city. Are they dangerous?"

"Well, sort of," Jack said. "Most of them aren't armed. They're just kind of wandering around, waiting for someone to help them. Eventually, they'll starve. It's like they're past the point that they'll fight for food or water. Once in a while, some lone man will come and cut out one of the women. Who knows? She may be lucky or not. It just depends."

Jack changed the conversation. "Y'all are welcome to spend the night. You'll be safe here."

Colt could already see Lila shaking her head when he replied, "No, we'll be moving on."

"Come on, Lila," said Jack. "I remember you didn't used to mind spending some time around here. If you're worried about Adam, he won't bother you."

Lila responded before Colt could. "Those were younger times, Jack. It's a different world now. Those days are gone."

"Aw, Lila…"

"How many men do you have here?" Colt interrupted.

Jack turned his attention away from Lila. "I have ten men counting me that stay inside. Adam probably has control of another twenty. That's the bunch that will be going to check on that food cache."

"Adam's men, who're they loyal to?" Colt watched the man closely.

"Well, not to me, if that is what you're asking. But he still knows where his bread is buttered. He won't cross me."

"I hope you're right. How many women do you have here?"

"None."

"And why is that?"

Jack smiled. "I get your point, boy. They cause too much trouble. This ain't a boarding house. Besides, women come to us—and there is never a lack of them. Seems when everyone else was stealing guns and food, we stocked up on birth control pills, and everything else you'd find in a drugstore. Then we hit the clothing and lingerie stores." His grin got wider. "We don't lack for company."

Colt shook his head. "Sorry, Jack. I lost one woman because I didn't protect her well enough. Actually, it may have been two, and I won't make that mistake again. You need to back off, and we need to boogie on out of here."

"Your choice," Jack said. "Although I think Officer Bentley can make that decision for herself. She always did. So, if she wants to stay, she can."

"Yeah," Colt replied. "You know, we all think we can take care of ourselves, and then all those damned clichés start kicking in. Murphy's Law and all the corollaries, the X factor, You Just Never Know, and then Pride Goeth Before the Fall. All of which can be summed up in two words."

Lila interjected, "Shit happens."

"Succinct and accurate," he said, smiling at her.

As they went out the door, Colt said, "See ya, Jack. Do yourself a favor and don't give us trouble."

"Let me know where you settle," Jack said. "Maybe we can help each other time to time."

———

FOLLOWING a trail north around the bluff, Lila stopped as soon as they were out of sight. Turning toward him, she grabbed his shirt in her fists and kissed him hard.

"You'll fight for me and try to keep me safe and you'll not share me with anyone else? That sounds nice. Do you love me, then?"

"Honestly, I don't know. But we have a lot going for us if we can just survive, and a long-term contract with you looks good to me. We'll see how it shakes out. One thing, though. I don't own you. Anytime you want to walk, just tell me first. I'll hate it, but I'll let you go. Just don't lie to me or make any promises that you can't keep. I'll do the same with you."

She kissed him again, softer this time. "This may be a surprise, but you do."

"Do what?"

"You do own me, so get used to it."

He smiled. "Kinda sudden, isn't it?"

"Not really." She gave him a serious look. "If we'd met and dated for a year or so, would we know each other any better than right now? After what we've gone through? I don't think so."

After a few minutes, Colt looked up and down the trail. "How well do you trust this Trader Jack?"

"I said we used to bust him about once a month, and it wasn't for selling cookies without a permit. It was a fun place to hang out, and at that time in my life, I didn't like the town boys. They were too tame."

"Someday you'll have to tell me about your adventures at Trader Jack's. And thinking of Jack, is there any reason we should use a trail he recommended to us? A trail that he took very special pains to tell us about?"

Lila took a quick look around. "Dammit, you're right. He did try to make sure we knew the right trail."

"Nice guy, right? It makes me wonder why he gave us all the stuff he did just on the promise of a food cache that may be blown all to hell."

Her eyes narrowed. "You mean like, maybe he planned on getting it back?"

"Exactly."

Thought turned to action, and they turned west immediately, finding a game trail up and over the bluff. Once on top, the landscape was all cleared pastureland, bordered with thick stands of trees and brush. There was a lot of concealment around the edges, and that was something Colt liked.

Lila stood next to him with her hand on his shoulder, catching her breath after the steep climb. She shifted her pack to a more comfortable position. "We need to find a campsite soon." Her hand was now rubbing him under the heavy backpack.

"Why? Are you tired? Is your wound hurting? There's a lot of light left."

"Dummy."

NINETEEN

COLT STOOD in the morning mist, listening to the sounds of the awakening forest. A cool front had moved in during the night, giving them relief from the oppressing heat of July. He chuckled to himself as he scanned the tree line and pasture around him. Lila still had her watch that showed the month and day. It was incredible how quickly time lost meaning when all you had to do from day to day is survive.

On one level, he loved the near solitude of the country, and couldn't understand why more and more people had seemed to gravitate to the city and suburbs. Then, when tragedy struck, those same people went running back to the country, thinking she'd nurture them in some way. Too late, they found Mother Nature was as unforgiving as the stone-gray walls of the city structures.

Movement across the field in front of him caught his attention. He saw several small deer walking unconcerned across the grass and into the trees. He was glad to see them, knowing they'd be a food source. He was also glad they didn't seem spooked. No one was hunting them —at least, not yet.

At a slight scuffling sound behind him, he turned and found Lila coming up to him. She handed him a plastic bottle of brown water.

"I put some of the pre-mixed tea in the water," she said softly. "It kills the taste of the purifier."

He nodded his thanks while scanning what he could see of the land to the north and west. They still didn't trust the water, even out in the country like this. Later, if they lived long enough, he knew they'd be able to drink from most of the streams and lakes, because by then, their bodies would be used to all the pathogens and 'critters' in the water. But not now or anytime soon. He was convinced the unclean lake water had sickened his children and eventually killed them.

She leaned against him and sighed. "Nice morning, isn't it? You look like you're lost in thought. Anything you can share?"

Colt put his arm around her and squeezed. "Actually, I'm just relaxing. It's been a wild few days. Hell, it's been a wild few months. I'm just relaxing and taking stock."

"Can I make a suggestion? Don't leave camp without at least your pistol."

The illusion of a relaxing camping trip out to the 'boonies' was shattered when she handed him his holster belt. He noticed she was fully armed and ready for the trail. While he was daydreaming, she'd struck the camp and got the packs ready. She was carrying his rifle but didn't hand it to him.

"I'll give you the rifle whenever you get the 'monster' on."

Trader Jack had given him a proper pack made of

lightweight aluminum tubing. It was a lot easier carrying all their gear and the sleeping bag rolled up on top. One modification they made to this pack was the quick-release panel. Once he had the pack on and all four straps were attached to the metal disk on his chest, all that was needed to release and drop the pack was to hit himself in the chest. The heavy pack would drop away instantly.

"Old Jack sure gave us a lot of stuff," Colt said.

Lila laughed teasingly. "He probably thinks of me as a daughter he never had with all the off-duty time I spent out there, just hanging out and listening to stories. He's harmless."

"Really? Is this the same Jack that you used to bust all the time?"

"I think he knew that was just business. He didn't hold it against me."

"Well, I think Jack wants you stretched out on a bed in his environmentally controlled cave house. That's what I think."

As they stepped back to their campsite and got him into his pack, she said, "You know, things are going to be bad for guys now."

"You mean, other than dying at an alarming rate?"

"Well, other than that," she said. "Since everything fell apart, men seem to think it's open season on women. Didn't you notice how, when we'd see people sneaking out of the city, it was usually in pairs? Or groups, evenly matched?"

"Well, that's kind of how the good Lord wired us, isn't it?"

"Okay," she said. "If a woman is 'wired' kind of like... oh, let's say...your ex-wife? Things were easy for slutting around when things were normal, for both men and women. Discounting the morals and emotions, the physical consequences just weren't that great. But tell me, who do you go to now for stuff like birth control or feminine hygiene products, or the morning-after pill? That is after Jack runs out of stolen supplies, of course."

Colt rolled his eyes.

"This disaster is hitting us in a lot of different places other than just food and water."

They were moving along the edge of a pasture, close to the tree line and speaking in low tones.

"So," he said, "what you're saying is that what was once thought of as old values are important again, one woman and one man, fidelity, trust, and all that?"

"Yup."

He stopped when he saw movement ahead and then started up again when he saw a hawk lifting off from the ground with its morning meal.

"It was always important, Lila. Just some people didn't think so. If it helps, you saw I didn't do anything with Jen. There hasn't been anyone since all this crap started except you. Not even Beth."

"Not even Beth?" Her voice was light and mocking. "You've got to be kidding. The woman you just can't wait to see? Then, what's the attraction with her?"

He chuckled. "You're just not going to let that go, are you?" Continuing, he said, "I don't know. She was there when my kids died and helped me through that. Jen just walked away."

"God, that's cold."

"So, I guess it's like you and me. We just clicked. We helped each other."

"Aren't you going to ask about me and my history?"

"Nope. It doesn't matter to me at this point."

"It sure as hell does matter, and for your information, I could have matched your past until I was captured. I've always come across as too macho for most men."

"I like a strong woman."

"I know," she said. "You've been proving it every day. There's one other reason I'm staying with you."

"And that is?"

She chuckled. "I just like the dickens out of you. That and I think we've been honed by the fires into a matching pair."

He shook his head. "You know, I promised myself to Jen once upon a time. Then, after the kids died, Beth kind of picked me up by the hair, dusted me off and got me going again. I wasn't strong when I should have been. We promised a partnership with each other. Then, I was shot and captured and I lost her. Months later, here I am with you. Be careful, Lila. I don't seem to have a good track record with women."

"Alright, we won't talk about the past, Colt. I'm just eternally grateful we found each other. What we need to do now is stay alive."

―――――

THE SUN WAS high and the mist and fog had burned off leaving them covered in a sticky, cloying heat. They crested a tree-lined hill, and as the wind shifted, the stench of rotting corpses hit them full force. It was not a new smell for either of them, but unexpected. Standing with their hands covering their mouths, they saw a ravine stretching out before them that was alive with buzzards, coyotes, dogs, and small varmints—and dead bodies.

They spent a while scouting the area. Close in, the

stench was unbearable. Farther away, it was awful. Finally, when they'd seen all they could stand, they moved upwind from the dump.

Lila finally asked, when they were far enough away to breathe normally, "What do you think?"

"I think it's trouble on a stick," he said. "But, not unexpected."

"Meaning?"

"Remember all the people that fled the cities? There had to be thousands of them. Where did they go? It takes about two weeks for a person to starve, and other than the varmints we saw in the ravine, I haven't seen any cattle, horses, goats, or anything else big enough to eat since we left Springfield."

"Deer," she interjected.

"Yeah, we did see those. The burial pits are the only way. Since there isn't much of a way to bury a lot of people without heavy machinery, this is the only choice."

Lila moved up to him, and he held her close.

"I guess it's been kind of abstract to me. I knew people were gone that they'd run away. It just didn't strike me that they were dead. I mean, yes, we've seen a lot of killing over the last months, but that was just gangs and Homeland Security. Not real people."

Colt shrugged. "That's not the part that worries me. See that little one-lane dirt road that comes up and ends at the ravine?"

When she looked up at him and nodded, he said, "Some of those bodies are fresh, and the tire tracks on that lane aren't grown over with grass. Someone is using it often, so let's get out of here."

They'd only walked a few minutes when they heard the low growl of an engine coming up through the trees.

"Well, someone has fuel left," Lila said.

Hiding behind a limestone outcropping surrounded by scrub cedar, they watched a dirty white pickup come into view. Gears whining and grinding, it slowly made its way up the steep lane toward the dump. When it got closer, they saw the cab had three men in it. The bed of the truck was full of bodies. As the truck passed, it was obvious they all had died of gunshot wounds.

Colt held his finger to his lips for silence. He pointed at her, then at the ground, meaning stay here. Then he dumped his pack on the ground and followed the truck. At a sound from behind, he turned and saw Lila a few steps behind. Rolling his eyes and giving her an exasperated look, he turned and followed the truck.

From their vantage point, they watched the pickup back to the edge of the ravine, and the men pile out. It only took a few minutes for two of the men to toss and roll the bodies out of the truck. The driver of the truck was huge, and when he took his cap off to wipe sweat from his forehead, Colt suddenly stiffened. Startled, Lila reached out and grabbed him.

When he started to get up, she grabbed him and pulled him down again. Violently, she shook her head. Together, they watched the men pitch the bodies into the ravine and leave.

"What?" she nearly yelled at him after the pickup had left. They were standing toe to toe in the dense shade of the trees. "Were you trying to get us killed?"

"Did you notice anything about those guys?"

"Yeah, they were Blackboots, and that's a little disturbing. I thought they stayed in the cities."

"Do you remember me telling you that Tyler had sent Jen's old boyfriend to look for Beth's farm?"

She thought for a minute. "Yeah, you told me. Was one of those men Sammy Boy, as you called him?"

He nodded. "The really big guy that watched the other two men dump the bodies."

"Wow, he's a monster. So, what? That's old news, Colt. It's water under the bridge, and the ship has sailed. All of that. Tyler and Jen are dead, and from what you've told me, this Sam character will probably die of some exotic disease. It's done."

He had to smile at that. "Maybe," he said. "But, in the midst of your attack of the clichés, you might think maybe he found the farm, and that's where all those bodies came from."

"It still doesn't matter. I didn't see any women in that last load of bodies. We just need to find the farm ourselves so you can check on this Beth chick and make sure she's okay. Then we need to boogie on out of here. Right?"

He turned and walked back toward the rock where they'd left their packs.

She followed close behind him. "Right? That's what we're going to do? Dammit."

TWENTY

THE FARM NESTLED between hills in a natural, hollowed-out bowl left by a river long since changing its course. The stream, or creek as Lila called it, was now about a half mile away.

Apparently, it had left rich soil in its wake. Shaped like a horseshoe, the small valley was about a half-mile across and a mile long, with an open end toward the east and the river.

The farm was an assortment of scattered buildings and garden plots. There were windmills scattered around, and the reflection from what they thought must be solar panels blinked at them. From their vantage point, they could see several men working in the gardens. What looked like the main house rested with its back against the bluff for a windbreak and smoke was rising from a stone chimney. That is how they'd found the little valley. What bothered Colt was that Trader Jack was right—anyone else could find it, too.

"What do you think?" he asked Lila as they leaned

against a tree. Their packs were in a pile just behind them, and their shotgun and rifle leaned on the packs.

"It looks like a real nice setup," she said. "But I think they've been raided already."

"See, all they have are gardens," she continued. "Most of these little farms would have some milk cows that double as beef later, calves, maybe a horse or two. I don't see any. There aren't any chickens, ducks, goats, pigs, or any other small animals that I can see. Not even a guard dog. Nope. They've been raided, and I'm betting it's been pretty recent."

"So," Lila said, looking at him expectantly. "Are we going down to see if your girl is there?"

"We'll watch. If we see Beth, we'll go down. Otherwise, you'll get your wish and we leave."

Lila leaned against him. "Colt, can you understand that I've committed to you and that I'm uncomfortable with you wanting to see Beth?"

He turned from watching the farm and looked at her for a long moment. Her eyes were starting to tear up when he said, "Look, Beth helped me when I needed it. I count her as a friend. If your roles were reversed, I'd be checking on you. I can't help that, Lila."

"Now I know why you wouldn't let me have a rifle with a scope on it."

The sound of a truck approaching interrupted them. Since it was the second time he'd heard the sound of the engine, Colt decided it was a diesel since that would be the most common fuel used in farm country. The same pickup they'd seen before pulled up, and several women got out of the back bed of the truck and joined the men in the gardens. Oddly, they didn't see any interaction between the men and women. No hugging, kissing, or 'hi how are you'—just nothing. The last woman to get out of the truck was short, blonde, and wore a loose print dress. She headed straight toward the house with a dejected look about her.

Beth.

Colt felt sick as Lila slowly cursed beside him, and she introduced him to many terms he didn't know. It didn't take much imagination to know what had happened.

"Well," she finally said. "If that big bastard is Sammy Boy, he sure doesn't change his M.O., does he? Why in the hell can't they just get their own women? There are plenty around."

"I should have killed him the other day."

Lila shook her head. "Yeah, sometimes I've got all the sense of a rock. You need to remember that and override me once in a while."

The truck left, and they used the concealment of the woods to come up behind the house. They eased up to the front porch and still concealed, saw Beth sitting in a rocker. She was crying. Colt motioned for Lila to speak to her, thinking a woman's voice wouldn't startle her.

"Don't look this way," Lila said.

Beth gave a small start and then nodded.

"Is there a way inside your house that we won't be seen? We just want to talk to you and help."

Not saying anything, Beth sat for a moment and then got up and went into the house. They could hear her closing curtains on the windows facing the porch, and then in a few minutes, they heard a window open by the back corner.

Moving up to the window, they first handed their packs to her, and then Lila shimmied into the house.

Saying a quick 'thank you' to Beth, she turned and offered a hand to Colt.

When they were both inside, Beth closed the window and pulled the curtain across.

"Hi, Beth."

Beth gave a gasp and backed up rapidly until she fell against the bed that dominated the center of the room. Her mouth was open, but nothing was coming out.

"I swear to God, Colt," Lila said, grinning and shaking her head. "You have that effect on every woman you meet." She looked at Beth's expression again and then started rummaging in her pack. "I better get her some water."

Suddenly, Beth launched herself toward Colt and leaped into his arms with her legs locked around his waist.

He heard Lila mutter to herself while she watched them hugging each other, "Never fails."

A few minutes later, Colt asked, "Is there a chance anyone will be coming in to see you?"

"Not right now," Beth replied. "We eat in one of the other buildings or sometimes out front in about an hour. I don't have to be there."

Colt asked, "Lila, do you want to keep watch out front?"

"While you're sitting on a bed with her? No," Lila said caustically. "I really don't."

Colt introduced them.

"I'm with him," Lila said pointedly.

Beth gave her an odd look, and the two women stared at each other a moment. Amazingly, both started to smile.

"I understand, Lila. We can all move to the front room," Beth replied. "No one will know you're here."

Colt and Lila took turns filling her in on everything that had happened to them. After a few minutes, they both turned to Beth.

"So, what's going on here?" Colt asked.

It took her a few minutes to tell. Zeke and his bunch had rescued her and brought her to the farm. Then, they'd gone on to Lake Stockton. They told her there was another safe place there.

"Everything was fine until about a week ago. That's when the Blackboots showed up." She looked at Colt. "And Sam."

She continued, "We didn't have guards and none of our people were inclined toward that, so they just waltzed right in and took over. They killed the few men that tried to fight. When everything settled down, they took all the animals we had for meat, right down to the last rabbit, and then told us we'd be safe from them if we just farmed. They'd get their share whenever it pleased them, of course. I didn't know what to do and rationalized that things wouldn't be too bad if we just did as we were told. Boy, was I wrong. Colt, I remember you telling me once about the analogy of the 'frog being slowly boiled in water.' Well, that's what happened here. We honestly thought we'd be okay, that we could just pay our tax, so to speak, and go on.

"Yesterday, they came with guns and loaded all the women into the pickup." She looked up and then gazed at the floor. "Including me."

Lila sat next to her and hugged her hard.

"They stripped us...it was awful," Beth said, crying. "I can't begin to..." She glanced at him. "Remember, you promised me that last bullet and you weren't here, Colt. I needed you."

"I know, but in a way, I'm glad we didn't carry through with that—we wouldn't be holding you now. You don't have to tell us anymore. We know all about Sam and the Blackboots. We know what he does."

Beth was crying harder, looking at Colt. "I remember what he did to Jen and you. And I remember how you hated her for it. I'm so sorry."

Colt was just sitting there until Lila, with tears in her eyes, gave him a look that woke him up.

"Beth, it's okay." He took over hugging her from Lila and soon they were both holding her. "It's not the same, and I don't blame you anyway. I hated Jen because of what *she* did to the kids and me. Sam was just the horse she rode to get where she wanted to be. All the things that happened with Jen seem like another world and another time."

After a few minutes, the women went into the bathroom. Colt strolled to one of the windows and looked out between the curtains. Deep twilight was upon them, and someone had started a fire in a pit in the center of the compound. It looked like they were roasting a small pig above the fire. What he assumed was most of the people were sitting around the fire in lawn chairs.

Lila and Beth came out looking fresh. Both had combed their hair, and Lila had changed into jeans and a blouse. He could see Lila's bandaged shoulder through the blouse. Looking outside, Beth said, "I wish you could speak to the men. They're in the same boat as you were with Jen, and they just don't know how to act or what to say. I know they want to reach out to each other, but just don't know how. They're my friends and are hurting."

Colt shook his head. "Maybe I can tomorrow. Right now, we need to rest and get some food in us." He paused. "Did Sammy Boy say when he'd be back?"

"Tomorrow, about noon. He said there were some new recruits, and he wanted to introduce us." She started crying again.

"Not going to happen," Colt said. "Are there guards?"

Beth had calmed down enough to talk. "Three or four, I think. They stay up in the tree line and watch. Once in a while, one will come down, but not often."

All three of them stayed inside and ate from their meager stores. Beth went outside and got some of the pork and then brought it inside.

When Colt stretched out on the floor, Lila said, "You didn't eat much."

"I'm going out later and don't want a full stomach."

Lila stared at him a long moment, long enough that Beth picked up on it and watched both intently. Finally, their silent communication was over, and she said, "I don't like it. Is there another way?"

He shook his head. "You watch from here. If anyone comes down, you need to take care of the problem, understood?"

When she nodded, he relaxed and drifted off to sleep. Before he slept, he could hear Lila and Beth talking in low tones.

———

LILA SAT UP SHARPLY, which startled Beth awake. They'd both fallen asleep on the couch in mid-conversation. Glancing around, she saw Colt was gone and it was getting light outside.

"Where's Colt?" Beth asked.

"He went hunting," Lila said, knowing Beth wouldn't know what she meant.

The two women went out on the front porch. The fire pit was trailing a little smoke, which mingled with the early morning mist. Looking around, Lila thought the peaceful scene was one of the best in her memory, until an anguished scream shattered the peace and quiet.

The sound started with a guttural shout and ended in a high-pitched squeal. Then, the silence was deafening, as everything seemed to pause to listen for a moment.

"What was that?" Beth breathed softly.

"It's getting light, so hopefully it was the last of the guards."

"That's Colt out there?" Beth bolted up out of her chair. "We have to go find him. He may be hurt."

"Believe me, Colt isn't hurt."

"You knew what he was going to do, didn't you?"

Lila looked at her with a grim expression. "It had to be done."

Beth shook her head. "Weren't you worried for him? What if he'd been killed or hurt?"

"Of course I worry—all the time. But, Beth, there's something you need to understand. Colt isn't the same man you knew. And thank God for both of us, he'll never be that man again."

She sighed. "I never really had much of a chance to get to know him anyway, Lila. There just wasn't time."

The scream woke everyone, and most congregated around the front porch, wondering what was going on. Beth told them Lila was a friend and that everything was alright. They were about to start breakfast when someone gasped and pointed.

The group watched as Colt came walking up to the group, loaded down with four rifles and assorted handguns and knives. He dropped it all on the ground and stretched his back.

Noticing the blood on his shirt and covering his hands and arms, one of the men asked, "Did you kill a deer? If you dressed it out, we'd better go get it before the varmints do. We're short on meat right now."

Colt studied the man a moment and then looked at Lila. She knew he wouldn't be able to explain to the farmer what he'd just done.

"No," he said brusquely.

Walking inside, he started stripping off his shirt. "I need to clean up." He smiled quizzically as both women started moving like a well-trained unit. Beth led him into the bath and turned on the shower.

"You've got running water? And hot water?"

"We do as long as the windmill keeps turning for water and what little electricity we need."

Lila brought in a spare shirt and said, "You're out of luck on pants."

They were both trying to help when he said, "Ladies, it's a little crowded in here, so unless you want to take a shower..."

As they left, Lila said, "I guess the man wants to be alone."

Beth made a very unladylike noise. "I doubt it."

In a few minutes, Lila watched as he walked out onto the porch and joined everyone. "Okay," he said. "We need to talk ambush."

AS COLT FACED the small crowd of people and saw their expectant faces, he thought of a similar situation at the stadium in Springfield. God, how he wished that group of fighters were here.

"Alright, folks, I know the situation here after talking to Beth. There's no easy way out of this. To paraphrase a passage in the Bible, there's no point in worrying anymore because 'The Philistines are among us.' From this point forward, you're going to fight, so get that in your head. You men won't be used as slaves, and your women won't be used against their will." He looked at the women and made eye contact with a few. "Never again."

He said, "If there are any who refuse to stand and fight, I need you to walk away right now."

One man spoke up. "But what can we do?"

"I've learned this the hard way and from experience," Colt said. "There's *always* something you can do, even if that choice includes dying. The women of this group can tell you there are worse things than dying."

Everyone stayed. Colt was proud of them until an errant thought crept in. All but one stayed at the Alamo, too.

He and Lila spent the next hour showing them how to use the weapons they had and then dispersed them in pairs to different locations around the barnyard.

Now, all they had to do was spring their surprise on the Blackboots.

———

THEY WAITED an hour before they heard the sound of trucks. Trucks? Two farm trucks pulled into the farm lot and then parked sideways across the open end by the road. Colt knew it was a maneuver to keep anyone from escaping by the road. When the men dismounted on the side away from the house and barns, he knew the ambush wouldn't work the way they'd planned. He needed something to occupy the Blackboots' attention, either a diversion or flanking attack. Turning to look for Lila, he saw she was already hustling around the side of the house and into the trees. Trust her to know what to do.

At a word of encouragement from him, Beth stood, took a deep breath, and walked out to meet the Blackboots. He followed closely behind.

Sam and two of his men stopped a few feet from them. One of the men was Trader Jack.

"You just made a bad trade, Jack," Colt said.

Trader Jack started looking around. "Where is...?"

"Where are the rest of the women?" Sam's harsh voice interrupted Jack as he looked at Beth. "You were supposed to have them ready to go with us."

If anything, Sam was even larger than he remembered, but it looked as if he were going to seed—a little more paunch and an overall softness were apparent. He could see Sam looking him over and could tell that Colt having a gun bothered him. At a gesture from Sam, Trader Jack and the other man spread out a little.

Colt's first thought was to shoot the men immediately, especially Sam. But Beth was beside him, and he knew that action would end in a bloodbath as the men behind the trucks opened fire. His only option was to buy time until Lila could get into position.

"You won't be getting any more women, Sammy Boy. Not after today."

"Oh? And why is that, tough guy?"

"You won't be leaving. We'll throw you into that body pit your men are trying to fill."

Sam flinched but still didn't recognize him. "You called me Sammy Boy. Now, where have I heard that? You don't look like one of these damned farmers. Just who are you?"

"I'm not a farmer, although I wouldn't mind it. You might say I'm an independent contractor."

Beth was slowly retreating to get behind Colt. She pressed up against his back like she was looking for protection and he could feel her hand close on the spare .45 wedged in his belt at the small of his back.

Sam was still trying to place him. "You do look familiar."

Recognizing Colt, the other Blackboot was trying to get Sam's attention.

"Think about Jen and your little commune by the lake," Colt said.

Sam's eyes widened, and he started to smile. "It's the *yuppie* who couldn't keep his woman home."

"Boss," the Blackboot finally spoke urgently. "That's Blaine. He was the leader of Colonel Tyler's conscript killers."

Sam became a little more attentive. "Well, maybe we'll just hold him for Tyler. It looks like he must have escaped."

Colt smiled at him. "Tyler's dead, along with his whore. They got blown up at the airport."

"What?"

Trader Jack interrupted, "Boss, I don't see Lila. She could be a real problem."

"Who in the hell is Lila?" It looked like Sam was getting confused.

On his right peripheral, he saw movement up the slope. *Finally.*

Sam started in on him with a taunting voice. "Was this little lady hiding behind your back your woman? That is too bad if she is because she's mine now. It seems like I'm always taking your woman."

"Not this time."

"You might as well give her up. I'm the better man, you know. I was before and I am now."

"Hardly," Colt said. "The last time I didn't fight, and I should have. I won't make that mistake again."

"You're going to fight me? By yourself? I've got you by a hundred pounds."

Sam shook his head and continued, "It wouldn't have mattered, even if you'd fought for her. Jen was exactly where she wanted to be, and you'd have lost...even if you won."

Colt thought he saw movement on his left by the tree line. *Well, now.*

"You boys are really considerate," he said. "Wearing black, I mean."

The men looked at him.

"It'll come in handy for your buryin', Sammy Boy."

Sam leaped forward with a roar and swung a round-house blow at Colt. He slipped the punch, and as it sailed harmlessly over his head, he buried his right fist in Sam's side, just under the short ribs and then hooked him with his left in the same spot. The larger man went to one knee, his face a rictus of pain.

Colt stepped away and looked at the other men. "This is between your boss and me. It's personal."

The first punch will win many fights, but Colt knew he was in for a battle. Sam was huge and strong, but slow.

Like most really big men, Sam hadn't actually had to fight much. He mostly intimidated those around him. Once he joined with Homeland Security, conscripts did all his fighting for him.

Sam came up off the ground, and then being more cautious, threw a straight jab at Colt's face. When he stepped away from the punch, Colt slipped on a rock and went down. With a shout of triumph, Sam dove on top of him. They scrambled a moment, with Sam winding up on top of Colt. Just as Sam was about to throw another punch, Colt hooked his heel around the other man's chin and flipped him backward.

Both men jumped to their feet and stood looking at each other. Colt had landed two more blows on the way up. Sam was panting from exertion, and Colt waited calmly for him, breathing slowly and deeply. With hatred boiling over, both men charged together, grappled for a moment, and then traded punches for a few minutes. Both men were bloody and Sam ripped away his torn shirt, showing his muscular torso. He posed for a moment, showing off his physique.

"You can't hurt me," he said.

They came together again, and Colt kept working on the larger man's midsection and ribs. He was able to slip most of the punches, but enough had landed to make him respect the man's strength. At one point, Sam backed away, holding his side, grimacing in pain. Colt followed and hooked a right just under his heart, then elbowed him in the throat.

"Damn you," Sam gasped. His face was ashen, and he went to one knee again. He tried to get up and fell back to his knees.

Thinking the fight was over, Colt turned to speak to

the other men. A shot rang out behind him and he whirled to see Sam sprawled on the ground, a knife falling from his nerveless fingers. Beth stood holding the .45. As he looked at her, she started to warn him, and he turned toward the other Blackboots. He palmed his pistol and nearly dropped it because of his bloody hands. He turned and shot one of them as the Blackboot raised his rifle. A blow to the hip turned him, and he saw Beth firing into Trader Jack, who backed up and sat down with a surprised look on his face.

When Colt looked at her, she must have read his mind. "Arnie taught me."

Trader Jack was lying on the ground, trying to hold in the blood spurting between his fingers. "I told you," Colt said.

He could hear firing beyond the trucks. A couple of the farmers had realized the situation, sneaked around the other side, and opened up at the same time as Lila. The Blackboots never had a chance, and as he watched, several made a break for the woods with the people from the farm following closely behind. The shooting stopped a few minutes later.

Beth's people were moving forward, collecting guns and throwing the bodies back onto the trucks. The men and women were side by side, and he saw a couple stop and hug each other. Maybe the battle was retribution for them, and a catharsis that would allow them to go forward. Lila came strolling toward him, slinging her rifle over her shoulder, barrel pointing down.

He noticed she had a concerned look on her face and he was barely able to understand her when she said, "Colt, you'd better sit down."

He felt his .45 slip from his fingers and watched the

little puffball of dust as it hit the ground. Colt looked at his hands and saw they were bloody and swollen. *Never dropped a gun before.* Feeling lightheaded, he could feel wetness on his side and in his pants. Looking down, he saw he'd taken a round in the side and hadn't realized it. The bullet had hit his belt, right at his hip, and left a bloody gash. As he went to his knees in the dust of the barn lot, he heard Lila scream.

"Beth. Get over here."

Colt's mind was a jumble of thoughts. Sam wasn't worth much, but he sure could punch. *I should have just shot him.* He must have blacked out because the next thing he remembered, some men were carrying him to the house. The jostling pain cleared his mind for a moment. Lila was on one side of him, and Beth on the other. Hobson's choice—chose one and hurt the other. *Unacceptable.* He took the manly way out. *I'll just lie down and rest...*

————

COLT GRADUALLY CAME AWAKE and realized he was lying on a cot, covered with a blanket. Hearing voices, he tried to turn his head but found it was too much effort. He could tell it was Beth and Lila sitting at the table by their voices.

"He'll make it, won't he?" Lila asked.

"Oh, he'll be just fine in a few days," Beth said. "The bullet left a nasty gash, but it's not deep and cleaned up well. The rest of his condition is just from the fight. I think he's just really, really tired."

"God," said Lila. "He was bloody all over. Why did he

fight Sam? That was so stupid. I couldn't believe he didn't just shoot the man when he had the chance."

He heard Beth sigh, and was surprised he could easily tell the difference in their voices. "It was to buy time, I guess, so you could get into position. But, regardless of that, he still had to do it. That man took a lot from Colt. Killing him just wasn't enough."

"Yeah, we've all lost a lot, Beth. Thanks for saving Colt's life at the end of the fight."

"That was *my* payback."

"We have a lot in common, don't we?" Lila's voice was nearly too soft for Colt to hear. "He's a good man, Beth." It sounded to him like she was crying. "Look, I need to leave. With your nursing abilities, Colt will be just fine. It will be better if I'm not here when he wakes up. I'm sure he'll be up and around in a few days."

"So, what're you thinking, Lila? Is this that point in the romance novels we used to read that one of the women leaves for the greater good? Or, when Colt leaves, and one of us goes chasing after him? I don't think this problem will be so easily resolved."

Beth seemed to hesitate a moment. "But why are you leaving, Lila? With the Blackboots out of the way, at least for now, I think we have a real chance to make things work on this farm."

"Oh, come on. Beth, I've seen the way you look at him. It's a crazy term in this new world of ours, but you love him. I know you do."

He heard a long sigh from Beth. "I do. But, Lila, *so do you*. You two are so comfortable together, it's obvious to anyone. He cares for you."

She continued, "Just look at us...I'm little Suzy Homemaker, and couldn't fight my way out of a wet paper bag. And look at you—an Amazon goddess mixed with a Valkyrie warrior. Hell, if I leaned that way, I'd be all over you myself. He won't want to let you go."

Lila laughed. "Is there some point here except to know we're both up shit creek without a paddle?"

"Yes," said Beth. "I want you to stay. With him. With me."

Startled, Lila said, "What? Uh, Beth, that's—"

Beth interrupted, "Look, he needs both of us. Hell, after what he's been through, he *deserves* us. Don't you see? Together, we make the woman he needs. Together we're a team. Jen and her betrayal hurt him terribly, and the guilt over the loss of his children is eating him up. He thinks they died because of his failing them, and we need to get him past that. Once he gets by all the anger and hurt, I think he loves both of us. If the situation were normal, that would tear him apart, and us, too. But things are far from normal anymore. I think that if we make him choose between us, the winner only gets half the man. That is our first priority, to make him realize he doesn't have to choose."

"Beth, I swear, you could talk the stripes off a skunk. Do you really think that kind of arrangement would work?"

"It will be tough, but yes, I do. And it can't be like divorced parents sharing custody of the kids. It has to be the two of us, together with him. All the time."

They were silent for a while, but he could hear their breathing and an occasional sip from a glass or cup. He could smell coffee. Finally, as he was about to nod off again, he heard...

"Okay, Beth, I know this is crazy, but we'll give it a try. I know that I don't want to be alone anymore, and I sure as hell don't want to get knocked over the head by some randy farmer wanting to start a family."

Beth snorted into her coffee. After she coughed for a minute, he could hear her hands scrambling around on the table. Then she blew her nose.

"God," she said. "I've never had coffee up my nose."

Lila continued, ignoring the interruption, "And I think we can get along. So, I guess we're just down to logistics. How do we share the boy? How are we going to do that?"

Colt struggled to stay awake for the answer. He wanted to hear the answer. Hell, he *had* to know the answer, but drowsiness overcame him.

He was smiling as he dozed off. *"I'd rather be lucky than good, any day of the week."*

————

FOR THE SECOND TIME, Colt came awake gradually and listened to the sounds of the house. Glancing toward the window, he could tell it was late afternoon. Soreness and stiffness prevented him from moving much, so he lay under the sheet and enjoyed the quiet. It was windy outside and he could hear the pines whispering in the breeze. In the distance, the faint echo of someone chopping wood mingled with the sound of two women talking. He would have felt relaxed in the comfortable bed if not for the other noise that bothered him and got his attention. The odd, out-of-place sounds always stand out. The noise he heard sounded like a window frame sliding open, and then closing slowly. Someone was trying to be quiet.

A floorboard creaked at the door to his room, and he opened his eyes.

"Hello, Blaine," Tyler said.

Colt started to get up, and Tyler pointed a pistol at him. There was a wildness in his eyes that hadn't been there before, and he still had that superior, smug look. "Just lay there, Blaine. It looks like you get to die in bed. A few weeks ago, neither of us would have guessed that."

"I thought you were dead," Colt said.

"Oh, did you now? How stupid do you think I am? Did you honestly think I'd take the risk of digging out that basement door? There was no need."

"I was hoping you would. How did you get past the guards?"

"They're farmers, Blaine. I didn't even have to kill them—just walked on by."

Colt moved as if to ease his position, and Tyler said sharply, "I told you not to move.

"You know," Tyler continued. "We kind of suspected the basement door would be booby-trapped. But Jen insisted she go and check it out. I really liked her, but she got to acting strange at the end. She just didn't look at me the same. Odd, don't you think? It was almost like she had a death wish."

Colt felt a twinge of regret for what he and Jen used to have a lifetime ago. "Yeah, maybe she grew a conscience."

Tyler laughed quietly and then shook his head. "I don't think she ever had one of those."

The sounds from outside were getting louder and he could hear laughter and someone cleaning off their shoes on the porch steps. From the sounds, he could tell Beth and Lila would be coming inside.

"Well," Tyler said, raising his pistol. "I wanted closure and I guess this is it."

The sound of the gunshot clapped loud in the room and brought both the women running inside. Colt swatted at the burning hole in the sheet that was covering him. Beth's hands covered her mouth in shock, her eyes wide from the adrenaline rush of fear. Lila brushed her aside, holding her .45 in a two-handed grip. Her gaze met Colt's, saw that he was okay, and then she looked at the body on the floor.

Lila nudged the body with her foot and then looked up at Colt.

"Tyler?"

"He came to say goodbye."

A LOOK AT BOOK SIX:
AFTER THE FALL

SOMBER AND HOPEFUL—OUR BASIC INSTINCT TO SURVIVE IS EXEMPLIFIED IN THIS APOCALYPTIC AND ACTION-PACKED TALE.

John Trent survived the hordes of mankind pouring out of cities—looking for food, clean water, and any other dream that made sense—and the starvation and disease that followed.

Now in the aftermath, a small community in the Ozarks is trying to rebuild, despite Raiders trying to kill them off and hungry movers wanting to take over. So, when John reports to his Army commander and is tasked with saving this small town, he jumps at the opportunity to set flame to evil for good.

In a constant fight for survival, battle-hardened John learns to care again. He learns to love again. But first... he must defeat a ruthless adversary whose treachery knows no bounds and secure the survival of a town that represents one of the last few hopes of survival.

AVAILABLE AUGUST 2023

ABOUT THE AUTHOR

Darrel Sparkman is an award-winning author of novels, novellas, and short stories. He's been included in three western anthologies, worked as a feature writer for *Saddlebag Dispatches* and blogged a short time for *Sundown Press*. His ideas come from a diverse past of serving as a combat search and rescue helicopter crewman in Vietnam and volunteer Emergency Medical Technician First Responder. He has worked as a professional photographer, computer repair tech, and was once part-owner of a commercial greenhouse operation and flower shop.

Darrel is enjoying semi-retirement and finally has that job that wakes him up every day—with a smile on his face.